FIREBALLS WERE COMING STRAIGHT FOR THEM....

They sped at an incredible rate, the wind roaring with their passage. Blade's horse reared, and he fought her heaving panic to bring her back to all fours and get her out of the fireballs' pathway. There was a moment of soundless agony. Blade could feel the mare trembling as she balanced on her hindquarters. Could see the fireballs coming in at them like comets. Could feel his hands frozen in an attempt to bring the mare down. Could see Lady Nolan riding in, throwing herself at the headstall to pull the mare back to the ground.

They all came together at once as time suddenly resumed. The mare came to earth, tearing her headstall out of Lady's hand.

The Protector looked up, her jaw dropping open in astonishment. "What is that?"

Blade shoved his boots deep in his stirrups. He looked up and saw it also—so massive that the fireballs it had thrown seemed mere sparks now. It was dark with an orange corona, and it was curving along the horizon toward them. The wind sucked in, hot and dry, as he stared at the inescapable apocalypse descending on them. . . .

THE
MARKED
MAN

CHARLES INGRID

DAW BOOKS, INC.
DONALD A. WOLLHEIM, PUBLISHER

1633 Broadway, New York, NY 10019

First Printing, December 1989

1 2 3 4 5 6 7 8 9

PRINTED IN THE U.S.A.

Chapter 1

He spotted the body half-hidden under the rotting hulk of an '02 hovercar. Mesquite and oleander had crowded the car until the corpse was only one of the dark and twisted shadows in the dirt. The dead man wore patrolman's clothing.

Blade reined in. He sat still for a moment, and watched the ears of his gelding flick back and forth. A raucously chattering crow circled low and flew in to shred at the victim's sprawling arm. The horse's ears pricked, then relaxed. Satisfied that they were alone, Blade swung a leg over and dismounted. He dropped the reins. The crow protested his approach and left with a flap of tattered black wings.

The body had been dead a while. Two days, probably, from the smell and lividity. The throat had been worried at by crows and ants and sowbugs, but it looked to be the death wound. The ragged edges had not been slit cleanly—something had torn it open.

Blade wiped his hands on his knees, then absently touched the chevron scar marking his brow. There were a lot of things out here which could have killed the man, but he didn't like speculating.

He straightened up. A wind smelling of sea and salt tugged at the long white scarf about his neck. On a clear day like today, from where he stood on the ravaged coast of the Los Angeles basin, Catalina could still be seen. Blade toed the body. "You're a suspicious son of a bitch," he said to himself. But patrolmen didn't stop to check the view, and, from the grooves in the dirt, the body had been dragged in and hidden. Predators behaved differently than murderers.

5

Blade got the groundsheet out of his bedroll. The gelding rolled a white eye at him, reacting to the stench of death amid the already pungent odor of the disintegrating car. He sidestepped when Blade attempted to mount up, malodorous bundle under his arm. Thomas cursed the horse and pulled himself up anyway. The groundsheet would absorb most of the smell for the time being. He'd be down at the big house soon where Charles would not be pleased to know that someone or something had taken out one of his patrolmen.

He took the horse around in a cautious circle, examining the ground and brush for more information, then reined about toward his original destination. He almost overlooked the snare lines set in the heavy brush above what was obviously a jackrabbit run.

Blade did not get down to look at the snare. He knew nester work when he saw it, but he wondered whether discovering the snare was coincidental or important. Charlie didn't like nesters and neither did Blade, and it would be convenient if the blame for the patrolman's death fell that way. Thomas distrusted convenience.

The canvas-shrouded body stuck out awkwardly across the gelding's withers. Its shadow crossed the snare as the horse shifted uneasily. Blade made up his mind, clucked the horse into a trot, and headed for the big house.

The big house was a magnificent, if timeworn, manor house of stone and flagstone and red-tiled roofing where sparrows and pigeons quarreled among the eaves. The crescent drive was hand-cut across the grounds and the sun glittered off the '96 Cadillac coach sitting in the driveway, its antique carcass waxed to within an inch of its metallic life. Thomas thought briefly of its biodegradable counterpart which he'd left moldering in the foothills. He squeezed the gelding into a lope.

A man broke into a greeting run from the driveway's far end. "Thomas! They've been asking for you!"

The crescent drive and the stables just downhill bustled with life. There were small carriages and carts and horses picketed all over the grounds. Blade smiled wryly. All the secretive plans of the past years were up in smoke now. The head groom reached for his gelding's headstall. "Looks like you've brought an uninvited guest."

Thomas dismounted, took his hat off, and settled it on the saddle horn. The sea wind dried his fine blond hair quickly. "From what I've seen, there's no such thing as an uninvited guest. Who's here?"

"Every governor and mayor Charlie could call in. They've been sitting in the big house arguing for the last day or two."

"Where's Charles now?"

"In the schoolhouse. He told me to tell you, no trouble." But the servant did not look very menacing as he delivered his warning.

"You're a little late on that one, Weber. Take that bundle down to the cold house and see if you can make it a touch more palatable. And don't let Veronica see it."

The groom nodded. He stroked the gelding gently with his third hand. "Who was it?"

"One of the sentries. Now I can't tell you any more, so don't ask."

"All right, then. What did you bring for a wedding present?"

Blade patted Weber's shoulder. "Now that would be telling." He pivoted on a boot heel, then pulled on his yellow-gold mustache. "Not a word until the kids open it . . . I've got three more laser disks. The machine still working?"

"Impeccably. About the only thing around here, besides me, that does." Weber watched as Blade took off his saddle pack. Hoisting it over his shoulder, he made his way to the group of outbuildings used for schoolrooms.

The doors and windows had been left open to catch the breeze off the ocean cliffs. He took a moment to collect his wits. He could hear the drone of young voices in response to the lecturer. It took him back a few years as he moved quietly within the shadows to stand where Charles Warden could not see him. The teacher of the class, an elderly man, sat tucked up in his corner as though trying to avoid notice altogether while the Director of Water and Power was speaking to his students.

The DWP had begun to run a little to fat, Blade noticed, but was still an imposing man. The children seated at small desks and on the floor ranged in ages, sexes and races, and with few exceptions, had their attention fixed on him. At his back was a multicolored plastimap of the old United States.

Blade smiled in spite of himself. So this wedding was to be the launch of a number of pet projects. Charlie was inside the schoolroom now, hoping to whip up the imagination of future cartographers.

"What good does it do, sir," a reedy voice piped up, "to know their names if the states aren't there anymore?"

"Ah, but that's the point," Charlie said. He paced back and forth in front of the children. His neck was florid above his collar, a sure sign of excitement. "We know that much of the country was devastated, both by the "Star Wars" reprisal and by the plagues that followed—but we don't know who's there and who isn't. There are bound to be pockets of people who still exist."

"What happened?"

Charles paused a moment, looking into the face of the solemn girlchild who asked him. She knew the catechism, of course, they all did, but large-eyed Alma seemed in quest of an ultimate truth. The DWP cleared his throat. "We don't really know. We can guess. Two incoming asteroids of tremendous size struck North America. Attempts to deflect or destroy them evidently set off the "Star Wars" defense network accidentally. That, in turn, set off limited nuclear war. And, that in turn, set off nuclear havoc in third world countries such as India and South Africa, which had unregulated and unauthorized nuclear weaponry. After the destruction and what we called nuclear winter, we know that parts of China and Russia managed to survive—parts of Europe are rumored to have made it, too. And South America. We lost the African continent, of course, but we still get radio signals we cannot quite decipher or locate. So you must know your countries, states, and counties as they were, until we can get the mappers out and back again to tell us how our world is *now*. For the first time, we have a stable enough population here to let you go, if you want to."

"Anywhere?" A small dark boy, legs folded gracefully under him, spoke up.

"Wellll." Charlie turned around and looked at the map. He pulled at the slateboard and brought down a map of California. His back to the children, he began to delineate areas with a blunt finger. "We know, of course, what the asteroid strikes here and here left—"

"Us!" the children shouted out.

"Well, it left this massive fjord over what used to be Santa Barbara, and this crater here in the greater L.A. basin was made on the bounce—Nevada took the heaviest brunt—and the nuclear strike wiped out most of the bay area here and the upper part of the state and the far east coast here. Chinese Vancouver took over the greater Seattle area, but we have a massive break from upper Washington all the way down to San Francisco. This area was never densely populated and we don't know what happened after the radiation and plagues." Without skipping a beat or turning around, he said, "What do you think, Thomas?"

The children let out squeals of surprise and delight as he stepped out of the shadows, dust motes swirling about him in diffuse sunlight. "I think," he said quietly, "that anyone who goes out to map the world will be a great adventurer."

Charlie smiled broadly. He added, "I'll turn this class back to Protector Wyethe."

As the spindly, white-haired man stood up from his stool in the corner, the DWP caught Blade's attention and guided him back outside.

"What do you think?" Charles Warden asked him as they stepped away from earshot of the classrooms.

"I think you ought to be ashamed of yourself," Blade answered. "Sending lambs out into the wilderness with the wolfrats."

Charlie gave him a resentful look and a sigh. "Has to happen sometime. You know it and I know it. What we don't know can kill us."

"What we do know can kill us. I brought in one of your outermost sentries with me."

"Who?"

"No one I trained. Weber took him to the cold house. He's not in good shape, even for a corpse, but his throat had been ripped out."

Charlie's eyelids flickered. "Predators?"

Blade shook his head. "I don't think so. I think a lizard got him."

"*Shit.* Don't say anything to Ronnie or anyone else in the house, will you?"

Blade quirked his brow. He felt that oddly shaped scar pucker as he did so. "That depends on who you've got in the house."

"I've got everybody in the house, dammit, and you know it."

"I know it now, but this isn't what we discussed months ago. We discussed discretion—we discussed out-and-out secrecy. You're going to have unwanted visitors, if you don't have already."

Charles stopped in his tracks. His bulky shoulders tensed and shifted under his shirt. "I have my reasons, Thomas."

"Of course," he said smoothly and proceeded to the elegantly carved oaken doors of the big house. Beyond, the sounds of laughter and muffled talk, even the clink of fine crystal pre-Disaster glasses could be heard. "Coming in with me?"

"No. I need some time with the body. Keep Ronnie busy and stay civilized."

Thomas watched him walk around the far end of the house. There had been mullioned windows here, in the front, but for defense they'd been boarded up long ago. No one could watch him as he stood there until he could shake off his vulnerability, don bravado like a fine cloak, then kick the door in.

Someone screamed. The sound climbed, then truncated. The crowd in the foyer turned, drinks in hand, saw him, and faces brightened. Thomas recognized what Charles would call "his political crowd." He threaded his way through. A male voice followed after. "Veronica! Hide the virgins."

Laughter shrieked and blushing faces turned away from him. But they shrank away from him rather than brush shoulders, this crowd. And why not? They were more than a little afraid of him. He was, after all, the executioner.

He passed a tray of lemon drops. He was uncommonly fond of lemon drops. He dipped a hand in and filled a pocket. He caught a fleeting glimpse of himself in a gold-veined mirror. The tail of his white scarf floated behind him, caught in the draft created by his swaggering gait. His fine gold hair was cut a little too long over the ears and brushed the collar of his battered brown leather jacket. The hairline was too far back, revealing too much of a lean face. *Twenty years from now,* he thought, *I'll be bald as an egg.* The notion made him frown as an elegant woman in a dress of Alice blue emerged from an alcove at the foyer's end.

Henna accented her long brown hair. One slender hand curved about a champagne glass, as she hooked the other along his outstretched arm and brought it down gracefully to her level. "Thomas! Behave yourself. Charles is worried enough about things without you."

He kissed her temple. "But, Auntie, isn't that why I was invited?"

"Lord Protector," she said smoothly, the tone of her voice reminding him of both his office and his duty, "you were invited because we love you. Now come with me and let me present you." Her nose wrinkled slightly. "Really, Thomas, couldn't you have stopped at the bathhouses on the way in?"

"Water and time are money."

"Ummm." She didn't sound convinced.

"I'll get there as soon as I can," he reassured her, as they walked into the great room of the house.

The wedding of Charles and Veronica's daughter had brought out the big cannons, Blade could see. The mayors he knew because of his circuit riding as judge and executioner, but the others he knew only by repu- tation. As his gaze swept across the room, he saw no fewer than five Protectors. Those, plus himself and Wyethe in the classroom, meant Charlie had called in the entire group. The county barriers and the people living behind them were vulnerable to any attack, physical or psychic, that might be launched on them. Blade felt his jaws clench in anger.

The cattle baron from Santa Barbara gave him an acknowledging nod. Thomas noted that his new jacket had been smartly cut to both accommodate and hide his tail as neatly as possible. His perpetually bald wife had a new wig as well. They were lean and tanned from hard work, but their clothes spoke of prosperity.

Veronica did not miss the look nor did she miss Charles' entrance from the rear of the manor house, his face pale. "Boyd, I can see you and Delia know Thomas. Take him under your wing, will you? I have some other things to do and he's not a social animal."

"Just an animal." Thomas smiled engagingly, but it did little to change the pallor of Delia's own expres- sion. He could not blame her, really. The last time they'd met, he'd been there to put her eldest son to death. He looked past Delia to watch Veronica corner her husband. The DWP looked unhappy for a fleeting second.

Before Boyd could react to his newest duties, Delia's lip curled and she began to speak. Or tried to. Her voice was drowned out by the squeals of the children as they caught sight of him, a pack of them emerging from the kitchen and racing across the massive room heedless of the crowd they scattered. Wyethe must have let them out for good behavior.

"Thomas! Thomas! Thomas!"

The corner of his mouth quirked. He was always undone by the children. They knew him for what he was. It was fortunate the adults didn't—they attributed Thomas' popularity to the toys and odd things he was always bringing up from the ruins. It was the children who knew how to spot a free soul and unfettered heart when they saw one.

He flipped the ends of his scarf back over his dark brown leather jacket as he got to his knees in order to talk to the clamoring children. Quiet Alma, as soulful as her name, smiled up at him and touched the patched knee of his riding and tracking trousers. He patted her hand back. Behind her, Stefan watched solemnly, his hair white-blond, courtesy of his Russian blood. His mother had come over on a boat fifteen years ago, most of her fellow voyagers dead from the journey, too frail to last the arduous trip from their snow-blasted lands. She'd worked in Blade's county for many years and he'd taught Stefan to shoot. But when he'd lost his mother, he'd come here. The DWP took in all orphans. He gave Thomas a quiet nod. But the others were anything but quiet, bouncing and cheering his presence.

They drew Veronica's attention away from Charles and she said, "Honestly, Thomas. When you're ready, I'll have you announced."

He looked up, irony mirrored in his brown eyes. "I think everyone here knows my name already."

She made a noise of disapproval and stalked off, her heels making a staccato noise on the flooring. He

watched her go, knowing that her agitation was not
caused by him but by what she'd just learned from the
DWP. Amid soft laughter, Thomas shrugged and turned
back to the children who were tugging on the strings
of his saddle pack. Even the bride and groom were on
their knees like everyone else, her swirled party dress
crumpled under her. He reached out and touched the
girl on her shoulder where the gown exposed soft skin.
"Jennifer . . . you'd better get up before I get in
trouble. That's no way to treat such a pretty dress."

Blondely beautiful, the twelve-year-old wrinkled her
nose a second, then nodded and got to her feet. The
groom, thirteen-year-old Ramos, darkly handsome even
though his features had not quite delineated themselves, stood up bearing Thomas' pack. It was his right
to ask, and so he did.

"What did you bring?"

Thomas shook his head. "A wedding present, but
you won't know what it is until you open it. Bad luck,
you know." He fought the impulse to reach out and
brush Ramos' straying black hair from his forehead.
Young, both of them. He sighed. The world around
him seemed to go in pairs, and now it was pairing off
younger and younger—although these two were special indeed.

"Thomas!"

He craned his neck and saw Charles bearing down
on them through the crowd. He grinned at the children. "I think I'm being called."

Ramos bore the pack off to the ballroom, where
long tables held packages of glittering splendor and
threw the canvas pack to the head of the table, where
it reigned by virtue of its own difference. The boy
stroked the pack before bolting off to join the herd of
children as they clattered past him, headed toward the
kitchen. Alma lagged behind for a moment. He threw
her a kiss.

"Go on, big eyes. I'll be here for the party."

The child nodded, then turned and raced after her
friends.

Thomas watched wistfully before turning back to Charles who said, "Was it necessary to kick in the door?"

Blade reflected for a moment and decided that it probably hadn't been, but it had seemed appropriate at the time. "It wasn't latched."

"No, but your boot left a notch in it. Antique, Thomas, a genuine oak antique, and you left a mark in it that—"

"Will always remind you of Jennifer's wedding day," Thomas interrupted smoothly. "Congratulations, Charlie." He played out the lie that they had not met outside the classrooms, though few seemed interested in their conversation.

"Thank you." The big man paused. "Come in the study with me."

The way he said it, Thomas knew he didn't have a choice, and he followed in his friend's wake, trying not to walk on his heels. Macaulay's *The Way Things Work* was open on the massive desktop. Thomas knew Charlie had been attacking another knotty problem.

Charles gave him a glass and tapped an aromatic, amber liquor into it.

"Must be serious," Thomas said as he took the glass and sat down. The sweet smell of herbed stuffing issued from the couch. "You've given me the serious stuff to drink."

"You're right . . . one of Denethan's raiders tore his throat out. That was Franco, one of my best."

"I didn't train him." Charlie's glance flickered over Thomas as he answered that, and he knew the DWP had identified the arrogance in his tone. How could Franco have been one of the DWP's best sentries if Thomas had not trained him?

Charlie drained his shot glass. "Have you heard anything?"

"Heard anything about what?"

"Thomas! About the wedding, on the streets or anywhere else."

"No, but then, I already knew. What's this all about? You've got a block full of carriages and now you're worried about discretion? Who in the hell gave you permission to call in the Protectors? Worried about the Lizard of Oz?"

"Water rights give me the permission. As for the Lizard—is nothing sacred?"

"Lighten up, man. *The Wizard of Oz* is a brilliant political satire. And if I hadn't found the disk for it, none of you would even be dissecting it for dinner conversation today." Blade grinned humorlessly. "And if it applies to our nemesis from the Mojave, so much the better."

Thomas eyed Charlie as the burly man sat down in a leather chair. Air wheezed out of the chair discreetly as the DWP squeezed in. Blade sipped the whiskey and waited for the mellow sting to leave his tongue before adding, "Isn't that why I'm here? Isn't that why all seven of us are here, at one time, in one place, as seven Protectors haven't been since the early days? Because you're afraid—no, petrified—that Denethan will somehow find a way to come at you and your little Adam and Eve."

"It's no joke, Thomas."

"I wasn't making a joke. We all know that Denethan would love to take out our two genetically pure beauties before they have a chance to bear children who might—just might—bring back a pure human race. I saw the guards up on the hills. I rode right through them and I'm here to tell you that if Denethan uses his wind raiders, we're dead meat, just like the sentry I brought in. All seven Protectors, the children, and every one of your hypocritical wedding guests."

Charlie took out a handkerchief and mopped his sweating brow. His thick salt-and-pepper hair was plastered to his skull with perspiration. His full neck bulged outside the confines of the tight neckline, adding purple to the scarring on the side of his neck. Blade, finding himself staring, looked away, out the window, to the windmills busily churning in the sea breeze off the cliffs. He was aware of the increase in tension that followed his words.

Charles said softly, "I know you're angry because I didn't follow your advice."

"That wasn't advice I gave you. I thought we were taking security precautions and making plans for their future."

"I had to do it differently, and I won't have you calling my guests names."

Thomas took another draft. "The fact is, we're all here to celebrate the mating of two pure specimens—when it's our own mutations that have kept us alive this long. Genetic splicing came along just in time to keep the disaster from annihilating us. And now you and the others are busily trying to undo what made us survivors."

Charlie looked at him bleakly. "I suppose you side with Denethan."

Thomas glared back. Then he tossed off the last of his drink. "I'll pretend I didn't hear that. I'll pretend it's because you're under a lot of stress that you suggested I have anything to do with that reptilian monstrosity in the Mojave. Because if I didn't have a good imagination, Charlie, I'd have to take you outside and carve you up, just out of principle."

Charlie let out a gusty sigh. "You know I didn't mean it. But you're right about one thing—I'm scared. I wouldn't have all the Protectors here at one time if I wasn't—and if it wasn't for the future of the human race, you guys wouldn't have agreed to come. Jesus." And the aging man buried his face in his hands.

Thomas relented. "He's heard, Charlie. Denethan's tentacles stretch all over L.A. The only question is: did he hear in time to do something about it? We don't know, and we won't until something happens." Thomas stood up abruptly and poured himself a refill. "Where's the ceremony? I saw the Caddy out front."

"At the sea bowl." Charles raised his face. He mopped it quickly, but his eyes had reddened.

"Good choice. Lots of nature. I like it there," Thomas said thoughtfully, as he moved past his old friend to the picture window. "We might have a chance yet."

"Do you think so?"

Thomas' answer was interrupted by Veronica, as she opened the door and stuck her head in. "Art Bartholomew is whipping everybody up over the water share allotments again." Veronica's icy blue stare pinioned Thomas for a minute, then she smiled. "Being a good boy?"

Thomas shrugged. "Give me a break, Ronnie."

She flushed at her nickname and left them alone in the study. In the sudden silence, he could hear the scold and song of the birds outside. He turned back to the DWP.

"What's this about Bartholomew?"

"Politics. You wouldn't be interested."

"Why don't you just cut off his water altogether? He's got a well, he'll get along for a while. Give him an appreciation for the system."

"I've never used water to make anyone toe the line and it won't be done in the counties as long as I'm DWP. And Art has a fine appreciation for the system. He wants to be Director of Water and Power when I pack it in. That's why he's here, drinking my booze and celebrating my daughter's wedding."

"Just as long as you duck when he decides to bury the hatchet." Thomas finished off his drink.

"Tell me I'm doing the right thing," Charles said heavily as he got to his feet.

"You're doing the right thing," Thomas answered automatically. He paused. "Politically. The people out there have a right to be polarized into this. But as for the kids—I think I'd just take the two of them and tell them to make love and babies for the rest of their lives. No muss, no fuss. This," and Thomas indicated the celebration with a wave of his hands, "this is going to pull Denethan's attention to us."

"I can't do that. They have to be gotten out, and gotten out now. Ten years have passed, and the plague is showing up again. Nesters, mostly, but I can't afford to lose anybody."

Thomas grew silent. The eleven year plague was a

mutating virus that attached itself to the DNA—inflicting even worse abominations on them than genetic engineering had—and it was uncontrollable. Luckily, short-lived, but women and men once infected had to be sterilized or pass on genetic changes too monstrous to face. Nesters lived outside the system, by choice. "Then send them away quietly. Why wine and dine all your friends and enemies?"

"I don't have much of a choice." Charlie's neck, where he had his immature gills cut out, pulsed. "Politically." He opened the study door. "Shall we go?"

Chapter 2

"What is an Art Bartholomew?" Thomas asked, easing his way from the muffled quiet of the study back into the cheerful din of the outer rooms.

Veronica pointed her chin at a warty little man on the far side of the room, talking enthusiastically and waving his hands. He had attracted a crowd of his own, much like dung attracts flies. Thomas pulled at a corner of his mustache as Veronica said, "I told you not to invite him, Charles."

"I couldn't very well leave him out. Besides, this is an opportunity to get some things settled without having to put them to a vote. You might as well come, too." He looked at Blade. The scars above his collar line pulsed slightly.

"Right."

Bartholomew's voice seemed to rise with every step closer they took, as though their approach enflamed him. Charles was at the edge of the crowd when Gray Walton took him by the elbow.

"A word, Director, if you please."

Gray Walton was black, and his brown eyes shone with a keen earnestness from his burled skin. Charles stepped back away from Bartholomew's audience. "What is it, Gray?"

"My daughter gave birth yesterday."

"She did? Congratulations, man. . . ." Charles paused, seeing the too bright gaze in Gray's eyes. The two turned away to exchange quiet words Thomas was not privy to. He edged past them to listen to Bartholomew.

"Water isn't politics, he says. Bullshit. If it wasn't, he wouldn't be Director of Water and Power. The problem is to use it politically. Take water rights away from the nesters and let them dry up and blow away in the wind."

"You know that's not policy." Thomas raised his voice as the man paused in his tirade.

"Policy? The policy is nothing more than situational ethics, anyway."

"Nothing is ever black and white."

Bartholomew fixed an intent gaze on him. Then the warty man smiled. "You, of all people, should be first to judge."

The crowd parted a little at seeing Thomas in their midst. Blade felt himself smiling. "On the contrary, Bartholomew. As executioner and Protector, I'm the last one to judge a situation. I only come in when the accusation has been proved or disproved, a neutral party. I truth-read and I carry out the sentence, but I make no moral decisions."

"And that leaves you innocent?"

"No, it leaves me disinterested. Which leads me to ask: what do you hope to gain from additional damming in your county? As I recall, you have fairly heavy rains, but with a lot of runoff. In order to deny water rights to the nesters, we'd have to build an earthen dam . . . then you'd have quite a little reservoir of your own. No way to test the water or filter the contaminants out of it—but you wouldn't have to come to the DWP then, would you? Unless, of course, your people want clean water."

Bartholomew closed his mouth tightly for a moment, then said, "I won't countenance such accusations by responding to them."

"I bet you won't." Thomas turned away. He bumped into Charlie's bulk.

"Defusing the situation?"

"Trying to."

His friend made a funny sound at the back of his throat, a half-growl. "No duels this time."

"Who, me?" Thomas spotted a clear area by the patio doors, which were open to gather in the late afternoon breeze. He headed for them. In his wake, he heard a strong female voice saying, "Soap's your best insecticide. Nothing dangerous and it kills the infestation all the same."

"Not these bugs it doesn't. I picked one off my bushes the size of my thumb . . ."

Charlie followed him out to the patio. They stood, facing into the wind. Blade watched the windmills generating energy for this tiny square of civilization. After a long moment, he said, "As long as the wind blows inshore, Denethan can't launch his wind raiders. The minute it changes . . ." and he let his voice trail off.

"Have you felt anything yet?"

Blade looked at him. "Why me? You've got six other Protectors here to ask."

"Because you're more sensitive."

Thomas thought of a scornful reply, then discarded it. Instead, he took a meditative breath. He had not felt the black wave of dispair and fear that Denethan usually launched along with a physical assault for years. He did not feel it now. He shook his head. "Nothing. But that doesn't mean our lizard man isn't out there waiting and watching."

The patio doors reopened with a squeak, bringing both men around. This time they faced three governors, one of whom, from Thomas' own county, was on his tiptoes from drink.

"Valdees."

"Blade. So he roped you in here, too?" The chunky, graying man with skin like burnished leather lifted his glass.

"I sense a request," Charles said. He eyed the other two governors, the woman tall and lanky like her counterpart.

"We want the nesters cleaned out." Her voice was clipped, emotionless.

Charles answered, "You're talking murder."

"No. We're talking war. I don't advocate Bartholomew's method of taking away their water. That's cruel."

"And it takes too long," Thigpen added. He had not spoken yet, but stood back as if weighing the speech of his peers.

Charles shook his head. "I'm the Director of Water and Power. Water's life, and I'll give that to you. If you want death, you're going to have to find yourself a general."

"There's that," Valdees said. "You're quick enough to fight if the filtration station is threatened."

"But I don't want to do it as a full-time job. Governors, I invited you all here for this occasion to air some of these grievances. But I can't give you a snap answer for them, and I don't think you really want that from me, do you?"

Governor Irlene shook her head, her dark hair threatening to break free from its glittering net. "No. What we do want is a guarantee that you'll sit down and talk with us."

"All seven mayors and governors? Or just you three?"

"The three of us, first." Thigpen took a step forward. "The nesters are vermin. Something has to be done."

Charles nodded gravely. "Then we'll talk," he said.

The trio left as quietly as they had come. Thomas

took a deep breath and could smell himself. "That reminds me," he said. "Veronica recommended a visit to the bathhouse. Any hot water left?"

Something in his question struck Charles as funny and the man put his head back and bellowed with laughter. Blade could still hear him faintly as he walked across the lawn toward the bathhouses in the deepening afternoon shadows.

Charles joined him in the immense wooden tub, awakening him from a half-drowsed dream. His mood had become much more somber. He washed first on the deck, rinsed, and in a wreath of foam, sat down next to Blade. The water level immediately surged up, covering Thomas' reach for the dagger he'd brought in with him. Charlie said, "At ease," as if knowing he'd be armed.

Blade gave him a baleful glance. Then, after a moment, he said, "How come, if I'm a good fifteen years younger than you, you've got twice the hair I have?"

Charles grinned wickedly. "Ronnie and good genes," he answered.

They laughed together, then sighed.

Finally, the DWP said, "We're going to have to do something about the nesters. They're using up valuable grazing land and runoff water."

"And?"

"And they're unclean. And they've chosen to stay that way, and outside our laws. We're walking a fine line here, just to stay alive, and they've chosen not to be a part of that commitment."

"Show me a death warrant for each one and I'll take them one at a time. But I won't stand by if you declare war on them. What about the ones who are born on the other side? They didn't choose that life."

"Then bring them back."

"Maybe I will." Thomas stroked his scarred brow. "One of them, or a creature of one of them, gave this to me. A token. Could have taken my head off, but didn't."

"I know."

"But do you know what it means?"

Charlie shook his head, spraying water like a wet dog. Thomas paused, watching him, then said, "I don't know what it means either. But I do know they could have killed me and didn't."

The DWP answered only, "If the plague starts in, we may not have any choice."

Thomas decided not to answer him. They sat in the immense wooden vat until the water chilled.

The wedding day dawned fiercely clear and clean. Thomas left his hat with Weber to be brushed and blocked, took his gelding, and went up into the scrub hills surrounding the settlement.

He spotted the sentries long before they gave any indication of sensing him. One got to his feet, grunted his intentions to the second and moved out of sight behind a stand of blooming red and white oleander. He ground-tied the horse and made his way around behind their position. A swift movement and the garrote was around the neck of the chunky woman nearest him. Her hands went up and he twisted the loop a touch.

"Down there," and he nodded to the manor house, "down there, they're having a party. Up here, you're working. You're supposed to make sure the people down there are safe while they're having a good time."

A necklace of tiny crimson beads welled up from the garrote. The woman husked, "Who?"

"Blade," he said. "And be glad it's me." He brought the guard to her knees with a bit more pressure. "Next time, neither of us could be so lucky."

Her hands had stayed at her neck, fingers rigid and coiled, not to free the loop but to jab at his eyes. It was the only correct thing she'd tried to do. With a grim smile, Blade twisted the loop a fraction more and left her kneeling, dazed and clawing at the garrote that was biting into her fleshy neck. It was a spare.

* * *

Veronica was livid when he returned. "Where have you been?" The air was filled with the whickering of horses and the creak of harness as carriages pulled into the procession.

"Checking on the security. The wind's about to change, Ronnie, and when it does, we all need to be ready." His gelding skittered sideways under him. "Where's Charlie? We're riding shotgun."

"Oh, no," she said firmly. "You're driving one of the guests." She watched him dismount, took him by the arm, and led him to a small VW cart.

The woman inside, young and blonde, full-cheeked and with a thickened waistline, smiled prettily at him. Her rouged cheeks pinked genuinely as he seated himself next to her and took up the reins. His muscular thigh brushed her fleshy one.

"Sir Thomas Blade," Veronica said formally, the hem of her dress of antiqued ivory lace in danger of being stepped on by his gelding. She reined him back. "This is Shellyann. I told her you'd escort her today." She gave the gelding a no-nonsense slap across the nose as he clicked his teeth at her sleeve and left them to their own devices.

The line of coaches pulled away and he turned his attention gratefully to the trail ahead, as he clucked to the mule team pulling them.

"Lord Protector," the woman repeated softly. "I'm Shellyann. Is it true what they say?"

There were two kinds of women, thought Thomas. Those who were repelled and a little frightened by what he did, and those who were excited.

The last thing he felt like was flirtatious conversation. He allowed a glance at his carriage mate. More of Veronica's matchmaking, no doubt. "That depends on what they say."

"Are you in the ruins often?"

That surprised him, a little. Most of them wanted to know if he was really an assassin and executioner.

"Sometimes, on the fringes. No one goes In-City. Rest assured, madame, I do not glow in the dark."

Shellyann blushed again. The heat of the sun overhead and the weight of her party dress made her face dewy with perspiration. She looked away, saying, "I hope to test that statement myself . . . later."

Thomas clucked to the mules. One of the children's carriages, a van made convertible, was directly in front of them. The children hung over its sides, scolding and crying out to him, individual words melding in a din of enthusiasm. He thought he spotted a sturdy blond toddler who waved with more vigor than the others. "Is he yours?"

"Why, yes, I—how did you know?"

"Your waistline, Veronica's intentions, and his obvious love for you. Where's his father?"

"Dead." Shellyann looked at him. "But I am proven a fertile woman."

"Indeed." Blade sank into his own thoughts then, and the woman, with an expression that said she'd been insulted, lapsed into silence as well.

The road wound like a serpent across the peninsula. Eucalyptus limbs waved beside the path's edges and shed their scented bark, gray-green leaves fluttering in the wind. The grass was golden, dry, awaiting the beginning of what passed for a rainy season. Soon they would be brown, brittle, and dangerous. Blade had often warned Charlie about living in the foothills because of brush fires, but it did no good. Just as Charlie's warnings to him to stay out of the borders were ignored by Blade.

A cry to the fore of the caravan rang back, and Blade pulled his team to a halt, right against the bumper of the chop-topped van holding the children. The blond leaned over and cried, "I love you, Mummy."

"I love you, too, dear," she called back. To Blade, she said anxiously, "What's the matter?"

He stood in the VW. Ahead, he could see the point riders pulling their rifles as their horses milled about restlessly. The road hairpinned down and around. Soon, they would be making the immense horseshoe turn that led past an enormous, ancient campus, and on to the sea bowls. He didn't like what he saw. The riders were too nervous. The scarf pulled at his throat. "I can't tell," he said, finally. "It could be javelinas or maybe coyotes."

"Or nothing."

Blade doubted that. Although his mule team was calm, the horses ahead were too nervous, their nostrils cupped wine-red against the wind. He looked down at Shellyann. "Can you drive?"

"Of course. If I have to."

"Good. You know who I am. You know what I may have to do."

She lowered her eyes. "Yes, Lord Protector."

Charlie came loping down the road on his half-Clydesdale gelding, the reins of a riderless horse in his hand. He stopped alongside the carriage. "Care to mount up, Thomas?"

Thomas stepped off the door frame and swung effortlessly aboard the black mare. He nodded to Shellyann. "May we meet again," he said.

The woman's bow-shaped mouth tightened as they rode off. Overhead, thin wisps of clouds moved across the sky in a high wind. But Blade sensed a change in the air. As he drew to the fore of the line with Charlie, he saw one of the point riders tap a vial into the hollow barrel of his rifle. He recognized the chemical.

His head snapped back toward Charlie. "No defoliants."

"Why not?"

"For god's sake, man, the peninsula is just getting back to normal. Would you contaminate what you've worked for all these years?"

Charlie sat his horse heavily, his jowls working. Then he turned to the guard and said, "Put it away, Castro."

"Something's in the tall grass, sir."

"Then we'll flush it out."

"The chemical's quicker." Castro sat, stiff-necked.

"And more harmful. Do as I say."

Sardonically, the guard said, "Yes, sir," and unloaded the vial carefully. His flat brown-eyed gaze swept across Blade in amusement. For a fleeting moment, Blade wished this man had been guarding up on the ridge instead of the woman. This one, Blade would have killed cheerfully without a second thought.

Wyethe rode up in his Protector's robes, his elbows flapping and the high, thin strands of his white hair blowing in the wind. The sun had reddened his pale face. He squinted nervously behind his glasses.

"What's happening?"

"You tell me," Blade said as he stretched in his stirrups, trying to gain a better view across the tall grass.

Wyethe said, "I d-d-don't like it."

Charles made a strangled noise at the back of his throat. He settled for waving his point riders into the grass. The arrogant sentry rode in first, his back straight as a ramrod.

A silence fell over the caravan, and over the broken road, and across the grassy field.

It was broken by a high-pitched squeal of anger and Castro pitched headfirst over his horse as the beast bolted in panic. A pack of wild pigs burst out of the undergrowth, ill-tempered and in a hurry.

The javelinas swept over him, squealing and grunting, their slotted feet and tusks tearing him to ribbons. He screamed once, tossed out of the grassy cover like a rag doll, but he was done for before Blade could reach him. In a wave of bristles and tusks, the beasts snorted and broke over the road, scattering riders on unnerved horses while the mule teams lifted their heads wisely and watched the javelinas disappear downhill into a gully.

Blade ground his palm onto the saddle horn. The rider, whoever he'd been, had been a lean and dangerous man. The javelinas had saved Thomas the trouble of doing something about him later. He watched the beasts grunting and disappearing into a gully.

Charlie steadied his pistol on his left wrist and fired, bringing down the boar at the rear. He signaled his guard. "Go get him, Stein. The wedding table can use some fresh meat."

His man nodded.

Wyethe shivered. Lady Nolan rode up then, on a mincing, cream-colored mule with one brown eye and one blue one, uncannily like those of his rider. She tilted her straw hat back. Wisps of light brown hair escaped as she did so. "What is it?" she asked.

"Javelinas. Gone now."

She wrinkled her nose slightly and looked at Blade with the blue eye. He had the eerie feeling she equally thoroughly examined Wyethe with the brown one. "We'd better get this procession underway. I don't like the barometric pressure."

"It's dropping?"

She nodded. "Rapidly."

Charles overheard and understood immediately. He waved the procession on. To Blade, he said, "What about Stein?"

"He can catch up with us. The carriages are slow enough."

The seven Protectors eventually grouped at the head of the caravan, each drawn by his or her Intuition. If they had lacked such Intuition, they would not be Protectors. Four were women. Three men, and two of them older, white-haired, or bald. Of the men, only Blade was virile and vigorous. Three of the women were young enough . . . but none of them really caught his eye.

And yet Blade understood more than most that it would be disastrous if he did not marry and procreate soon. And if it were with another Protector, so that their talents might be passed on, so much the better. Thomas flexed his neck and looked up at the blue sky.

It was not that he had not had his dalliances. It was only that his heart had never seemed too interested in what the rest of his body was doing. He found it highly ironic now that he was leading a marriage procession.

In two hours, they had reached the crest and were heading down its winding road to the immense leveled-off field before the sea bowls. Blade reined back. Blue sky had fled, pursued by gray. His ears registered the dropping pressure and he swallowed carefully to ease it. His scarf lay limply about his neck. The sky rumbled.

Lady Nolan let out a high cry, punctuated by, "Here it comes."

Charlie wheeled his horse. He gave a piercing whistle. "Head 'em in and get set up in the buildings! Hurry!"

Whips cracked. The mules broke into a run, their sleek pelts glistening with sweat and a patina of fine dirt. The carriages rocked unsteadily behind them. The children hung over the sides of their vans, whooping with excitement. The train of the bride's white lace dress streamed out a window. Blade watched Veronica gallop past, keeping pace, her face pale, for she knew the danger.

Wyethe muttered, "D-D-Denethan."

Lady Nolan fought her mule to a standstill as his stablemates went hurtling past. "Mindstorm," she said. It meant a storm of black panic and fear, driving strong men to irrational acts. For some paranormal reason, it would also create a turbulent weather front. Blade had seen strong winds and even rain accompany a sending from Denethan.

No one of them was strong enough to block Denethan. It would take all seven.

"Not here," Blade called. He spurred his black mare at the heel of the caravan, and followed it to the outbuildings of the sea bowl.

It had been built before. None of them were exactly sure if it had been for religious ceremonies or entertainment, but the massive park and aquarium structures had stood the test of time well. Inside, one of the restaurant's kitchens had already been cleaned and stocked for the wedding banquet.

As for the bowls themselves, the locks and equipment and pumps were complicated enough that they were no longer maintained, except for the very outermost pool, at the edge of the docks. Blade hadn't been there in almost a year. He liked to think the sea bowls had been constructed for religious purposes.

He reined the mare to a halt and touched her lathered neck. The beast minced a sidestep or two, as the other six joined him.

Charlie waited, on foot, poised as though he was seriously considering running away and joining his guests in the temporary safety of the building.

Lady Nolan looked at him. "Go inside, Charlie," she said softly. "We'll hold it off here as best we can. Get the wedding done." The rising wind tore her hat from her head, and only its ribbons tied about her throat held it.

"But I need at least one of you inside as a bodyguard."

"Charlie, if you can't trust your own guests, then we can't help you. We need all seven to stand against the storm . . . and even then, we might not be enough. You know that. Marry the children and send them off while we have a chance."

He couldn't meet her eyes—either of them—and turned away abruptly.

Blade dismounted and held Wyethe's mousy brown stallion as the Protector got down. The older man clamped his jaw tight against his fearful stuttering.

The sky blackened. Phosphorescent bolts stalked overhead, sizzling and striking at one another.

"Jesus," said Alderman. "When did he learn to do that?"

The plump, brown-skinned woman named Oletha muttered grimly, "He'll have our range soon."

"Clasp hands."

Blade's hand was squeezed tightly by Wyethe on one side and reassuringly by Lady Nolan on the other. He planted his booted feet firmly on the asphalt. His intuition sent his thoughts questing deep into the earth. Man sculpted creations of natural elements . . . he could feel the power and memory rooted in them. Blade felt the tiny bridges and interferences of synthetics. He had no power over or from synthetics. That was Denethan's strength, he'd been told. Blade gritted his teeth. His heart began to pound in involuntary reaction to the despair aimed at them.

The mindstorm broke. It lashed and battered at their minds, frizzling the synapses of their brains, short-circuiting their rationalities, searing their dreams. He felt Wyethe's palm go sweaty.

The air crackled. He smelled ozone. He shut his eyes against the intensity, but the blues and greens of the lightning burned through his lids.

Lady Nolan said tightly, "Let it go no farther than us." Each slow word was paced by a hard-fought determination to speak.

They made a shield against the sea bowls. The storm whirled and funneled down at them, at their very toes, lashing across the broken parking field. Chunks of asphalt exploded and flew off into nothingness. Stalking men, stick figures of lightning, ranged about them.

Blade realized that Denethan would kill them all to get to the children. Sweat dripped down his forehead and cut a path over his taut face.

Alderman went to his knees, slack in the lineup of Protectors, his bald pate crimson with the sudden pounding of his blood pressure.

Power speared Blade. From the blackened sky, a funnel dropped and began to twirl its deadly way toward them, the field and lot churning at its base. On its heels came the roar of a power mightier than anything he'd ever felt before. He dropped hands instinctively and stepped forward.

Lady Nolan let out a tiny cry of fear.

Blade looked into the storm. He unwound it in his

mind, feeling the fury of it and trying to send it streaming away from them. He held up his left hand and then, in defiance that smacked across the field, slammed his right fist into his palm. "Storm break!"

He had broken the line. The Protectors at his back might not stand without him. He most certainly couldn't stand alone against Denethan. But he threw his chin up. Overhead, the clouds boiled. Patches of blue broke through, and his scarf bannered from his neck.

"Thomas! Come back! He's too strong!"

Thomas grinned. He stood rooted in his elements. The enemy had parapsychology and he did, too, and more, he had the witchery of his elements, his time, behind him. He felt the storm give and then the fear drain as though he stood alone, a lightning rod that grounded Denethan's hatred. He stretched his hands up and felt the last vestige of his intuition crackle outward, smashing the black funnel whirling toward him.

Oletha gave a cry and fainted dead away.

Charlie held up a punch glass. "To the Protectors!"

The hall rang with the toast. Blade felt himself blush beneath his weathered tan and was glad that few would be able to discern it. Lady Nolan, recovered from the outlay of psychic energy, arched the eyebrow over her brown eye.

"Modesty, Thomas?"

"I know, it ill becomes me." Thomas stood uncomfortably in the banquet hall. Veronica had taken his hat and he felt overexposed. He nodded toward the children, who stood shyly, their hands clasped, surrounded by adults and watched at a distance by their friends, separated for all time by a ritual they scarcely understood. "I think I'll wander around for a while. I'm not needed here anymore."

Nolan placed a hand on his arm. "Be careful," she said. "You have no reserves left."

The corner of his mouth quirked. "Neither does Denethan at the moment, if we're lucky."

"An assassin doesn't rely on Intuition," she said. She sniffed. "Now I've mothered you enough. Go on."

It was late afternoon when Blade stepped out into the sunlight. A cold wind smelling of sea and fog blew up the hill. It was the scent of the sea that drew him.

One of the secondary sea bowls had been filled. Thomas approached it cautiously, by way of the tunnel of the amphitheater. He ran a hand through its salted water.

The water was bitter and acidic. It stung his hand and he drew it out quickly. Nothing of the Pacific could live long in this water. One of the pumps, perhaps, was fouling the chemical mix. He passed that bowl by and went down to the grand one, the one that opened onto the Pacific itself. He stepped back and sat on a concrete and aluminum step. The aluminum was corroded and pitted. It dug at the smooth denim of his jeans.

He watched the sea bowl. It had a movement and life all its own. He'd spent one summer exploring the area and knew that down below was a huge window through which the secrets of the sea pool could be seen. But if he went down below, then he couldn't watch the surface up here.

And, he told himself, *nothing swam there anyhow.* He knew. He reached up and gently unwound the long white scarf from about his neck.

His gills sprang pulsing to attention.

He was tired. His Intuition had been drained away to return when it would, a fickle thing, like that of most Protectors, but better than having nothing. He sat, his hands loosely resting on his knees, staring into the hypnotic flow of the water.

Like a bright lance, the last glow of the sun off the water blinded him. Thomas sat up straight. He wondered how long he'd been sitting in the stands. *Long enough,* he thought, and stood.

A star danced on the brow of the water. It drew him. Blade wandered down the asphalt pathway to the water's edge where the water gate was open. Whatever creatures of the sea were once penned here had long ago been freed. Three summers ago he'd stood here and had been privileged to see a wild porpoise swim in, circle, and then swim out.

He anchored himself at the sea bowl's edge, scarf fluttering forgotten from his left hand. The star was the sun's reflection in the mirror of the water, the water that called to him now. His gills feathered in the salty wind. He breathed deeply, using them as they had been intended.

Blade shivered. *Why not?* he thought. He shed his jacket, kicked his boots off and dove in.

As he came up, the setting sun lit the water with fire, its rays shattered into a million hard diamonds bobbing on the surface. He sputtered—the Pacific was cold this time of year. He treaded water for a moment, his eyes dazzled.

And then he saw what had broken water in front of him, had come swimming through the sea gate and into the bowl, and was now watching him.

She was three times his size, nearly twice that of any dolphin or porpoise he'd ever seen. Her skin was azure blue and turquoise. The water sheeted off her like a gossamer veil as she tail-walked toward him. Blade had no doubt he was viewing a goddess. He held a hand up and she dove, spraying him with foam, and then arced up from below him, her hide grazing his hand as she surfaced.

They swam in tandem, dancing, he and the dolphin goddess. When she dove below, taking him with her, the salt water tanged through his gills and he wondered if he would live long enough to swim with her, embraced in her fins. But, unafraid, he sank in the dark sparkling water, whirling and twirling to the rhythm of her desires. When at last they gained the surface again, Blade broke into the air, gasping and gulping with exhilaration.

The dolphin smiled at him. She opened her jaw and took his hand in it gently, and bit down, her sharp teeth making a pattern of crimson diamonds down the back of his skin. The salt water stung in it. Blade shuddered as she let him go, knowing he'd been marked for the dolphin's own as surely as if he had been tattooed or branded.

A last whirl in the iridescent water, then she looked at him with an ancient wisdom, leaped the sea gate, and was gone.

Blade floated weakly in the water. He touched the chevron mark over his brow with a limp hand. He'd been marked for the second time. It was a mysticism, a spirituality he had not yet reached.

He swam to the concrete lip of the pool and pulled himself out.

Chapter 3

"To the newlyweds!" Charles said. His voice rang out gruffly over the muffled noise of merrymakers, but enough of them heard him that they echoed the toast.

Blade stood inside the restaurant archway, a blanket that smelled faintly of dog and mule thrown over his shoulders to dry him. He shrugged into it. Shock and giggles had greeted his wet condition.

From a shadowy corner to his right, he heard a whisper. "A jealous husband threw him in. Can you imagine? He just got here yesterday."

He turned an inquiring face toward the corner and the whispering stopped. "And so legends beget legends," he said wryly and strode into the main hall, ignoring the silence that followed him.

Charles captured him with a beefy arm. "Thank you, Thomas. That was nice."

"What was?"

" 'And so legends beget legends,' " Charles quoted. "An apt followup to my toast. I won't tell you what I heard about you falling in. Still wet?"

"Not quite. And I won't tell you what I saw when I jumped in." Irritated, Blade looked around for more interesting and infinitely more sober company.

But something in Blade's manner pierced Charles. He straightened up and set his champagne glass down. "The kids won't leave for a few minutes. I've got time. Come with me, and tell me what you saw."

In a quiet corner booth of the restaurant, Charles snagged Blade a cognac snifter off a passing tray and forced it into his hands. "I'm not as drunk as I appear," he said. "Nor you as foolish. I can't believe you decided to take a dive. What happened? Rumor has it you lost a fight with a jealous husband."

Thomas had replaced his white scarf. It rubbed over the delicate, sensitive edges of his gills as he turned his head and looked harshly at Charles. "I was alone, and I jumped. Maybe you've forgotten why we went back to the sea and what we owe it."

Charles sat back. His fleshy neck overflowed the neckline of the tuxedo and his scars flushed purple. "I haven't forgotten," he said haltingly. He rubbed his neck. "What did you see?"

"A dolphin as big as an orca. Incredible. She came in from the open sea, over the sea gate . . . she danced for me. Then she marked me." Almost shyly, Thomas laid his hand and wrist down on the tabletop for Charles to see. The toothmarks had dried, crusted blood on them, but the pattern to come could be seen. "Have you ever heard of anything like that?"

Charles sucked in his breath and shook his head. "Never." He commandeered the untouched cognac snifter. "Maybe it's better not to ask questions."

He quaffed the cognac and jumped slightly as a young voice interrupted, "Daddy . . . it's time."

Jennifer withdrew her hand from her father's shoulder. She looked a little flushed, and the hem of her wedding dress had been grayed by dragging it on the floor while she danced. She stared at Thomas with wide gray-blue eyes, and blushed.

"Jenny! Yes, of course." Charles got to his feet much quicker than his bulk and inebriation should have allowed. "Come on, Thomas."

The restaurant crowd pushed outside. Charles went to a canvas-draped shape on the parking lot and, with a snap of his wrist, uncovered the paralight sitting on the asphalt. It was a gleaming antique relic from days of old and looked hardly big enough to hold two teenagers.

Thomas sucked in his breath. "Charlie, the wind raiders—"

"Come on. Denethan's already had his try at us. You broke the mindstorm. He won't be able to muster up anything else for days."

Blade looked at his old friend. "You knew that. You counted on that, didn't you? Even if you had to sacrifice the seven of us." At Charles' back, Lady Nolan swayed, and she looked at Thomas with outrage.

"Grow up. We do what we have to. Anyway, the sun's going down. Ramos has been piloting for several years. Even I won't know where he's taking her."

Veronica had steered Jennifer out into the evening, and she stood, her hands showing elegant knuckles as she gripped her daughter's shoulders tightly. She kissed Jennifer. "You remember what I told you."

"I will, Momma. Don't worry." Jenny hugged her mother vigorously. "We'll be back soon."

He felt a little out of balance as the rush of Intuition flooding him made his ears pound.

"With children," dark Ramos said. He grinned suddenly. "Like puppies!"

"God, let's hope not," Wyethe muttered. He stood on his toes. "Let's get this thing in the air." His fine white hair fluttered about his ears.

The wedding guests stood on the edge of the broken field as the paralight buzzed into motion and sped down the lot. It lifted easily, wafting into the sunset.

Thomas blinked as the frail aircraft banked and headed north, up the coast. He knew the boy wouldn't fly much farther at night and that the fuel wouldn't let him get more than three or four days by horseback anyway. From there, they'd travel on foot to whatever sanctuary Charlie had found for them. He'd seen the packs on the floor of the aircraft.

Charles stood, his head craned back, as he watched the circling paralight. Jennifer's white wedding dress came floating out of the sky like a cloud and settled among them, to shocked gasps and a few titters. He smiled grimly as Veronica gathered up the dress and crushed it to her bosom. "Let's hope Ramos can steer by the stars like we taught him," he said to nobody in particular. "Come on, everybody! We've food and drink to finish off!"

At the door, Blade caught Charles by the elbow. "I'm leaving."

"So soon?"

He nodded. "You don't need me anymore. I'll take the black mare—she's fresher. You keep my gelding till I come by again."

"All right." Charles hesitated, then reached out and grabbed Thomas in an immense bear hug. "They'll be all right, won't they?"

"I'm sure they will," Blade answered. He knew then that Charles knew he was going to follow them, as far as he could, to ensure their safety. This was what his old friend had really wanted of him, and known he could not ask. For a Lord Protector to leave his county for the needs of a few, weighed against the needs of many, could not be asked. But it could be volunteered. Still, Thomas said nothing. It was better Charles not have his guesses confirmed if Denethan came hunting answers.

Chapter 4

From the look of it, the wedding reception was doomed to hang on all night and into the wee hours of the morning. That would make it more difficult for Thomas to evade the lovely thighs of Shellyann and leave the party unnoticed unless he left right now. Which was fine with Blade, for he wanted to stay as close on the trail of the paralight as possible. Charles followed him to the outbuilding being used for stabling where Blade ran his hand over his packs and discovered Charlie had brought along everything he might need to follow Jennifer and Ramos. There was even a crinkly bag of lemon drops. He said nothing about having been shamefully manipulated as he took the black mare's reins and led her outside, his friend at his heels.

They faced each other awkwardly in the twilight, the warmth of Charles' bear hug already stolen away by the wind off the ocean.

Blade wrapped his white scarf closer about his neck and ran his fingers about the collar of his jacket. The movement reassured him that he still had his three garrotes and two shuriken in place. Then he said, "I don't want to be seen following after. Pull your sentries in or make sure they're looking in the other direction." He would leave no witnesses behind to testify that he, the Lord Protector, had abandoned his post.

Charlie, however, took things in hand by summoning Wyethe and Alderman. When the two Protectors stumbled out of the building holding each other up and congratulating Charles on a splendid party, he interrupted brusquely, "Veronica says she's worried. I want to be sure Denethan can't bring in his wind raiders."

Alderman's shining head glowed with an alcoholic flush. His job presumably finished for the day, he hadn't stinted in partaking of the celebration. He stammered, "Projection. You want a Projection . . . Wyethe, I can't think!" The two men leaned against each other in confusion.

Thomas dug down in his pocket. His hand emerged wrapped about a smooth gray stone, a beach pebble ground down by sand and tide. He dropped the object into Alderman's palm. A spark arced between his hand and the other Protector's. "Here," Thomas said. "Use my pebble. Cast up a fog."

"Thank you, Blade," the old man got out. He made a fist about the pebble as though to keep its potency from leaking out. He and Wyethe strode shoulder to shoulder down the slope of landscaping toward the sea bowls, where it would be easiest to Project a low coastal fog. Blade watched them go, knowing theirs would have been illusion but now, based on his pebble and power, it would be real.

Veronica had been on edge all afternoon and he wondered fleetingly if it was due to more than hosting the wedding and giving her only daughter in marriage at such a young age. Ronnie's sharp blue eyes occasionally saw more than was visible to others. He caught Charlie's elbow as the DWP took a lumbering step after his weathermen.

"Where's Ronnie?"

"Inside, with the others. Leave her alone, Thomas, please. She won't tell you anything. This is just . . . a precaution. And it will give you better cover to leave." Charles put out his great, callused hand. "We'll be sitting down to council tomorrow. We'll come up with a workable plan for the nesters, but I won't do anything until you get back."

They locked grips. "I can't thank you enough—" the burly man began, and his voice choked to a halt.

"Then don't. I'll take extra water shares." Thomas loosened his friend's hand, took the mare's reins and swung up as the first wisps of fog began to creep up the slope. He shrugged into the collar of his leather jacket, felt the silken wrap of his scarf bunch up comfortingly, and did not look back even as Charles yelled, "Good luck, Thomas. The mare's called Cindy."

The mist shrouded the peninsula completely by the time he reined the mare to a stop on the low crest overlooking the massive trail which led north up the coast and bordered the disaster-pocked basin. It hid fields he had not seen in a decade, and he didn't know if he could bear to look upon them now, assuming fog did not hug them in its obscuring embrace.

No more defoliant, he'd said. *The land was just recovering,* and Charles had ordered the vials put away. Unconsciously, Blade patted his jacket, feeling the inside pockets lined with similar vials.

But Thomas felt no guilt as he looked the area over now. *A single man was not a bad trade,* he thought. He'd seen these fields burning, plowed with the bone shards of the dead, ten years ago, in the last great battle against Denethan, before both sides had downscaled to hit and run raids, the cost of out-and-out war being too great.

His fingers twitched about the reins. He could ride around, far around, out of his way, but the night would have brought the paralight down, somewhere close to Zuma Beach, he guessed, and the fog would both hide the children and keep them there for the several days it would take him to catch up. There were ruins beckoning to him from the other side of the highway. He eyed them warily. Without his gauges they could be death traps for him as as they'd been for those who had died within the area during the Disasters.

The mare stomped uneasily, as if reading his own edginess, then stepped out across the field, her legs pushing the mist into swirls of gray as she took the short way across in answer to Blade's desire. He gave her her head, even as the mists coalesced around them and his curse came to life.

There was a borderline between parapsychology and witchery, a border which no man he had ever known could cross, save himself. He knew of no one else who could cast a fog with a painstakingly charmed pebble or who could see what haunted him now.

Never look at a ghost directly, his old mentor had told him. Gillander had trained him well to follow in his footsteps as a Lord Protector. Neither of them had figured the teacher would not be around to see his pupil succeed him. Perhaps Cindy saw the ghost as Blade did, for her ears pricked, then flattened, but the squeeze of Blade's legs about her barrel kept her to an easy trot, as he did not look at the apparition, but to the left of it, so that it could approach his right brain sensitivity as he'd been taught.

But he'd also learned never to meet a ghost on its own ground if he could help it, and drew the phantasm with them to where the fields leveled off and the broken edge of asphalt bordered them. He fought the mare to a stop and kept her curbed against shying as the manifestation caught up with him, its image in his peripheral vision.

The corner of his vision shimmered as if caught in a teardrop. Through it, he saw the mists gather and solidify until a rawboned man stood there, one shoulder hunched against a wind that did not blow in Thomas' twilight. He had no colors but white and gray and darkness and was difficult to see against the road. But he was there. No doubt of it.

His trousers bagged at the knees, and the frayed cuffs of the jacket were rolled back, and Blade could even see the stretched-out elastic suspenders underneath the jacket. Gillander, he recalled suddenly, had been a ruin crawler, too, and the elastic suspenders were a proud relic of a hazardous trip. They could no longer make elastic. Gillander was not bald, but his hairline had receded perilously far, and his colorless hair stood in a thatch as though he'd just run his fingers through it.

The ghost pointed a finger at him. Almost simultaneously, Thomas' skin prickled. The black mare shivered under him.

"Made me run hard enough to keep up with you."

"You could have stayed resting," Blade answered mildly.

"With you about, treading on my bones? Hardly. I've waited a long time to catch you riding by. How long has it been?"

"Ten years, give or take a few weeks."

The ghost mumbled a bit. Its image wavered, then flared into substance and color. "Look at me," it ordered.

"And be caught by you? Gill, you taught me better."

"I hadn't time to teach you everything. Who's Lord Protector in my place? You?"

Blade didn't answer. His mare pivoted suddenly, bringing his line of sight straight into those intense gray-green eyes of the ghost. Having met the calamity, he would not flinch from it. He stared until the phantasm gave, blinked, looked away. Not until then would Thomas acknowledge the patch of skin on the back of his neck that had gone ice cold, and the beads of sweat under the band of his hat.

"You are strong," Gillander said, and it was his voice that remained insubstantial. "You'll have to be."

"I know."

"What's it been like?"

"Since you've gone?" Thomas considered the ghost's question. He answered slowly, "Heaven and hell. We prosper, we dwindle. And the mutant keeps his distance, but harries at us."

"Do they know what to do with you?"

"I guess," Thomas answered flatly. "They made me executioner."

"Hah! Figures. They could never see beyond. Projections, Truth-reading, Thought-influence or Blocking, a little Precognition. What you can do, my boy, goes beyond that."

"Sometimes."

Gillander shrugged. "That's as may be. The sixth sense is a tricky one, and magic even shyer. How about water?"

"Some. Charles is working on an answer to that."

The ghost rubbed its forearms as though cold. "The ground is dry," it said. "My bones are brittle. This is a poor place you left me."

The tone of the apparition's voice bored through Thomas. He had not left Gill to die, he'd been driven off. But it was futile to argue with the dead. Thomas had much that Gillander's phantasm coveted.

The ghost sensed a lack of sympathy. It shrugged, pointing out a track across the ruins. "Are you going In-City tonight?"

"Perhaps. I haven't been here in a long time."

Gillander's thrice-broken nose twitched. "No wolfrats out yet. You might have some luck, Thomas. Be careful you don't catch more than you bargained for. You're being followed."

"I know," Thomas said levelly to the first and then reacted speechlessly to the last, touching his heels to Cindy's flanks, whirling her, but seeing nothing in the night.

The after-essence of his aged mentor was smiling when Thomas turned back, the black mare quivering between his suddenly tense calves. "You," Blade said harshly, "are only a retention of my memories. Wishful thinking. I'm tired of you."

Gillander shook his head. "Sorry, boy. I'm more than that. A manifestation of your curse, if you will. I no more wanted to be drawn up than you wished to be haunted. But here it is. Work with it or not, as you will." The ghost sat, Indian-style, upon the ground. Fog hissed and disappeared as though boiled out of existence.

"Who's following me?"

Patchy eyebrows raised. "Now you confuse me with Omnipotence. That I don't know, and you have a bit of time left. Spend it with me?"

"Do I have to cross your palms with silver?"

Gillander chuckled. "It would be difficult to try. Drop rein and sit with me, my boy."

Blade felt as though he had an iron bar frozen against his spine. The invitation went counter to every ounce of common sense he had. With a swiftness of movement as though cutting himself loose, he swung his leg over and dismounted. Cindy put her muzzle up and rolled her eyes, the whites showing, but stayed put in a ground-tie, as promised.

Thomas sat also. He reached out and his hand passed through the frayed cuffs and spindly forearms. He had expected it, but he had not expected the icy chill that accompanied the action.

Gillander put his hands out, palms facing. Thomas mimicked the action, his hands moving until almost, but not quite touching. As the warmth of his body touched the icy barrier of death, his aura flared out, and a corona of blue fire ringed the four hands.

"I have to move and move fast. The night Denethan attacked and you saved the perimeter—you moved time. I want to know how. Now tell me," Blade said, "and tell me true, or I'll find a way to rip the guts out of you as surely as I would Denethan's."

The ghost grinned.

Chapter 5

The sight of Gillander's bared teeth almost changed Thomas' mind. He shrugged mentally, and let his breathing even out and his thoughts shift into a more receptive mode. He felt his gills flare, prickling against the scarf. The auras of their nearly touching palms became clearer, more sharply defined.

"What do you wish me to tell you first?" the ghost asked mildly.

"Whatever you would have me know, Gill." Thomas bit back his sharper, more urgent needs.

"Then I would tell you that a Protector never, ever, leaves his territory. You are tied to it. Your energies are rooted there."

A sharp pebble under one lean hip ground at Blade. He nodded in answer to the ghost. "I know."

"Then you may not realize this. You're a naturalist, my boy. Your energies are grounded, bled out by artificial things. You feel it without realizing it—that's why the ruins excite you. There you're as blind as any man, walking the edge, and your blood runs hotter, knowing the danger."

His head shook in denial, an independent movement that Thomas had not ordered.

A whuff of disapproval as the other's aura flared, orange-red, against his hands. "The more fool you."

Blade felt his gaze narrow despite his attempt to stay aloof yet receptive. "I'm an enforcer as well as a Protector," he said sharply. "My skills in that domain move with me."

"A murderer." The ghost sighed. The scent of his breath, faintly foul, drifted past Thomas' face. "Not what I would have taught you if I had had the time."

"Then teach me now."

"Impossible!" Gillander clucked his tongue over his teeth, making a sound as physical as if he still existed in flesh and blood, bone and ivory. "Still . . . what are you doing tromping on my deathbed?"

"Trailing."

"Someone important, I gather. Most important if you want to know how I moved time itself."

Blade said nothing. The ghost reared up high, elongating itself in the torso until it towered above his body. He did not even look up, forcing Gillander to shrink back in order to meet his eyes.

"For god's sake," his old mentor sputtered. "Do you think I would tell your secrets even now? To whom? I hate Denethan more than ever. Out there, on that hillside, my bones rub cartilage of his folk . . . my flesh decayed next to their scales. I smell the stink of their wrongness. They are not even human!"

Thomas relented. He said only, "I'm following hope."

The night grew very chill about them, though the fog from the coast gave them a wide berth and hesitated even to cross the broken road track Blade could see clearly through Gillander's opaque form.

"Saaa," murmured the old man. "Babes. Charles found his genetic pair. I knew we were close . . . and he's sent them away to hide them. How are they traveling, Thomas? Did you brew up this mist? It stinks of the sea."

"No." He felt his face twist in a smile. "Wyethe and Alderman."

"Ha! I'd like to give those two old farts an ache in their joints for that." Gillander wavered a little. Red flames came to life in his eyes, then died out. "But I interrupted you, boy."

"I'm trailing a paralight."

"It'll be beached, then. Just enough range to get them away from Denethan's gliders, probably." Gillander sucked hollow teeth in thought.

"Yes."

"How many riders?"

"Just two."

The flame points winked up again. "You'll never keep up by horseback. That contraption travels as far in an hour as you can in a day."

"There's a lot of fog this time of year," Thomas answered noncommittally.

"You'll need more than fog to keep out of Denethan's way. Ah. Now I know why you palaver with ghosts. Do I hear Denethan following? No. But I have no ears for wind raiders . . . I can only hear what strikes the ground. Hoofbeats. Yours and those of that other who follows you. Perhaps I'm wrong. Perhaps fog will stand you better than I thought. Although . . ." and Gillander's reedy voice hung on the word.

Blade's attention wandered. The ghost seemed mainly lonely despite Thomas' original hopes for real information. The broken cityscape beckoned. Under slabs of concrete and rusted wire forms stabbing the night like lethal spears lay the secrets of a dead city. And despite what Gillander had offered earlier, wolfrats were running across the horizon. He saw the flashes of their red eyes, tiny pinpricks of rodent hunger, as they loped across concrete canyons. A coyote yipped once sharply, as if in defiance, but even a coyote did not dare the ruins alone when the wolfrats were out.

The ghost noticed what drew his gaze. "The ruins make you itch, don't they? You were always as curious as a catling, Thomas." At the sound of his name, Blade looked back, caught by the power of the ghost's voice. "Want me to keep on teaching you? Then I offer you the thing you want. That's right, my boy. Listen to me well."

Sparks rippled about the corona of their upheld hands. They broke off and drifted away, fireflylike, until they hissed out as they reached the curling edges of the mist.

"You want to trail without being seen, keep up with the wind, and learn the secrets of the land. I can give you the ghost road, boy. My gift to you—an' my curse, too. But when you take the ghost road, power changes. You don't need to worry or wonder about paralights or wind raiders."

Blade's legs had gone numb. "Ghost road?" he repeated.

"That's right. You want it, don't you? I can tell."

He wanted nothing like it, knew nothing of it to know if he needed it or not, but he'd given Gillander too much of his trust and now the phantasm had him, gripped his being tightly between psychic teeth.

"It'll take you where you want to go, and when, and even a few places you don't! You've got to be careful. The resonances will be able to find you there—you'll be open to 'em, Thomas. I can't protect you from that—I'm a resonance myself. You'll be walking the bones of the dead, boy, drawing up their hatred and their joy and their fear to fuel you. It's a tough road to walk. You lose yourself, bit by bit. And there are things, Thomas, which transcend our normal dimensions and can find you on the ghost road. Pure evil, most like, though a good un gets through now and then. It'll kill you if you walk it too long, and twist and turn you long before that. Walk it too long, and you'll be one of the primeval ones, and the only fuel you can draw on is the hate and fear."

Thomas started thinking about the shuriken in his left cuff, the special one, made of cast iron, guaranteed to ground any vibration. Warrantied to drain away ghosts, a lightning rod for the supernatural. The blue-orange corona of their hands trembled as his fingers twitched. Gillander clucked again as if he read Blade's thought.

"Not nice. But you need a trial, I know. A lessoning. Walk tonight, Thomas, on the ghost road. The wolfrats won't even scent you. But watch your back, because the ghosts will."

The corona flared suddenly, arcing out until his eyes watered from the glare and he shut them tight, tears leaking under his lids, the flare blasting through his eyelids which bled red from the inside. Then it got dark and very quiet.

Thomas woke still and cold, legs aching from being folded under him. His eyes were crusty and he rubbed them gently, feeling the grit sting as he buffed it away with cautious fingertips. The ground was dank. The fog had gone, and the black mare grazed on scattered tufts of grass. Moonlight swayed overhead as he got to his feet, staggering like an arthritic old man. Lady Nolan had warned him about psychic backlash, and he'd just had a doozy of one, glad that it had been confined to hallucination. One booted foot was still numb and he stamped, trying to wake it into pins and needles. He tramped on something, caught it in the air as it flew toward his face, and opened his hand to look at it.

Your key, Thomas, to the ghost road.

A bleached-out skeletal finger rested in the palm of his hand. The bones of the little finger, misshapen through natural propensity—a crooked finger. A memory flashed through Thomas of Gillander matching hands with him, and the mentor's crooked small finger.

"For shrewdness, my boy," the spindly teacher had told him when they'd both been younger and Gill still alive. He had visions of Gillander clutching the dowsing rods, crooked little finger stuck out stubbornly from his right hand and framed by his worn sleeve cuff.

Of all the finger bones buried on this war field, how many would be crooked? He did not feel like calculating the odds. It did not matter. He knew whose bones he had. He could feel them radiating the hate and despair of matter bereft of soul and consigned to decay in the earth.

Thomas clenched his hand about the gift. He slipped the finger bones inside his jacket where they rattled next to a vial of poison. With a slap to the grazing mare's neck, he warded her quickly with a few mesquite twigs and left her there within a triangle of protection. His numbed foot quickly came to life as he jumped the broken track and made his way down into the fringe of wreckage, willing to sacrifice some time exploring the ghost road in the hope of finding something to use against Denethan and his minions.

Light was always the problem in the ruins and being on the ghost road didn't change that. The best finds were underneath, below concrete slabs that might shift weight even as he sidled below into caverns of darkness that held stillness and death. Thomas disliked the inconvenience of carrying a lantern or torch, but he had little choice if he wanted to see what he might unearth. He swung underneath a jaw of concrete and dropped into the darkness, scattering a wolfrat's nest as he hit. It was empty and its stench burst cloudlike about him. He choked as he kicked free.

A tangled square of metal tried to bite into his ankle, He picked it up. The makeshift torch illuminated painted letters: E R NCH ARMS. Time and erosion had made the rest illegible. This building was likely to have been a dwelling, then, rather than a place of business. Thomas liked dwellings though he found most of their contents incomprehensible, ground to dust, and what had survived that, undecipherable. He dropped the crumpled sign and moved farther into the ruin.

The building had been thoroughly looted already. The stalls held little but rusty scraps of the cars stripped apart here, though the concrete still retained oil and grease spots, soaked into the cement. Signs of ransacking were everywhere amid the spoor of wolfrats which littered the garage flooring. He had a little time if he was cautious—the giant rodents would not be hunting here in their own warren. They would be coursing above—but would soon return, and if they came back hungry, his future held dire portents. Thomas raised his torch a little higher. The pillars bore the signatures of the gangs who had reigned here. Thomas scratched his chin. Before or after the demise of the building?

He fingered one of the markings as he passed it. The paint was still slick, viable, the signature meant to last the test of time. Charlie had an archivist who could probably read it, but the paint had long outlasted the regime of the signer.

Even here, in the bottom of the building, Thomas could see layers of life. What had happened here, just to this one building? Had it been in decline or had it been brought down by one of the Disasters?

Before Thomas could search further, he heard the click-click of nails trotting along the concrete. Torchlight reflected in beady slants of crimson as the wolfrats returned to their tunnels.

As big or bigger than a coyote, the rodents trotted along their hunting grounds, scaled tails sliding behind them. Thomas froze, then reached for his shuriken and tossed it, hoping to bring down at least one of the rodents before they charged him.

With a whisper like the wind, the shuriken sank deep into the rodent's body. It keeled over with a shriek. Thomas sucked his breath in. How could he affect them from another dimension—and how vulnerable was he to the hunters? The pack halted uneasily and cast about, their rodent teeth showing like sabers as their lips curled back. They milled about yet could not see him though he stood less than ten feet away and their stink nearly choked him. Crimson beams flickered toward him. They sensed him, he knew they did, and he knew Gillander had lied to him about this. Part of the trial, he supposed. He put his hand inside his vest and cupped the bone. He sifted through its anger and dismay until he found a flicker of hope and drew on that.

The hair rose on the back of Thomas' neck. He dropped his torch and stamped it out, as the flame seemed to draw the rats' attention, and the glowing eyes blinked, shuttering him away from their sight. Then the death squeals of their wounded companion grew louder as a packmate decided to feed. In a frenzy, the pack turned on its own and tore it limb from limb.

He did not know if he was grateful or had merely lost his mind. And he did not know if he had the strength to walk on the bones of the dead.

Denethan awoke from his nap as the moon rose and saw his men seated around the fires, drinking beer and fermented asses' milk. They looked as one to him when the firelight illuminated his profile. He could see that they had worked diligently even during his rest . . . catapult towers lay ready to be installed, to launch wind raiders soaring off the cliffs.

Their whispers hushed, so that they could hear him speak.

"I have failed," he said. "But my powers have shown that this war will be won by warriors, and we are all warriors here!"

They shouted in agreement.

Their noise pleased him.

"We are not less than the wind in the desert."

"No!" they answered him.

"We are not less than the sand on the beaches."

"No!"

"And we are not less than men!"

"No! No! No!"

Denethan raised his palms. They quieted. "You've sworn blood oath to this raid. We all know that many of us here will not return. Take care, even so. My powers tell me that the plague is about. Take no prisoners except the children. And take pride in what we are about to accomplish!"

They jumped to their feet and their cries echoed. Denethan bowed his head and returned to his tent. The night air chilled him, and he was weary. The Protectors had grown much stronger than he'd expected. They had turned aside his Projection and one . . . yes, one had even been mighty enough to take up his thought and create new strength. He vowed they would not prove strong enough to stop him.

The black mare sensed Thomas as he crossed the broken track, and she put her head up with an inquiring whicker. The moon appeared to be no lower in the sky as he kicked apart the mesquite twigs forming a ward on the horse, and picked them up to return to his pack to be used again. As he slipped the twigs in and fastened the flap down, he paused in thought. Had time actually stopped while he was on the ghost road?

"How did you like the ghost road, my boy?" a reedy voice inquired at his back.

"You're not there," Thomas said without turning. "You're the product of psychic burnout."

"You're angry with me."

"You lied to me! I brought down a wolfrat."

"Just a tiny one. So I misled you. I'm a ghost, after all, and jealous of the life and spirit which animates you, no matter how much I loved you in life. Remember your lessons. Use the bones I left you. When and if you wish to travel the ghost road, meditate on them. Do what I showed you. Just remember—the ghosts can reach you. They'll leech the life out of you, if they can. But you're a smart boy, and quick, too. Oh, and remember that time is like the snake swallowing itself. There is no time for you on the ghost road, but you are dying with every step you take."

Thomas turned then, and saw the wispy, amorphous form of Gillander drifting next to him. "Nice," he said. "How long do I get?"

"I don't know. I've never had to worry about it before." His mentor smiled. "So don't push it, Thomas."

"Right." Thomas turned back to the mare and swung up.

The ghost trotted to keep up. "Leaving so soon?"

"Thought I might," the executioner said. "We both agree I'm being followed." He paused, then added, "Thanks, Gill. And rest in peace."

"I'll try," the ghost shouted after him.

Brush along the ridge crackled as Thomas crept along it and then lowered himself into position. He could hear the sound of hoofbeats drawing near. Only a fool rode in the dark—or someone desperate to catch up with him.

He fingered his throwing star. The night flared with the heat of the trailing horse. He could hear its lusty breath and the creak of leather. When it got close enough to smell, it would be within striking distance. Thomas tensed.

His nostrils filled with the stink of horse and lather and he rose from the brush, his arm going back in a smooth motion.

The wall-eyed mule half-reared in startlement, and the woman on its back pitched head over heels to the ground.

Chapter 6

She was too busy falling to kill him and for that Thomas was grateful. Unable to stop the release of the throwing star, he gave an extra twist with his wrist, sending the shuriken off its target by mere inches. As it soared into the night, the mule came to ground and stood protectively over its mistress.

Lady Nolan rolled to her side, gasping for air. In a moment, her face reddened and she got out, "Shit. And I was worried about you."

Thomas moved then, knowing she'd identified him and he was no longer a target for retaliation. He lifted her to her feet. "Are you all right?"

"No thanks to you." She rubbed one buttock.

"What are you doing out here?"

She looked at him in the dusky moonlight, her blue eye paled to silver. "Nice reception."

"I lost my best shuriken because of you," he pointed out, "and you wouldn't have been too hospitable to me if you hadn't been in midair."

"Perhaps." Her slender hands went back and she retied the traveling scarf that held back her hair. "However, I was following you. Therefore, I wouldn't have been too surprised if I had caught up." Her brown eye glinted at him.

Thomas caught her mule's reins and the cream-colored beast put up its head, giving him the same blue-eyed, brown-eyed stare.

"Thank you," he said tersely.

"You're welcome. I figured you wouldn't even be able to put wards up. Fog or no fog, Denethan's crew is bound to be out here, somewhere." Lady took her mount's reins from him. "I suggest we move off the bones of the dead."

Thomas backtracked, hoping for a gleam of metal in the moonlight. The Protector watched him a moment, then sighed.

"Your favorite?"

"My most accurate."

"Heaven forfend." She held out her right hand, fingers twitched, closed her brown eye, and the shuriken came gliding slowly out of the night. She caught it and tossed it deftly to him. Her face paled with this telekinetic effort.

Thomas replaced it in the collar of his jacket.

"No thanks necessary," the woman said, as she put boot in stirrup and mounted up.

Blade grinned. "And none given. But you keep showing off and neither of us will be in any shape to set wards."

Over a low-banked fire that held off the chill of the fog, Thomas said quietly, "Now tell me the real reason you were following me."

She looked up from the battered tin mug she cradled in her creased palms.

"And tell me the truth," he added, not saying what he meant, but her eyes widened slightly.

"Because you'd hate to have to kill me? Blade, you have depths I never imagined." She sighed, pushing her booted feet forward and crossing them at the ankles. "There are now five Protectors."

He straightened. "What happened? Who did we lose?"

"Nobody, you nit. But you abandoned your post—and so did I. For the same reason, I imagine . . . following the children."

An intense heat boiled up inside Thomas. "Damn Charlie—"

"No." She held up her right hand. "I had no idea he'd spent the day manipulating you. I had decided on my own. Jennifer is too young to send off that way and Charlie wouldn't tell me where he'd sent them. Quaker County is small enough that Oletha can cover them as well. I had—" She gave a low laugh. "I had an unquenchable desire to be a midwife."

Thomas shifted uneasily.

"I know," she said gently. "You travel alone. But when I found that sentry bound and gagged . . . I knew when I touched him you'd done it. So I sat there on Murphy—" At its name, the mule's long ears flicked, then it went back to grazing. "I sat there and tried to figure out what the hell you were doing. Then it came to me that you were doing what I was doing. Only you're more ruthless about not wanting any witnesses."

"Oh?"

Lady smiled. "I was just going to sit and have a mug of tea with the sentry—and drug his cup."

"Poison beats a chop to the neck for subtlety any day."

She looked away. The firelight made the round planes of her face even softer, almost cherubic, but Thomas realized that when he'd lifted her off the ground earlier, she'd been much lighter than he expected, and well-muscled. Her beauty was in curves rather than well-defined bone structure.

"I'm sorry."

"Oh, you don't have to be. We're in a dirty business, Thomas. I know that. Although I don't think the DWP has ever had quite as efficient an assassin as you are."

"Thank you."

She looked back quickly, muttered, "Good god, you think I'm complimenting you," and emptied her teacup out. "I'm going to take advantage of what's left of the night."

Thomas watched her settle back onto her saddle and blanket. He kicked apart the coals to settle the fire down even more, and lay back himself. Perhaps in the morning he'd think of a solution to his problem.

He shrugged into his worn leather jacket. Vials clinked together in the inner pockets as he did so, and among them clicked the finger bones of a dead man. When he slept, he dreamed of nothing, not even ghosts.

He awoke to the mule's bray. It sounded akin to the wail of a dying cat and hung on the fog-damp air of the morning. The beast had put its all into the gut-wrenching noise and stood exhausted, sucking air back into its lungs. Lady Nolan bounded to her feet, kicking aside a tangle of saddle blanket. She went quickly to her mount, slipping one arm about its neck and pinching its nostrils shut with her free hand as she brought its head to her chest and cradled it there as if in apology for gagging it.

Blade felt the tingle of power down his spine, that black unreasoning fear which gave Denethan's attacking raiders the edge in any fight. He rolled to his knees and cast about.

Lady felt it, too. She looked at Thomas, as wild-eyed as the beast she tried to calm. "Denethan."

"Has to be. On the wind." He made a lunge for the black mare as she began to lift her head for a whicker.

"How do you know?"

The mare shivered under his touch and stamped in the dust. He didn't know how he knew, he did just did, and he bit off, "That's his fastest way in."

Lady took her hand off the mule's muzzle, shaded her eyes and then pointed. "Catapults off those peaks, riding the thermals in—"

Thomas looked in the direction she indicated and felt his blood chill. To have launched so close to Charlie's—Denethan must have built catapults at the base of the peninsula. How could he have gotten in so close without being challenged?

He uncoiled. He was wasting time wondering about the mechanics of the invasion. The giant batwings sculling closer to them would have them spotted soon, if they didn't already.

"Across the track," he hissed to Lady. "Under the concrete."

"Rats—" she began in protest and then broke off.

She kicked her dun-colored saddle under the furze bushes lining the campsite. Blade followed suit. He'd taken the nosepiece off Cindy, letting the headstall hang about her throat as if it were a catch instead of a bridle, Lady had done the same, so now they gathered up the loose reins and hustled the mounts across the broken roadtrack and into the shadow of the ruins. Cindy did as bade, but the mule planted front hooves stubbornly and refused to duck in under the overhang until Lady stepped back and planted a swift kick against its lean haunch. With a half-bleat of protest, the mule joined the black mare. Lady crowded in next and stood shoulder to shoulder with Thomas.

"You can't blame him," she muttered. "Mules have more sense than horses. None of us should be in here."

Thomas was unslinging his pack from his shoulder. He plucked out a vial and opened his rifle.

He ignored Lady's wide-eyed stare.

"You can't do that—it'll do no good without a direct hit and even then—if you hit a wing instead of the fuselage—the vial will simply bounce off."

Thomas did not look up as he dropped the vial into the firing chamber. Then, carefully, he searched a vest pocket until he came up with the ring he was looking for.

Even in the shadow, the exquisitely cut marquis diamond flashed.

"My god. That thing's worth a fortune."

"It will be if it saves our hides." Thomas raked the diamond edge across the handblown glass vial. It rasped as it etched a Vee cut into the glass. He went back over the etching several times before he was satisfied. "Now," he murmured. "If it survives the firing, it should be weak enough to shatter on impact—any impact."

Lady Nolan had a hand up to her mouth and was backed up against her mule's flanks. The two chemicals inside the vial boiled about each other in a lethal dance. With a grunt of satisfaction for the mayhem he was about to cause, Thomas lifted the rifle.

The wind raiders drifting across the morning swirled and eddied, cankers on the face of the sky, great blots of corruption, meeting wing tip to wing tip as if conferring, then looping about. They flew unerringly toward the ruins, but in spiral search patterns. He calculated their most likely path.

Pleased, Thomas said, "They're just reconnoitering. They didn't spot us."

"Then let them go."

"No. They're between us and Zuma Beach."

"Zuma . . . the children? You know where they are?"

"I can guess where they are . . . or were, until the fog lifted." Thomas watched the raiders swoop about again. He began to squeeze the trigger.

"You can't possibly get them both."

"I don't have to," Thomas answered absently, his concentration on his target. "Bring one down, the second will come to us—or head back to report. Either way, the odds are more to my liking." He heard her begin to pace, then blocked her out. There was nothing in his sight or mind but the corridor his missile would travel and its intended destination.

The two wind raiders began to pull together as if magnetized. He squeezed the trigger back and felt the rifle jump in his cradled hold as it fired. Without looking, he wound back into position and tapped the firing chamber open for another vial.

"Jesus, you're a bloody bastard," Nolan was in the midst of saying. "no wonder you keep the glass smiths busy—" when the bullet struck and shattered and both wind raiders were engulfed in a cloud of noxious smoke. They tumbled to the earth like singed butterflies.

"Both of them," Lady breathed in astonishment as the raiders hit the ground, and Blade saw a dark figure tumble out, get to its feet, and run.

He dropped his rifle and sprinted after it.

"Thomas, no!" she cried, and the enemy stopped, turned, and angled toward the sound of her voice.

A sane man, or a sane *human*, would have kept running for freedom. *But not one of Denethan's ilk,* Blade told himself as he circled. *Stay clear of its teeth and claws.* He sped across the open ground, closing on his target. He pulled the throwing star from his collar as he jumped a wicked-looking chunk of asphalt. Quarry in his sights, something from below hit him in midair, shoulder into his torso, driving the wind out of him as he hit and rolled.

Two! Thomas cursed himself for not having seen the second one escape the noxious cloud of the wreckage. He had no time to worry about Lady Nolan as the being clutched him tightly and brought up its feet to begin clawing at his stomach. Blade kneed him in a region generally vulnerable and the lizard man recoiled with a hiss of pain. Thomas shuddered in revulsion and fought against the band of muscle holding his arms down, shuriken still gripped uselessly in his hand. They tumbled about on the earth—the field of bones —and Thomas saw a broken end spearing upward, out of the dry ground as if blossoming from there.

He wrestled his own lean bulk against that of the other, even as the lizard man snapped in Thomas' face, carrion-smelling fangs missing his cheek by a fraction of an inch. As he bucked backward, he ground his heels in and propelled himself upward. His attacker lost his grip, falling back, and Thomas lunged forward.

The being fell onto the bone with a scream and a bubbling hiss. The lizard man convulsed, his clawed feet drumming in pain.

Then the being looked at Thomas, and he saw the poison sacs behind the ears begin to bulge, and the lipless mouth pucker. "Mercy," the being croaked, even as Thomas brought his hand up and slashed the throwing star across the exposed throat. Unspat poison drooled from the enemy's lips as the being's head lolled to one side and his thin, oddly formed chest sucked in for one last breath.

Thomas got shakily to his feet. He looked at his

shuriken, where a nasty green film stained the metal. He started to wipe it off, then changed his mind. A poisoned edge might come in handy.

A high shriek tore the air behind him. Thomas whirled, Lady Nolan brought to mind again, and made for the concrete cave. A second shriek tore out of the darkness and a figure came stumbling out, sank to its knees, then toppled over. Thomas slowed to a deliberate walk. The creature struggled to pull a charm from around his neck and just as stubbornly, the charm twisted to garrote him. Thomas caught up with him where he lay, spent, lips gone ashen. He kicked the creature once, in the ribs. The vicious blow spent what little breath the being had and he expired with a rattling gasp.

Thomas looked down. This beast was even more vile than the other . . . the visible skin was patterned in beige and gray scales. He could see little human remaining in the being except for the wide open blue eyes, now glazing over in death. The creature wore a leather overvest and thin cotton pants, ballooning about its travesty of legs. Around its neck, the thongs of a medallion it wore had constricted until they cut into the wattle of reptilian skin. Lady Nolan had strangled it with its own amulet.

Thomas reached down. He snapped the amulet off and then ground it into dust beneath his boot heel. A sooty, oily smoke puffed out and dissipated. He spat. It was just as well Lady had killed him—Denethan's man would never have suffered interrogation.

The Protector stumbled out of the cave a second later, her face gray from her psychic endeavor, her hands shaking. Thomas went to her and took her elbow quickly, steadying her.

"Is he?"

"Yes. Both of them." He helped her to sit down in the sunshine and fresh air. The black mare whickered after him inquiringly, and he led both mounts out. There had been quite a struggle inside, from the torn and bruised grass and the dirt kicked up. The mule had a welt down its right foreleg. Thomas examined the cut. His forte was not Healing and he could not ask Lady to expend any more energy. He would have to keep it clean and hope the wound did not fester, but Denethan's carrion-eating troopers carried a poison of their own in their claws.

Lady Nolan looked up as he reemerged. The color had returned to her cheeks, but she sat hunched up, her arms about her knees. Her blouse had been torn and she'd knotted it together, but sat hiding the tear like a mortal wound, hugging it from sight.

Thomas decided to examine the body instead. Revulsion soured the taste in his mouth.

He toed the body over so as not to see its face any more, its saurian travesty of a human expression, with eyes as startlingly blue as those of the child bride he was trailing.

"It's not worth it," he said.

Lady Nolan cleared her throat. "What?"

He had been thinking aloud, but turned toward her. "I said it wasn't worth it. Better to die out as the human race than become *that*."

She got to her feet and stood unsteadily as if facing a high wind. "Then," she said with determination and drew herself up. "We'd better find the children before they do."

Chapter 7

Thomas looked over the bodies. He'd retrieved his rifle and the tack. Beyond, the two wind raiders burned, the smoke rising from them foul and rank smelling. He breathed deeply and felt his gills stir beneath the scarf as if to cleanse the odorous air. "We'll leave the bodies where they fell." The palms of his hands itched in agreement. He had no desire to touch the lizard folk again.

"The blood scent will draw the wolfrats."

"Exactly. They won't leave a trace. As for the raiders . . ."

Lady uncoiled and stood up. "They'll be in ashes soon."

The feather-light touch of power, however unwanted, scaled his spine. He cast about, looking over the hillocks, greenery starting to wilt in the sun's warmth. Far away, corrupted shadows drifted over the hills. "Damn." He grabbed for Cindy's reins.

"What is it?"

"More raiders. Come on." He headed back toward the cityscape.

She set her heels. "I won't go back in there."

"What choice do you have?"

The cream mule stamped a hoof and one ear flicked forward and then back. For a second, Thomas had the weird sensation that the beast was part and parcel of her ability, like an antenna probing the world. She was still pale. Her fingers plucked unconsciously at her knotted blouse. Then she reached out and took her mount in hand. "If you don't feel it, I can't tell you what it's like—but I can almost hear them, Thomas. Like an echo from yesterday."

He fell in step with her, saying, "Sticks and stones can break my bones, but words can never hurt me."

She flashed a look at him. "Any child can tell you words form the major part of his arsenal. But you know that."

They reached the edge of the overhang. Thomas looked over his shoulder. He could just barely see the batwings now. He slapped a hand to the mule's haunch as the animal slowed to his mistress' reluctant pace. "I hear them, too," he said softly. "But they can't touch us."

Or they would not be able to until he took the ghost road, and if Denethan's pursuers were hot on their heels, it was a course he might be forced into. Yet he would be exposing himself to mysteries he had not explored and did not know the rules to, except that his own life fueled every step. But he clamped his jaws shut as Lady Nolan led her mule into the shadows. Time enough for her to know later.

He angled their flight north and west, determined not to let Denethan's men drive them out of their way. As the sun climbed, and the blue sky filled with its brownish haze, Lady became more and more taciturn. They wound their way through leaning walls of concrete and wood, wood so frail with dry rot that when the mule brushed one beam, it disintegrated into powder and splinters. Lady froze as the debris showered her, nostrils pinched as she held back a cough.

Thomas looked up as a batwing shadowed them, then sailed onward.

She cleared her throat. "Did he see us?"

"I don't think so. We'll be underground again in a minute." He nodded ahead to a yawning gap in the ruins.

She shuddered. "The wolfrats will be out soon."

He thought, *Sooner than that—it's always night down below*—but said nothing to her. His leather jacket creaked as he reached up to pat the black mare's shoulder.

On the heels of his silence, she added defiantly, "You don't care, do you? You've a reputation for exploring the cities."

"I've a reputation for a lot of things," he answered. "Less than half of which is true. But I do explore when I can, under the right circumstances."

Darkness swallowed them, but it was fleeting. She blinked rapidly to adjust to the dappled lighting. The tunnel was open-roofed in spots, so he did not bother with a torch. He would have put a hand out to steady her, but she put her hand through her stirrup and leaned on the mule instead. She stumbled anyway and as he threw a hand out to help, she peered at him through the murky visibility.

She laughed. "At least I can testify that you don't glow in the dark."

He flushed, knowing that Shellyann had been discussing her hopeful prospects. "Not yet. But I suggest we wait until we're done here. I don't have my gauges with me . . . this area could be quite hazardous."

"Life is hazardous. This is damned dangerous."

He had no defense there. A sound echoed behind them and both mule and horse pricked their ears alertly.

"Coyote," Lady identified.

"This time of day?" Thomas turned and sighted back the way they had walked. Memory of the coyote he'd heard at night stirred inside him. He reached out, shoving at Lady's elbow. "Run for it. Go as fast as you can."

Still she hesitated. "Why?"

"Coyotes stay out of the ruins—that's the territory of the wolfrats. Unless that coyote is being driven to trail a prey. That's one of Denethan's tricks."

She began to stumble forward into the patchy dark of the tunnel. She spat out a pungent curse and added, "They were right about you. You're trouble."

"But worth it." Thomas grinned fiercely and broke into a jog to keep up with her. The tunnels were mostly laid with ties and rails, but a few spurs were bare, always leading back to the main corridor. The yip-yip-yaroo at their heels grew fainter. He began to think they had outrun the trackers when Lady threw up her hand and came to an abrupt halt.

Fresh air dried the sweat on his face. He took the time to run an inquiring hand down the black mare's left foreleg. She'd tripped up badly in the murk, but he felt no heat in the leg nor did she wince as he probed it deftly. The mule licked at his scratch, but the edges of the wound looked clean, despite the reputation of lizard scratches. Without looking up, he said. "Okay. Whenever you've caught your breath."

"I'm not leaving without *her*," Lady answered.

Thomas looked up sharply and shouldered her aside. Huddled in a beam of light that broke through from a fiberglass corrugated roof, was a dirty-faced girl. He hadn't heard her sniveling over the animals' and his own panting, but now that his senses were alerted to her presence, her sounds of misery were deafening.

"Sweet heaven," he muttered. "She's a nester, a squatter. Leave her be, we've got enough on our hands as it is."

"She's in trouble."

"She's an outcast and she wouldn't be here if she hadn't chosen to be."

"She or her family couldn't pay Charlie's water tax, that's what you mean."

He was shoulder to shoulder with Lady Nolan and now leaned on her ever so gently. "She chose to be here. We haven't the time to argue the justice of it now. The rest of her tribe will slaughter us and suck the marrow out of our bones after they've roasted us. Come on."

Lady looked at him in the thinning darkness. He kept his face still, but the gaze of her eyes pierced him. "You'll kill her," the Protector said, "after we pass through, to keep her from talking."

He shifted weight. "That's the law for nesters." Then, softly, "At least it'll be quick."

"She's a human being."

"So are the kids we're trying to catch up with."

"And," Lady said, her voice lowering in emphasis, "she's in labor."

He saw the awkward thrust of the girl's body, her knees spread as she squatted in the shaft of light, chewing on her knuckles and staring fearfully toward them.

He looked away. The girl let out another muffled groan and began panting rapidly.

He couldn't close her out of his senses. "Oh, shit," he said, and dropped the mare's reins. Almost as one, he and Lady moved forward to her aid, Lady talking **rapidly.**

"We can't leave her here to the rats or Denethan's coyotes."

"We're not taking her with us."

Lady said nothing, but her mouth set firmly as she reached the girl's side and smoothed back a mane of tangled hair to reveal the teen's haggard face.

Thomas stood over them. If the girl's family had fled their holding, unable to pay for even enough water shares for their own gardens, then where were the rest of her kin? As he watched the swollen belly ripple under the rags of her garments, he thought it more likely she'd fled on her own—unable to prove who the father of her baby was. Unlike Shellyann, who could take pride in her maternity as a proven woman, this runaway likely had been soiled with nester seed.

An even worse sin in Charlie's quest for genetic purity.

The girl stopped panting, her temporary paralysis fled, and like a snake, she lunged toward the pointed stick that stood leaning in the corner.

Lady drew back, startled. The tapered end jabbed the air where her blue eye had just been.

"Git away from me!"

"We want to help."

Even illuminated by the rays of light filtering down, the girl's face was so filthy he could not tell the color of her skin. She gave him a feral, sideways glance, even as she jabbed her crude weapon at Lady's face a second time. Then a paroxysm of labor struck and she doubled over, unable to hold the stick steady. It clattered to the ground at her feet. She began to pant and Lady reached out to hold her shoulders steady. Thomas could sense the warmth and calmness she sent out for the other's comfort. The girl would have none of it. She struck out with a strength born of desperation and Lady Nolan went rolling.

Thomas charged at her and half-picked her up, pinning her arms against her sides. She rolled wild eyes at him, then dropped her chin and began to sob. He loosened his grip and she withdrew an arm cautiously as Lady got to her feet.

The girl traced the chevron scar on his left brow. "You've been marked by *them*," she said so quiet he didn't think Lady could catch her words.

"What? What do you mean?"

She looked at him shrewdly. "If you don't know, you'll know when *they* want you to." She licked dry lips. "Help me. Please." Another pain shuddered through her and he lowered her into the cradle of Lady's arms.

"How long have you been out here alone?"

"Four, five months. I ca—can't remember." The girl bit her lip.

"Couldn't prove the sire?"

She looked up from between strands of matted hair and tossed her head contemptuously. "Oh, I know who's the father all right. But when I told, they didn't believe me. Made it harder for all of us, so I ran off."

Lady had a smudge on her cheekbone where the girl had hit her. Her lips thinned slightly as she looked up. "Tell me," she said. "I'm a Protector. You're doing well, but if—"

"I'm not for dying, not this time." The girl's eyelids flickered. "But it's my own dad that got me pregnant."

Lady sucked in her breath sharply, but there was a wet mushing sound, and the ground beneath the squatting girl's feet grew damp and glistening.

The girl let out a startled chirp. Lady smoothed her brow and said, "That's the waters. It won't be long now."

Thomas stepped back to give the two room. He drew his knife from his wrist sheath. Lady's glance frowned briefly at him. "To cut the cord," he said defensively.

The runaway put her hand upon Lady's wrist. "I trust him," she said softly. "He's been marked."

Thomas moved away to pace uneasily.

He did not know if either Lady or the girl could hear it over the groans and pants of labor, but the muffled yowls of the coyotes drifted through the tunnels toward them. Whatever ground they'd gained was rapidly being eaten away. The miracle of birth was going to be the death of them all.

Chapter 8

A Protector of a county is just that, a protector. Sometimes an enforcer, particularly for the politics of water, but most times a judge, an arbitrator, and a shield. A Protector came to his duty with no name but the one he or she'd been born with, forsaking his own family, for the greater one of the community. Thomas had chosen his last name for his avocation and been awarded his knighthood for performance above and beyond the call of duty—but Lady had been so named at birth, and her surname of Nolan had been taken from that of her mentor.

Thomas stood now, at sentry, listening to the rhythmic panting of the girl behind him. He'd stood through enough births to know this might not be an easy one—that women sometimes broke their waters, then suffered through another day of labor, but he also knew he could not wait. The moment he heard the howls grow closer, when and if the howls grew closer, he would end the young mother's agony, his difficult choice already having been made for the good of the majority.

And he knew that Lady Nolan knew his decision as well. She coached the girl now, he could hear her calming voice though his own senses were pitched toward the outer world and the enemy trailing them. The hypnotic lull of her voice occasionally broke through his concentration and he found himself breathing in time with her. He pivoted toward them in irritation just as the girl let out a low wail and Lady gasped, "Thomas, help me! I'm exhausted."

He lowered himself at Lady's side. He could see a thatch of hair crowning, and knew the girl wailed because the birthing was stretching tender skin. He entwined his arms about Lady's, reached out with knife point and gingerly nicked the membrane, knowing that a clean cut would be better than a tear.

Lady cried out in triumph, "Now, push!"

The girl did so, and the baby's head came free. Thomas jerked his hands back as Lady reached for the infant. The Protector leaned on him or he would have thrust himself away, as a cold chill swept over him. He swallowed hard though his mouth had gone dry.

"Lady—"

"Not now, Thomas." She gave the young mother a too bright smile, her voice frayed. She was more spent than the mother. "The worst is over. One more push and I've got him."

"It . . . feels good to push."

"I know. Just go with it—now."

The baby slipped out, covered with the waxy coating some babies have, tiny thatch of hair sticking up on end, private parts red and swollen with the indignity of birth—all that Thomas had seen before. What he had not seen before was a babe with three legs . . . or perhaps that grotesquerie was a tail . . . and the wail that burbled out of its frog face was scarcely recognizable as a human sound. Unconsciously, he held the knife ready.

Lady Nolan took it from his numb fingers and deftly cut the cord. "Lean back, and take a breath. Then we've got a few more pushes."

"The baby?"

The woman was still. She'd taken off her traveling scarf and now wrapped the child in it for warmth. The girl leaned back against the tunnel wall. She turned her pale face toward Thomas as Lady swaddled the newborn from view. "What is it?" she asked, her voice edged in panic at what she'd read from Thomas' expression. "What's wrong with my baby!"

"Nothing, little one." Lady attuned her voice to its most soothing modulation, the strain showing in her face.

"It's the eleven year plague. Nothing else explains the monstrosity."

"No!"

"It has to be," Thomas protested.

"Father mated daughter . . . that's reason enough." Lady lost control of her voice. She looked to the girl, "But he's alive and that's all that matters. *Life*."

Cat-quick, the disheveled girl snatched the child from Nolan, child and knife, and unrolled the bundle which began to cry in distress. Her voice joined her son's in fear and horror. Too swiftly for either of them to prevent it, she struck with the knife and the child's cry stopped abruptly. She ripped the bloodstained scarf from the body and let it fall to ground. Her own body shuddered and expelled the afterbirth, one bloody monstrosity deposited on the cavern floor next to another. She bound herself as Lady Nolan let out a soft moan and toppled to the dirt, spent beyond her psychic reserves, all so that this mother and child could live. He swept Lady's hair from her face and checked her neck pulse. She'd be all right. He looked up to find the girl with the knife at the ready.

Thomas stood, keeping himself loose and prepared for action. Light angling in, illuminated her gamine face. She put her chin up. "Don't be following me."

"You can't go far. At least stay with us long enough to get out of the ruins."

Her lip lifted in an animal sneer. "I don't want to leave. This here's my home. I'm clean now, right? No more birthing monsters?"

"Maybe." His tongue felt like cotton. "The plague strikes differently. It could be you and your baby, or just the baby."

"I never heard of any plague."

He lifted his right hand. "They don't talk about it much. It comes in cycles. You're too young to remember. . . ."

"Don't come any closer. My lover will be coming for me."

"Your lover?"

She smiled then, and the smile transformed her into a sepia-hued madonna. The transformation confused Thomas long enough for her to reach out and touch his brow softly, murmuring a word as her fingers caressed his scar.

He heard her add, "You don't want to meet him just yet." The sound cut through the cord of his consciousness like a knife and he fell as though she'd stoned him.

He awoke to dusk, the yip-yaroo of the hunters ringing in his ears. He got to his knees and shook his head, groping for alertness. He heard Lady stir.

"Thomas?"

"I'm here. Are you all right?"

"Spent, that's all. What happened to you?"

"She nailed me," Blade lied. He had no more idea of what she'd done to him than why she put such store by his marking. He saw the knife lying on the ground in front of him and picked it up as he stood.

The babe and its afterbirth were gone, dirt scraped into a mound at the tunnel's side, a mound marked with stones and a pointed stick made into a crude wooden cross.

Lady, braced against the tunnel walls, put her hand to her mouth. "Oh, Thomas—she buried him."

The mound would not last when the coyotes came through. With a muffled curse, Thomas, his legs still weak at the knees, wove his way to the black mare. What in hell had that little bitch done to him? He pulled out his canteen, and the mesquite twigs that could carry the psychometric echoes of a telepathic warn-off. He returned, wiping his mouth from a long pull of the warmish water, and handed the canteen to Lady. As she took a similar drink, he squatted over the mound and set up the wards to protect it. When he finished, he ran his hand over the cross and pulled away a tuft of thick, brown hair . . . coarse and musky smelling between his fingers . . . and distinctly not human. Something else had been down there with them and the girl. He tucked it out of sight in his jacket pocket.

When Lady handed the canteen back, her eyes glinted moistly as she said, "Thank you."

He did not ask her for what she thanked him. A second howl pierced the silence. Lady scrubbed her eyes and said, "We've got to get out of here."

He shook his head. "Too close. We're done already."

"You can't be serious about making a stand here!"

"No." He reached inside his jacket again, and this time removed a dead man's finger bones. "But you may not like this idea any better."

The mule proved more stubborn. It stood with hooves planted firmly, long ears twitching forward and back, back and forward, as Lady pulled on its bridle. "Come on, Murphy. What's done is done!"

Thomas bypassed them, leading the black mare. A fine sweat dappled his brow. The road he'd opened before them crossed over the hatred and misery of a thousand million souls. The feeling of walking on it clawed at his guts. He didn't know what he felt, but he knew every step on the ghost road would weaken him. "You can't blame him, Lady."

"Don't want to blame him. I just want to *move* him." Lady backed up and Murphy, sensing the windup to a powerful kick in the haunches, hastily broke into a trot.

Thomas scratched his nose to muffle his response as Lady cursed and ran to catch up.

They strode in silence for a time. Lady's hair, without a scarf to hold it back, fluffed about her face, softening the lines of her chin and jaw even more. There was a thread or two of gray in her hair, but Thomas had seen the young go gray before and now he thought absently that she probably wasn't much, if any, older than he was. It was her talent for mothering that aged her. He thought about the flower-bedecked straw hat she'd worn for the wedding. She'd probably woven it herself with strong, capable hands.

She looked toward him as if netted by his thoughts. "Would you have killed it if she hadn't?"

His mouth pulled. "You always ask the hard questions, don't you?"

"Someone has to." The set of her face etched about her eyes, the beginning of wrinkles.

"Probably. It was plague-born."

"You don't know for sure!"

He put a comforting hand on the black mare's shoulder as the tension in their voices alarmed the animal. "The girl seemed unmarked enough. There was no reason for the baby to have been so deformed. All I know about the plague is what we all know—it's a constantly mutating virus that attaches itself to our DNA and changes it. It causes abominations far worse than the adaptive ones given us years ago. If it goes on unchecked, there'll be nothing human left of us. We might as well never have crawled out of the sea!" Unconsciously, he took his hand from Cindy and fingered the scarf about his neck.

Lady's mouth half-opened, but then she shut it firmly on whatever it was she had been about to say. Instead she said, "The only chance we have seems to be that it's a very short-lived virus. It attacks a few and then becomes dormant for another decade."

"It only needs to attack a few," Thomas said bitterly. "There're so few of us left."

"Life is still life," she argued.

He flicked a glance at her as she walked along,

the peculiar dusk of the ghost road paling her face. "I refuse," he answered, "to argue the quality of life."

"But you can't! You don't know what their potentials are, or what they think and feel."

"I know what I think. I know what I feel. That's enough for me."

"You really hate those gills, don't you?"

Her voice did not invite his answer, so he didn't, but he could feel his face turn hot. He tugged savagely on Cindy's headstall, pulling the black mare into the lead as the tunnel narrowed down and he had an excuse for walking alone. The aforementioned gills stirred, prickled into erection, and he ignored their throbbing in his neck.

Without those gills, he could never dance with dolphins. Nor could his ancestors have lived in the ocean environment until the earth had stopped revolting. But they were not what he would have chosen when the genes were being spliced. He might have chosen wings instead, to have flown above all this—

Lady stumbled at his heels. "Rats!" she said hoarsely, her throat gone tight with fear.

Thomas swung about. The mule threw its head up, shying away and bolting past him, its passage pinning the smaller black mare up against the wall. The mule stopped where the tunnel widened and came about, teeth bared, ready for a stand.

Blade slapped a hand up against his saddlebags, found the rifle sheath, and pulled it free. He pushed Lady behind him and could feel her trembling. He heard the rush of their clawed feet upon the packed dirt and rail way now, and the slither of their scaled tails behind them. As the pack rounded the bend, the dusk caught the glow of their slanted, crimson eyes.

He put a free hand back to pat Lady Nolan comfortingly. "Remember, we're on the ghost road. They shouldn't be any menace to us."

Her whisper back was tense. "Pat me there again and you'll have more than wolfrats to worry about."

Thomas chuckled as he opened the rifle's firing chamber, just in case, and tapped a vial into it.

The pack stopped just into their neck of the tunnel and milled about. They were a lean and mangy bunch, coyote-high at the shoulders, their tails dragging behind, scaled and scarred. They pulled back lips into rodent snarls, whiskers quivering as they sniffed the air. Predator primeval and it appeared they could hunt the ghost road as well as any other.

"They don't look unaware of us," whispered Lady.

"My thoughts," muttered Thomas. He locked the rifle into position and lifted it.

The lead rat, a beast of mingled gray and brown, with a white patch on his forehead that bled away into a transparent ear, put his muzzle up, winding the air enthusiastically. At his haunch, a brown and white spotted rat lifted its leg and peed upon the track, filling the tunnel with its pungent odor. The rats milled about their leader then, unsure about going either forward or backward. They mumbled jaws at each other, rodent tusks clashing.

The lead rat lowered his muzzle a tad and looked dead on at Blade. He could feel the heat of the beast's hunger. He knew the beast had to sense him. Perhaps Gillander's bones could shade the four of them only so well. Perhaps his blood still ran hot.

With a sudden squeal, the wolfrat launched himself at them, his packmates shrilling and charging behind him.

Chapter 9

"Damn you, Gill," Thomas said as he pulled the trigger and whirled to hotfoot it out of there. From behind his left ear, a wheezy whisper answered, "So I was wrong about the wolfrats. Sorry, m'boy."

Lady had already taken to her heels, beating on the haunches of the black mare and screaming harshly at the mule which retreated with a defiant bray. Thomas pointed to a broken bank, leading above despite its treacherous footing. "Up there!"

"Above?"

"You got a better idea?"

She didn't. She threw herself on the embankment to claw her way up. Behind them, the rats emitted bloodthirsty squeals even as the magnesium/water vial shattered in the tunnel and burst into a flare as the two mixed. White fire stabbed at Thomas as he whipped both the mare and mule out of the tunnel, their reins flapping as they bucked and crow-hopped over Lady and onto the lip of the embankment.

He took a running leap. His fingers found a purchase, and he kicked his boots up as the bank crumbled under his soles. Something caught at him and he looked back to see a rat fall back, teeth clashing, his boot heel scarred from one saber-toothed fang.

"Thomas!" Lady swung at him, caught his forearm and pulled with all her strength, both colored eyes blazing in determination.

He scrambled up beside her. The rats milled about below, working themselves into a frenzy to follow. The leader leaped futilely, his face blistered and bloody from the magnesium flare. Blade didn't have enough throwing stars to handle the pack. Close range combat looked more favorable, particularly if he could take them on as they came up the bank. He pulled his knife.

"I'll take 'em one at a time. You kick back the others, if you can."

Lady pulled on his arm. "Thomas, listen!"

Over the high-pitched rage of the wolfrats, he heard the suddenly crystal clear yip-yaroo of the coyotes.

"Jesus! Doesn't anything work on this ghost road?"

Gillander sounded peeved. "There's a knack to it you haven't got quite yet—"

"Shit!" he answered the ghost. "I haven't got the time to learn!" He took a swipe at the first rat clambering out of the tunnel after them.

It made a high-pitched chirp and lunged at his thighs, whiskers peeled back against snarling, pointed jaws. Its left eye was clouded and its gray pelt blistered. And it was hungry. Drool rolled off its saber teeth as it snapped at him. Thomas kicked it under its head and as it reared back in pain, he slashed across the exposed throat. With a peculiar sound, Lady kicked it off the rim and it fell, squealing and bleeding, among its packmates.

The wolfrats immediately attacked it themselves. Lady's face was greenish as she staggered back to him as they forgot their original prey.

"Let's get out of here," she begged.

Thomas threw a quick look over the edge to see how busy they'd be. The leader lifted his wedge-shaped head to return the look, then went back to tearing and crunching the carcass still quivering in its death throes.

"Looks good to me," he said, and followed Lady Nolan who'd already made a decision and was throwing a leg over the mule's saddle.

The black mare was not so accommodating. Thomas made a grab for her headstall, but the sound of the feeding frenzy down in the tunnel had made her wild-eyed and she shied away from his touch. Lady leaned in her stirrups to make a grab at the reins; she missed and nearly lost her seat. Thomas spread his hands and coaxed the mare nearer.

"Thomas!"

Lady's warning paired with the howl of coyotes. Thomas whirled. He could not see through the city-scape, but the beasts were close on their heels, they had to be!

He turned back around and lunged at the mare, grabbing the stirrup as she bunched up, ready to bolt, the whites of her eyes showing in maddened panic. He snubbed her with her own reins and mounted, loosening the reins as soon as he had both feet firmly in the stirrups. She gave a little hop, ramming the shoulder of Lady's mule.

The coyotes broke the shadows of the corner, dun forms fleeting across the eerie dusk of the ghost road. Their eyes gleamed yellow and green. They were silent predators leaping broken canyons. Their tongues lolled pinkly out of their grinning mouths. It was no longer necessary to howl to give away their prey—they were found!

"Get out of here!"

Lady looked at him, her face sheet-white. "Not without you!"

"You've got no choice. I'm in between and here's where I'm going to stay! Now, get! I'll catch up."

"No. Not without you!"

Thomas gripped the mare as hard as he could. He looked over his shoulder. The coyotes seemed almost to be in slow motion, bounding across the asphalt chunks of what had been a six lane road.

"Don't argue with me!"

"I won't go without you."

He slapped the ends of the reins against the mule's cream-colored butt. "Get out of here!"

The mule had more sense than its rider and charged into movement even as Lady Nolan shouted defiance and hauled back on its reins. Pink foam sprayed from its open mouth as the bit cut in.

Thomas slewed the mare around to face the coyote pack just in time to see them launch themselves at him. He reached deeper into the despair and hatred that was the foundation of the road, felt his chest grow chill, and his mind darken. But he had it—he had the fabric of the ghost road and wrapped it tightly about him like a shroud.

The leader came at him and a second leaped at the black mare's heels, wolflike, to hamstring her. He caught a glimpse of flashing eyes and ivory jaws. He threw his right arm up as he tossed the knife into his left hand and the mare let out a pealing whinny of fear.

Hotter than fire, the coyote passed through his form as though he wasn't even there. The predator tumbled to the lip of the ditch and bounded to his feet, head low and growling.

The entire pack ran through him, each beast a brand—and not one of them able to touch his flesh. Thomas kneed the mare after the mule and she plunged forward, her neck lathered gray and her hide shivering. The mule showed its heels to her and the mare plowed along in its wake.

"There," said Gill behind his left ear. "Satisfied?"

Behind came the sounds of coyote pack meeting wolfrat pack. Thomas shrugged deeper into his leather jacket. He did not understand what was physical and what was not on this ghost road—only that he could not trust his senses, any of them. And if he stayed in this dimension of cold unlife, he would need a death shroud indeed.

He rode hard after Lady Nolan and watched her brown hair streaming loose on the wind.

He examined the coyote dung on the patchy road and then stood up, eying the sun and clouds overhead. He said to Lady's blue eye, "Three days old, I'd say." He'd thought he'd never get warm again, but real time beat down on him and he'd not go back to the ghost road unless it were a matter of life and death. His heart beat sluggishly and his legs were still ice-cold numb from the knees down.

"So you were nearly savaged by a pack of animals three days gone?"

"Looks like it." It was warm inside his leather jacket. He thought of taking it off and lashing it behind the saddle, but things were too tense to risk losing it if he were unseated or lost the mare. He mounted up and scanned the curving foothills. "Zuma Beach is on the other side of that."

"Good. I'm for riding a little farther."

"Hungry?"

"God, yes." She swept her hair back from her forehead. "And I can hear Murphy's stomach cranking from here."

"The ghost road. It bends time somehow, I think."

"So this morning is actually two or three days from when we thought it was."

He shrugged.

"I thought you were supposed to save time."

"We made great time once we left the tunnel," he pointed out. It was her turn to shrug.

"Where are the children?"

"Who knows? From the dew on the ground, I'd say there's been quite a bit of fog through here. Maybe they're still grounded most of the day."

"And they're low on fuel." The two of them had discussed the backpacks Thomas had seen. Soon their quarry would be on foot and much easier to follow.

He nodded. Cindy fell into step with the mule. Lady rode silently for a handspan of yards, then said, "Would you have killed that girl?"

"Don't think so."

"But you said the baby was plagued."

"I'm no doctor. I don't know what went on inside her body. The baby was obvious."

She fell silent again for a while. Then, "I could be contaminated. Or you."

"Doubtful. The contagion takes more exposure than that."

"But the virus is airborne."

He looked over at her. "Are you afraid?"

"Shit, yes. And you are, too."

He felt the morning breeze through his thinning hairline. His wrist itched where the dolphin's teeth had scarred him. He rubbed it absently. "Not for myself," he said, reluctantly.

"Like Denethan?"

"Like me." He heeled the mare ahead of the mule, and left Lady behind as he followed the broken road toward the coastal foothills and the wide beaches he knew lay beyond.

When the mental whiplash flicked him, he thought perhaps it was her, lashing out in anger.

Then he realized that her Talent lay in Telekinesis and Healing. Not this attack that fried around the edges of his thoughts. He reeled in the saddle. Instinctively, he flung up an arm to protect his skull. He couldn't get a shield up; the ghost road had drained him dry.

"Thomas! What is it?"

The air crackled. He could barely hear Lady's alarmed words through the static. He opened his mouth to speak. His words sounded with the blue flash of lightning and ozone stink.

"Mindstorm. . . ."

Lady grabbed up the reins from him. He doubled over, the saddle horn gouging his rib cage.

Denethan was reaching for him. He could see it if he closed his eyes!

Blade shuddered. He knew he could break Denethan. He'd done it before. There had to be reserves inside him that he could tap. Desperately he reached deep into his determination. He half-formed a shield and hunched under it.

The two mounts stood in the road, the mare dancing nervously under her burden. He rolled an eye at Lady.

"The beach! Ride for it. Lead me."

Lady nodded. He lolled back in the saddle and let himself go to war.

Denethan straightened. His smile thinned. *He had him.* His coyote trackers had found something warm and vital—something so hot and pure that it was like molten rock. It had cooled, but now as he searched northward, he had felt it again—and it was his quarry!

He recognized the shield that had broken his sending before. Powerful, this one . . . the light to his dark, two sides of the same coin. He recognized the kinship immediately. The rock throne cradled his form, brought the sun's warmth to him, as the lethargy of nighttime crept away. His concentration waned slightly as his adjunct stole up to him and said, "The catapults are ready."

"Not now! I have him! Get away from me. Post a watch. Send me the scribe." All this through gritted teeth. Denethan dare not lose the contact, not when he had spent the better part of two days searching for it. Who was this unknown wrestling with him? He had Talent, no doubt of that—Denethan could not reach anyone without it—was he one of the fabled Protectors? If so. . . .

Denethan drummed his nails upon the rock. He could not have contact without Talent—and yet the better the contact, the better the ability of the other to defeat him. It was like a handshake . . . the more openhanded, the more sincere the gesture, unless the other got a grip on him that could bring him to his knees.

"I am here, Denethan," the scribe said mildly and curled up on a rock near Denethan's feet.

The man opened his eyes a slit and saw the scribe. The scribe was aged, had worked for Denethan's father. His thin hair was blue-white, his eyelids sagged over weary eyes, but the hand that held the pen was steady. Denethan closed his eyes again as soon as he ascertained that the other hand and two supple, bared feet were empty of weapons.

Although, as Denethan well knew, even a pen could be a weapon. His father's life had ended with one buried in his jugular.

He spared enough energy to signal the other to wait silently and record what Denethan said.

Chapter 10

Lady Nolan rode slowly. She let her mule pick out its own road in its wisdom and watched Thomas instead. His weather-beaten face paled as the trance dragged him under like a drowning man, and she wondered if he would awaken again. There were lines carved like deep crevices in his face and his eyes looked sunken. The ghost road had taken a terrible toll and left him almost defenseless against Denethan's psychic attack.

Never in all the learned history of Protectors had they dueled with an enemy such as this. She had felt it when Thomas broke Denethan's storm before and she could feel the incandescent energies now . . . she was like a moth twirling in the light motes before a lantern, drawn to it and knowing that for the sake of her life she must not enter.

She reached over and gently disentangled Thomas' now limp white scarf from around his neck. His gills were flared, rose-pink with exertion. She dampened the scarf with the meager supply left in her canteen and replaced it hopefully. Thomas' head bobbled about on his neck.

She watched anxiously for burnout, the sudden nova of power that could leave him a mere shell of a being. Her mentor Nolan had been destroyed doing mental exercises he was no longer empowered to do. Burnout was like the brilliant guttering of a candle just before it drowned in its own melted wax.

The sky darkened. Her ears popped as the air pressure dropped suddenly, and thunder rumbled. Lady looked about. Clouds of slate and ebony arced over the browning foothills. She smelled rain as well as salt air. But the swirl of activity covered a small area and she and Blade were its epicenter.

Lightning struck behind them on the road. The air filled with the smell of burning pitch. The ground thrilled as the shock wave rolled under them, and both mounts danced nervously. The display was not as dark and dangerous as that which had threatened them on the peninsula. Both Denethan and Thomas had to be nearing the bottom of their stamina.

Cindy stumbled, nearly pitching Thomas over her neck. He did not react to save himself—Lady caught him and almost lost her own seat. She looked about her in irritation, wondering if she should lash him to the saddle, and not finding a spare strap to do it with. She reined up Murphy, dropping back to the black mare's flanks to search Thomas' saddlebags.

She found the rope almost immediately. She pulled out the coil, relieved she would not have to paw through his personal effects further. He mumbled as she tied his wrists together and loosely tethered him to the saddle horn. She kept the end of the rope wrapped about her own saddle horn to jerk him free if she needed to. Better he should fall than be dragged by the mare if she bolted.

Irritation crawled up her spine. Sweat dripped down the back of her neck, under the mane of her hair. She blew, angling her breath toward her forehead, cooling her face briefly, wishing for her straw hat. If only rain would fall. A wind current tore through, expiring as quickly as it came up. She thought of the paralight on a storm-ridden thermal and fretted over Jennifer and Ramos. Several fat drops of water beat down and stopped.

The clouds swirled away, boiled off by a relentless sun. Did that mean Thomas held, or even was winning? She dared not guess, but kept the mule and the mare pointed relentlessly toward Zuma Beach. Her hair crackled in the residual static electricity that hovered about Thomas like an aura.

She was not used to extended riding, and her thighs chafed horribly as the high noon sun beat down on her head and they rode through the foothills, and down to the beach side. The ocean's sparkle hit her sight with a blinding flash of gray-blue, but its breeze brought a welcoming coolness to her flushed cheeks.

She pulled both animals to a halt. Thomas stirred for the first time in the last several hours. His lips were cracked. They were glued together and flakes sloughed apart reluctantly as he mumbled something.

Lady leaned close. "What is it, Thomas?"

"Ground. Ground me."

Puzzled, she straightened. Was that what he had said, or was he groaning? Why not, "Let me down?"

He convulsed. His feet came free of the stirrups. Uncertainly, Lady pulled the rope free, reached over and pushed.

He fell like a wet bag of grain. Sand clouds puffed up about his body. She watched a moment, then dismounted herself, her knees locking up for a moment. She staggered over and knelt beside Thomas' motionless form.

He didn't look as though he were still breathing.

"Shit." She tore at the neck of his shirt, laying it open so she could feel for a pulse in his neck. Beneath the white silk scarf, the gills fluttered madly, gasping for air. The rest of his body seemed not to be functioning. Did he dream he was swimming? If so, the dream would be fatal. She pounded the heel of her hand on his sternum. "Breathe, Thomas, dammit, breathe!"

Denethan had him. Thomas worried at the mindstorm that engulfed him, a maelstrom in his ocean of thought that threatened to suck him down and bury him forever, so far below the surface of consciousness that he could never return. He had to breathe and could not, to think and speak, and could not. He could not form a cogent thought . . . but he had to, it was the lifeline he needed to cling to.

He thought of the enemy. Denethan could not deny him that thought or he would deny himself—possibly even destroy himself. Thomas clung to it, a buoy in the miasma pulling him down. He fought the fear and panic that the other fed him—told his heart that it was strong enough to keep beating. He fought back to the surface, a long, slow fight that ached in his very bones. Gillander spoke behind his left ear . . . a niche reserved for haunts, Thomas supposed. "Remember your grounding, boy. You pull your strength from the earth. Denethan's a made-man. He pulls his from artifices. Get yourself to ground!"

The Lizard of Oz did not want to let him go, not yet, but Thomas had one last strike left in him. He lashed out, and as suddenly found himself washed ashore, in the midst of grit and sand. He could feel its burning warmth beneath him and reached out to anchor himself with Lady's strength, if she was still with him.

Denethan reeled back. The scribe motioned to a nearby servant and took up a bucket of water and a sponge and laved his face, the inside of his wrists, the nape of his neck.

"He was strong," the old scribe said.

"Yes." Denethan leaned back and half-closed his eyes. "Strong and hateful. Before I find the children, before I deal with any of the others—him, I will have to kill." He coiled in the sunlight, drawing in energy for a new strike.

He lunged upward into her face so suddenly she screamed. His eyes opened, pupils rolled back in their sockets. In reflex, she slapped him across the face and fell back in the sand.

He sat straight up, threw his head back and collapsed. This time, he breathed. Noisily, gustily, like a spent runner. The mark of her hand was the only spot of color on his face.

He opened his eyes as she knelt forward. His parched lips struggled to form words. She leaned close to catch them. His life, their lives, might depend upon it.

His lips worked to shape words, "Lemon drop?"

Lady slapped him again, this time with pleasure.

Thomas chewed gingerly. The bread had gone stale after three days in the pack, but the smoked fish was none the worse and the cheese perhaps aged even smoother. He looked pensively across the beach to the markings of high tide. The paralight had been here. Been here, camped for two days by the looks of it, and flown on. Lady sat across the fire, her arms hugging her legs, rounded chin resting on her knees. The ocean appeared to fascinate her.

He cleared his throat. "I didn't know you cared—"

"Knock it off, Thomas." She nailed him with that two-color stare.

He shrugged, unable to meet either eye.

"You did a stupid thing, engaging him instead of just shielding. I thought I was going to be packing around a goddamn potato for the rest of the trip." She pointed a finger at him. "And we've lost Jennifer. So I don't want to hear it."

"Right. I apologize."

Her gaze softened slightly as he made an effort to chew the last crust of his sandwich. He washed it down with a swig of water and held his cup out for more.

"Just remind me to let you do some swinging next time we get cornered."

"Thomas!"

She threw the whole damn canteen at him with some most unladylike words.

*   *   *

He awoke on the beach, the night fog creeping in across the phosphorescent waves, cold seeping into his bones. He felt hot and his chest was tight, and as he looked across the water, he thought he saw a dolphin, tail-walking the foam. He wiped a trembling hand across his forehead. He brought it down covered in briny sweat. Lady's stubborn back faced him across the campfire's embers. She lay curled under a spare saddle blanket. The ghost road had played havoc with his senses. He wondered what effect it had had on hers.

He pitched his voice to reach her, but what came out was a dry croak that died in the heavy sea air.

He tried to roll out from under his jacket. His joints had gone to mush. All he could do was lie on the damp sand like a broken doll. He was in trouble, and he knew it. They called it breakout fever . . . usually adolescents got it when they were developing their psychic powers as they crossed into puberty. The worse cases either had the power burned out of them . . . or died. This was the psychic backlash Lady had feared.

A shiver convulsed him. He bore it silently, sweating and shaking. When it was done, he made one last effort to contact Lady before he passed out.

"Lady!"

His plea was nothing but a feather gliding on the wind.

Born to be a Healer, she heard it even in her dreams. "Thomas?"

She was making her way to his side when he slid under.

Chapter 11

Fever dreams.

No, not dreams. Memories.

Thomas had never seen a block prepare for war before. Men crawled like giant ants over the foundations and up and down the streets. He stood at the window, watching the supplies for fortifications being hauled away. Rusting car bodies, salvaged to use for carriages, were filled with sacks of sand to be dumped as barriers. He saw the frames roll by, thinking of all the pride of fallen men resting in those cars. The DWP liked to restore them and use them for dress carriages. Not now. Those frames awaiting restoration had other, less esoteric uses in store.

"Been thinking of a name, boy?" Gillander spoke from the corner where he sat, legs crossed Indian-style, a lap writing desk balanced on his bony kneecaps.

Thomas let a smile through as he looked back over his shoulder. "Not yet. Besides, it's a little early, isn't it?"

"Not necessarily. Last name for a Protector's like ordering a pair of boots while your voice is still changin'. Takes time to find the right fit and settle into it."

The tall boy returned from the window to sit at his teacher's side. "Maybe," he said, "but I won't need a surname until you retire and you've already told me I've still got a lot to learn."

"Now there's truth in that," Gillander agreed. "What's going on out there?"

"Preparations. Lots of them. I don't understand most of it. Sure hate to see those cars going for barriers. Wish they could use the melty ones."

Gillander wrinkled his face, long skinny nose moving with the grimace. "We've been smelting those things down for decades. It's vanity keepin' 'em round. More putty than metal in most of them bodies now, anyways."

"Charlie likes them."

"Charles would. They go with his high falutin' job."

Thomas lapsed into silence. "But water's important," he said, finally, mildly.

"Course it is. It's life! And keepin' it pumpin' through and clean and rationing it, that's the most important job around here. Allotting the shares and enforcing the law. But you see," and Gillander tapped a lean finger on the writing desk, "Charlie inherited that job. There's a few around here waiting to see if he's bit off more than he can chew. He's got to do more than parade around in his fancy carriages to convince people."

"You talk like Charlie has to fight people around here, too."

"Maybe yes, maybe no." Gillander looked at him shrewdly. "He's going to need a lean, mean bodyguard."

Thomas felt his cheeks heat up and he turned around, unable to continue meeting his teacher's stare. Had Gill seen him working out? It wasn't like he'd ducked out on his mental exercises or anything. Uncomfortable on the floor, Thomas surged to his feet and returned to the window.

"War is a fascinatin' thing," Gill commented.

A shiver like cold goose feet walking down his spine shook Thomas. He said, "And it's horrible, too." He looked at his teacher from the safety of the window. He felt the change sweep over him, the change that came when he realized he was remembering, or dreaming, instead of living this experience. His voice dropped suddenly, hitting an adult register. He groped for what it was he wanted to say. "What's it like being dead?"

Gillander grinned. The late afternoon light slanting from behind Thomas struck his eyes, making them reflect like cats' eyes, red pinpoints of flame. "It's having time to do things over, like havin' this conversation now instead of the one we had fightin' over your training for Charlie."

Thomas shook uncontrollably. "What's happening now? Am I dreaming? I don't understand!"

"No," his teacher answered sadly. "Not yet."

"You can't tell me—" his voice went up again, cracking. "You can't tell me what to do! I want to know how to shoot a rifle. I want—I want to know those moves with your hands and feet. I want—"

"You want to know how to kill," Gill interrupted.

"I don't want to sit around cobbling people's old shoes when I'm not being a Protector!"

"There's nothing wrong with being a cobbler. People need souls, too."

"Soles," Thomas shouted. "You mean soles!"

"Do I?" Gillander's form began to grow misty-opaque and disappear as though the angled sunlight ate it away. "Do I?"

Confused, Thomas threw himself at the door and tore it open. He bolted outside, gasping for air.

Outside the small building, it was night. He saw Charlie walking by with one of his overseers, saying, "They won't attack at night. They're sluggish at night. . . ."

Blinking at the sudden loss of the sun, Thomas turned around. He'd been fighting with Gillander over his training. Nervously, he wiped the back of his hand across his mouth. He had lost time somewhere—an hour or two of sunset and dusk—and perhaps he'd lost more than just time.

He cast about. Fires glowed on the hills. Fires for bivouacking troops, and for signals. Embers banked in the event of the conflagration of war.

Seeing him hesitating in the shadows, Charles turned and pointed at him. "Who are you?"

The DWP was a big-shouldered man, in his prime. His gills flared in challenge. Thomas straightened. He hid his gills under a muffler his mother had knitted. It was clumsy, hot, and chafing. This man wore his gills like epaulets, badges of honor and rank.

That was in the days before Charlie had his cut out . . . I kept mine because I liked swimming with the dolphins too much. . . .

"I'm Thomas, sir. Apprenticed to Gillander."

"Oh." The massive man looked him over briefly, then said mildly, "Shouldn't you stay close to your mentor, son? there's likely to be quite a power drain when Denethan hits."

Guiltily, stammering, "Y-yes, sir," and knowing there was no going back to Gillander. Not just yet.

The DWP swung around, rejoined his aide, and strode off to the big house chosen as headquarters for the line. Shortly, halfway up the lane, a slender woman joined him. She carried a fair-haired toddler. He put an arm around them both. Thomas heard, "Veronica . . ." drifting back on the evening wind, then nothing.

With a feeling that he only had his skin halfway on, Thomas made his way to a ridge and stood on it, looking at the approaches to the peninsula. Absentmindly, he patted down his blue-tick shirt. He usually carried a spare garrote or two. He was empty-handed this night.

But he wasn't himself. He knew it and could do nothing about it. As he overlooked the pockmarked basin, he heard it now as he'd heard it then . . . a wind raider skulking on the night breeze from off the peninsula, downwind, so as not to alert anyone. So as not to make the signal fires gutter low and then flare up with the message of its passing.

He had no time to scramble down off the ridge. Now, as then, he threw his head back and yelled with both voices, exterior and interior, so that everyone could hear. "Enemy, coming in, south downwind!"

And now, as then, the hills erupted in fire as the troops of the desert mutant known as Denethan made their own sunlight.

He himself, killed one of the Protectors with that scream of warning. No one blamed him for it. She was

an old woman with fuzzy iron—colored hair and a
knack for finding lost things. She'd been the one who'd
taught him to dowse water, a Talent that Charles did
not encourage because all water needed to be cleansed
and metered. In later years, Thomas would find dowsing invaluable as he also found Charlie did not control
the wilderness. He was not the one who discovered
her body—he could no longer remember who did—
sitting in her rocking chair, next to one of the armory
sheds, her tatting in her lap. Her head was nodding
upon her chest, and crimson leaked from both her
ears.

The Protectors were not allowed at the front. Thomas
remembered thinking that sometime around dawn, after the moon had smoldered and gone dark with the
battle, and lizard backs rippled around the tiny knoll
where he and his Protector had taken a stand. Gillander
grabbed up his sweating hand.

"Run for it, m'boy."

Panic-stricken, Thomas gazed across the enemy ranks.
He could, perhaps, make it back up the long sloping
field. But Gill was too spent, and Thomas was not
strong enough to carry him. "We'll hold them here,"
he said, and his words came out far braver and stronger
than he felt.

"No." Gillander shook his head. He tapped his
temple. "Charlie's bringing out the missile guns. They're
going to use the defoliants. Get out. Get out now, and
I'll do the holding."

This land would be ablaze—ablaze and toxic. The
small fires Denethan's men had set during the night to
keep their blood warm would be as nothing to what
Charles had planned. Even young Thomas could comprehend the horror about to erupt.

He turned and ran, without a good-bye. He ran as
he'd never run before, once or twice skittering past a
mutant soldier like a flushed rabbit, too quick to be
sighted or caught. He ran for Nolan and the other
Protectors, but mainly Nolan because he was good
with TK and if anyone could pluck Gillander out of

thin air, whisk him out from under the enemy's nose, Nolan could.

But Nolan had not survived the night's war either. Lady wept over him . . . funny, Thomas had not remembered her that well before . . . her eighteen lush years to his fourteen a threshold he could not cross then . . . and his only hope then had been to go to Charles.

Out of breath and with a stitch in his side that threatened to double him over, he found the ridge where the missile guns squatted and a handful of men paced at their bases.

Charles did not remember who he was. He looked at him evenly. Thomas had somehow grown in inch or two since their meeting last night. The big man's pepper-colored hair looked as if he'd just run a hand through it, and his eyes, once the color of freshly dried tobacco, now looked murky and tired. "What do you want?"

"I'm here to—to guide your placements."

"A little young for gun fire control, aren't you?"

Thomas gulped down the "yes, sir, no, sir" that became garbled somewhere in his throat where his gills intersected his windpipe and answered, "I just came in over the fields where the line broke late last night. *Do you want to know where they are or don't you?*"

Charles reached out with a massive hand and gripped his collarbone so tightly he could hear the bones move and he would carry the bruise for a month. "Tell me the truth" was all that the DWP said to his impertinence.

A soft cloth salved his wound now and he heard a gentle voice murmur, "You're just dreaming, Thomas. Come back to me."

He stirred in his wandering. He did not want to remember the morning Charles stalked the battlefield, unconquerable, beating back the lines of desert mutants, roaring his defiance at Denethan, repairing breaches, and Thomas strode shadowlike in his wake, searching the fields for Gillander.

The battle was over when Thomas found him. He sank to his knees beside the sere carcass that bore little resemblance to his teacher and cried. He beat his fist into the gory soil.

"You *moved*, damn you. You *moved*. I saved the knoll for you, but you *moved*."

The dead could not answer him back. And worse, the dead could not hear him explain why he had run without saying good-bye. He had never intended that to be the last time he ever spoke to Gillander.

A month later, his bruises faded to a sickish yellow, he packed up his kit and left for the ruins, in search of a murdering squatter who, it was said, knew a hundred different ways to kill a man. Only Veronica and Charlie knew that his prodigious TK powers had been dampened, lost, leaving him almost deaf and mute. He could Truth-read and Project, but the other Talents had been striped from him. That was okay. He still had his hands.

He found the squatter and brought him in for bounty, dead, but not until after a year and a half of scholarship from him. Then Thomas went back to the ruins, combing them, for the murdering squatter who had known a hundred different ways to kill a man had had a gentle, inquiring side to him, like Gillander, and had been searching for civilization in those times when his sanity came upon him.

When Thomas came back, it was to take up his role as Protector, having chosen the surname Blade for the weapon he most liked to use, and a chevron scar quirked his left brow sardonically.

He had not found any answers in the ruins. Or rather, he'd found too many: fire, quake, decay. And he had been found by something intelligent living on the north edge of the L.A. basin, where the Cleveland National Forest edged down to the foothills. Something that had reared at him out of the night, with a hoarse cry, and marked him as its meat.

Or disciple.

Thomas mumbled in his delusion and cried for the lack of knowledge. Lady Nolan reached across the sand and took his calloused hand in hers, and murmured soft words he could not quite hear.

Chapter 12

"You're deluded if you think Denethan is holed up somewhere in the foothills, sweating through breakout fever."

"I didn't say that," Thomas answered evenly, if weakly. "I said, he's as spent as I am. So the night and day we lost isn't. Hopefully."

His retort didn't mollify Lady. She viciously stabbed a stick into the campfire, stirring up ashes and embers. "Who told you to go on the offensive anyway? Did you think you could stick one of your knives into him?"

Thomas felt his lips curl. "I wouldn't waste one of my knives on him," he muttered.

"No? Then you had no business taking the offensive! If you can't handle it, don't do it! I can't—we—can't afford to lose you."

"I almost had him." Thomas, not listening, stared at the fire dancing on the sands. "I almost had him at the wedding."

"That was then! We were all linked. Yesterday he almost had you."

Thomas looked at her fiercely. "You don't think I can do it. But I can. We're bound now. He's like a shadow to my every thought and all I have to do is look for him."

Lady sat back and tucked her knees up. She was far enough back from the fire so her eyes were shadowed as she answered somberly, "You probably can. But we can't afford to find out. Your symptoms were those of breakout fever, but I've never seen that in an already realized Talent. Twins are thought-tied, sometimes. Why not mortal foes? So what are we going to do now?"

"We catch up with the paralight. The tide's wiped out most of the sign, so there's nothing to lead Denethan on if we're careful in the morning. We ride hard and hope our luck holds."

Lady mumbled, "If it weren't for bad luck, we'd have no luck at all."

Thomas grinned at her. "Toss you for the blanket? Or we could share it?"

She rose up. "It's my mule and my blanket. You got it last night because you were ill. Tonight you can molder on the sand for all I care." She stalked off, rounding the boulders that tumbled onto the sand where the mountain met the shore, to make her evening ablutions. Thomas watched her go, thinking that she probably had been lying to him when she'd said she preferred to sleep with her mule.

Probably.

The noon sun was hidden under a bank of clouds, the kind of clouds that leaned on Southern California oppressively until the sun burned them away into a kind of haze. There was no rain in them . . . they were dove gray against a nondescript sky. Thomas reined in the black mare and stretched in his saddle, eyeing the horizon from under the protective shade of his wrist. The clear, crisp days of February were nearly gone.

The mule rattled to a stop at the mare's heels. Lady's face, pink with sunburn, was framed by damp tendrils of hair.

"He has more sense than any of us," she remarked, also stretching in the saddle. "Another mile and he won't go for me at all."

Blade cast a glance at the cream mount which seemed

to know it was under consideration and looked up, eyes rolling. Its hide shone with lather.

"We'll break for half an hour. No longer." He swung down and Cindy quivered in relief. She lipped at her bit, foam dripping. He dampened a rag and wiped her mouth down, then cupped a hand and let her suck up a bit of water.

Lady said mournfully, "We're low on water, too."

"Not likely to find any around here. The ground's too thirsty."

The Protector looked to her left at the ocean, where water rolled gently with the tide, gray-blue under the overcast sky. "There's no drinking that."

"Not yet, anyway." He looped Cindy's reins over the saddle horn so she could wander and crop whatever shoots of grass she found in the wash cutting across their trail. The mule followed after, with a flip of its tufted tail.

Lady sat down abruptly, after first examining the dun-colored dirt for ants or other biting disasters. She settled her canteen in her lap and lifted her hair off her neck. "Thinking of Charlie's dream?"

"It's more than a dream—it used to be a reality, once."

"Once," she echoed. Her left eye, the blue one, seemed to catch a touch of the ocean's reflection. "You and he seemed obsessed with the past."

"If he gets the aqueduct repaired, he can bring runoff from as far away as Santa Barbara. . . ." Thomas twirled a pair of rods in his hand, preoccupied.

She fanned herself. "I refuse to argue politics with you."

"Politics?"

"Water is politics, Thomas, you know that. At least in our society. Charles may be DWP, but he's not above criticism. The aqueduct is a serious liability for him, particularly if he can't get it operating. He's had to delegate a lot of authority on other projects."

"And the more diffuse his power gets—"

She nodded, "The less power he has. I don't have as much faith in democracy as he does."

"Now who's arguing politics?"

"Not arguing, just commenting." Lady gazed serenely at the grazing mare and mule. She wet her lips from the canteen and gave a wistful sigh.

Thomas checked out the wash as well, noting the streak of green brush that ran down its eroded side. "Well," he said, "I wouldn't want you to be offended by my political opinions, so why don't you sit back while I do a little dowsing."

"Dowsing? Really?" She sat up straight and looked at him with a delighted expression. "I've never seen it done. Does it work?"

He shrugged. "No time like the present to see." He gave her a hand up. "Just don't jiggle my elbows."

Her eyebrow quirked. "Pardon me. I didn't intend to touch anything that was off limits."

Thomas felt heat washing his face as he approached the cut. He showed her one of the metal rods. It was two hands long, with a three-finger length at the end bent at right angles for a handle. He held the rods loosely in his fists, pointing ahead, parallel but separated. He began to walk slowly but deliberately across the ground.

As he approached the line of greenery, the rods began to slowly drift apart. He made no attempt to tighten his grip and did not stop walking until the swing was abrupt and complete.

Lady caught up with him. She looked down at the rods and the green path beneath them. She looked up at him. "It doesn't take an idiot to know there's been water through here," she said, "or there wouldn't be any vegetation."

"And it doesn't take a pair of dowsing rods either," he answered her. "But this is a wash—the rainwater came flooding through here and left. Or did it? If there's a decent water table level, we might hit some by digging."

She waved her hand down the length of the erosion. "Where might you suggest? Or are you the one going to be doing the digging?"

"I'll dig. But not here." He paced to the start of the greenery, settled his rods loosely in his fists again and began to pace the length of the wash. The rods would not stay parallel in his hold—they wavered back and forth—as Lady trotted next to him, saying, "It's psychosomatic."

Suddenly the rods swung violently outward, the one on his right bringing her to a quick halt. She looked downward at dirt as fine as ash, drifting over the toes of her boots. "Dig here?"

"Don't move." He shoved the drowsing rods into her hands and caught up with his black mare. His breakdown shovel was in the far pack. He returned, snapping it into place. Lady, somewhat apprehensive, had not so much as twitched.

Grinning, he shouldered her off the area. "You can breathe now."

She gave him an evil look as she moved out of his way. He began to dig.

By the end of their half-hour break, the mule had come back out of curiosity. Its nostrils were flared as it nodded, and Lady pushed it out of the way for the billionth time. She eyed Thomas in his hole.

"I'm not impressed."

"Oh?" Thomas paused, and wiped the sweat off his upper lip as it seeped into his fine mustache. The ends hung sullenly. He pointed at Murphy. "Tell him that."

She looked at the mule. "Him?"

"Him. Why do you think he's crowding you? He can smell it." Thomas drove the spade a little deeper, then lifted the shovel close to Lady's face. "Run your fingers through that and tell me it's not damp."

But she could see the difference in the texture. See and smell it. As she watched, Blade drove the shovel down three more times, and suddenly his boot leather began to turn dark as water trickled into the bottom of the hole. He quickly shoveled out the mud a few more times, then held his hand out and Lady helped him out of the hole. He grabbed hold of the mule's headstall. "Let it seep in and fill a little before you water him."

"Is it clean?"

"It's not toxic, if that's what you mean. Not out here. We'll fill our canteens after the animals have drunk and the silt settles down a little."

She looked after him. "You could put Charles Warden out of business."

Thomas stopped in his tracks, the shovel between his hands, as he began breaking it down. He met her gaze. "If I wanted to," he said. "But I'd have to dig a hell of a lot of holes to water Southern California."

The tension lines fled from her face with her sudden gasp of laughter. The mule nudged her aside and she turned her attention to wrestling with it until the water level came up enough to water the two beasts.

Lady packed the last of the filled canteens. As she fastened down the flaps on her pack, she said, "I thought dowsing was a folk art."

"It is. But the DWP has discouraged it." Thomas didn't look up as he shifted the contents of his pack about a bit, getting ready to put the dowsing rods away.

"I thought anyone could do it, if they wanted to."

His chin came up. He smiled slowly. "Like to have a go at it?"

"Daring me?"

"Why not?"

"All right." She took the rods from his grip. "What do I do?"

He led her into the wash. "Let's do an easy one first. The water hole's over there, ten paces. Let's see if you can locate it."

Lady rolled her eyes skeptically. He shrugged. "Hold the rods like this. Think: *water*. Then blank your mind. And don't try to move the rods. Keep your fists level and flexible. If the rods swing out, they swing out. If they don't, they don't."

"But I know the water's there."

He nodded.

The woman looked at him, started to say something, then firmly closed her lips. He noticed that they settled automatically into a half-smile, without conscious effort. Abruptly, he took his hands away from her fists. "Go to it."

She hesitated briefly, then strode out confidently. He watched her walking past, her tan blouse open at the neck, revealing fair skin that freckled faintly rather than tanned, her long, denim riding skirt down to her ankled boots, the color pattern of brown and blue repeating itself. An intentioned echo of her eyes? The rods wobbled a bit and he yelled out, "Hold them a little firmer." Then he watched her stride closer and closer to the hole, her strides becoming shorter and more hesitant. The rods stayed parallel in her hold.

At the pit's edge, she stopped and threw him a baleful glance over her shoulder. "Nothing happened."

He joined her. "Then I guess you're not a dowser." He reached for the rods, she held them out of his grasp.

"One more time."

"All right."

"Blindfold me this time."

"And have you fall into the hole?"

Her jawline tensed. "I've been wet before."

Wet, but not defeated. He fought the grin teasing the corners of his mouth. "All right, then." He reached for the white scarf about his throat. It was not there. Thomas looked down and saw his reflection in the still, murky surface of the watering hole. His grin fled.

"Where's my scarf?"

Lady gave him a puzzled look, small lines forming in the center of her brow. "In my pack, I suppose. I took it off when you were sick."

"Why?"

"You breathed easier. And I needed something to wipe your face down." She called after him as he headed for the mule and began rummaging through Lady's saddlebags, looking for the silken fabric. "What's wrong?"

"Nothing." His fingers snagged up the scarf and he drew it out of the pack, heedless of the disarray he left behind. He wound it around his neck, protecting and hiding his gills, and thus changing his reflection to mask what he saw as the inhumanity of his own image. He took the rods from her. "We've lost time."

"All right." She trailed him back to their mounts. "I say you cheated."

"And I say you can't dowse." He mounted up and kicked Cindy into a swinging trot, not caring whether Lady Nolan stayed with him.

He slowed down when the mare's neck became white with foam, and she put her head down, blowing in exhaustion. Lady Nolan reined in.

"We can't keep this pace up."

He looked out over an ocean turned sullen and gray, the sand rippling in glistening patterns as the tide shifted. "I told you it would be a hard trail."

"It's not the trail I'm worried about." She wrapped a leg about the saddle horn, her long skirt pulling back, showing a shapely, if pale, calf. Most of the women from his Protectorate had taken to wearing slacks for riding, or shorter skirts. She drew her hair back with her hands and twisted it quickly into a knot, tucking it into place at the nape of her neck. It wouldn't stay there, of course, three or four loping strides of the mule and it would come down.

Thomas reached into his inside jacket pockets. Vials tinkled and his hand brushed the ivoried finger bones several times—damn things appeared to change pockets at will—and he finally found what he needed. He stretched out his palm to Lady. Two long hairpins lay across it.

She snatched them up. "Wherever did you get them—" the rest of her words cut off as she pinned her hair back.

"I use 'em for lock picks. Take care of those two. I can't spare any more."

She dropped her hands back to her reins. With a slight shake of her hand, she put her heel to the mule's flank, pressing him back to the trail. By leading them out, she moderated the pace. Thomas watched her back—ramrod straight in the saddle, yet at ease, at one with the mule's rhythmic walk.

He put his hand inside his jacket again, checking the remaining hairpins. For some reason, the finger bones now resided in that slit.

The ghost road would save him—them—the hard trail days ahead. But he was feeling the toll of his fight with Denethan as much as his pressing need to find Charlie's children. He didn't think he could afford to travel the ghost road now. He remembered the death-like chill and despair too well. Was that where Denethan drew his attacking Projection from? From the hopelessness of a thousand million dead? Perhaps.

He remembered the flickering reflection of himself in the water, gills exposed. Denethan was hunting, and the eleven year plague had begun its cycle. And Thomas knew he couldn't afford not to follow the ghost road. He had to catch up with Jennifer and Ramos before Denethan did.

The bones were in his hand almost before he slipped his fingers inside his jacket.

Chapter 13

He didn't tell her until late afternoon what he had decided. A red-tailed hawk, too young to have the russet tail feathers accenting his speckled body, sailed the cooling thermals of the ocean. For a fleeting moment, his outspread wings spanned behind Lady's face, giving her an ethereal appearance. She had pulled the mule to a halt on the bluffs, and they were silhouetted against the lowering sun as though they rode the sky. Their trail had intersected the old Coast Highway and they now rode alongside its wasted track.

"No," was all she said. The denial was written in the sudden pallor beneath her sunburn.

"You're here at my sufferance," Thomas answered. He flicked Cindy's reins, and the black mare shifted uneasily.

"You can't leave me behind."

He did not answer. If he took the ghost road alone, they both knew that he could and would.

The hawk circled and disappeared, skimming the bluffs behind Thomas.

He waited for the tears and disappointment, but they didn't come. Lady lifted her head and pulled her shoulders back.

"You couldn't have come this far without me," she said.

"I'll be the first to admit it."

She eyed him closely, tiny lines furrowing between her off-color eyes. The hairpins still held her hair back, except for tiny wisps along her forehead that twisted in the breeze now, catching the last glinting gold of sunlight. "Damn it, Thomas. You've just been through breakout fever. Not too many grown men can boast that."

"I weathered it with your help. I'm not ungrateful."

"I don't want grateful! I want you alive." She slumped then and turned her face away, veiling her expression from him. "You're draining yourself. Psychic reserves are precarious, you and I both know that. You can't go on forever."

Thomas felt a stab of guilt for treating her coldly. She'd been an able partner thus far. If anyone was responsible for slowing them down, it was himself— yet he was punishing her for it. He kneed the mare alongside the mule.

"Then come with me."

She shook her head. "I don't think you can maintain the road for both of us. You think you're well, but we won't know until you're tested, and then it could be too late. Thomas, breakout fever could well have burned you dry." She dared to look back at him then.

Her words jolted him. He had never suffered break-out when young . . . he'd been apprenticed to Gillander when he was ten. He'd seen other boys come and go . . . he'd never wondered why. Breakout could kill, yes, he knew that, but he'd never come to the realization that it could also sear the power out of him, leaving him just another mutated husk of a human.

"I dowsed the water—"

"I was measuring you. No Talent used there, and I'll be damned if I know *how* you did it."

"I'd feel it if it was gone."

"Like Nolan? He never knew he was finished until he tried the impossible and it killed him. I can't let that happen to you!"

For a moment, the fever memory of a younger and weeping Lady interfaced over that of the one pleading with him now. He shook free of the memory and the feelings it evoked. "I'd feel it," he repeated.

The mule stamped. Its movement brought them closer together, knees touching. He grew aware of her scent—orange blossoms and hot sun as well as mule—as he leaned nearer.

The corner of her mouth quirked, as if she could read his sudden thought. Lady said softly, "I've never known a burned-out psychic who wasn't impotent as well."

He reached out and pulled her from the mule into his arms, saying, "I think we can settle that issue here and now."

No fog came in from the ocean that night. Firelight glowed off the banked embers, illuminating the black mare as she slept, head down, and the mule as it determinedly chewed a few thistles. Lady rested her head on his bare shoulder, murmuring, "Now we're even farther behind."

"And this time it is most definitely your fault." He tucked a strand of her hair behind her ear so that it could no longer tickle his neck.

"My fault! You grabbed me."

"Yes, but you just sat there waiting to be grabbed."

She put a knuckle into his ribs. "I was arguing. You were the one who got—"

He put his hand over her mouth. She subsided. He said softly, "We're not going to make very good time joined at the pelvis."

"I know that," she muttered through his hand, her breath coming in warm, moist bursts.

"Then we'll sleep a while, and take the ghost road."

That truly silenced her. He added, in his most gentle voice, "We've no choice."

She nodded, and threw her arm over his stomach, her touch light and comforting. He lay still, waiting for her to say something, then realized he was listening to her low and rhythmic breathing. There was a dampness on his shoulder where she leaned her head, but he could not tell if she had kissed him—or if she had cried a bit before she fell asleep. Thomas clamped his jaws shut tightly and tried to find sleep himself.

The ghost road was darker than he remembered, colored pale ash and charcoal rather than sepia. A spear of ice pierced him from his bowels to his throat, but he said nothing. Lady looked at him curiously as they crossed into the shadow rim of the other world, her hands in the air fussing with her hair. She finished pinning the loose strands back and remarked, "It must make a difference what hour you summon it at. We were nearly in daylight last time."

"It's time displacement. Anyway you look at it, it shouldn't make a difference." Thomas looked about. He would have, and did, trust the live Gillander with his life. The dead one, he had doubts about. He didn't like the twilight effect casting too many shadows to hide too many possible enemies. He tucked the ends of his scarf into his collar, felt the comforting coils of his garrotes and dropped his hands back to the reins. He wondered how long he could stand the cold. "The choice has been made."

Lady clucked to the mule and Murphy stepped out

smartly along the broken highway that hugged the rugged coastline. The black mare fell in behind. Thomas took advantage of riding at Lady's rear to loosen his rifle in its sheath. He tapped the firing chamber open and dropped a small but potent vial inside. He closed the chamber slowly and hoped his companion did not hear the distinctive click it made when it shut. If she did, Lady said nothing. She put the mule at point and held it there.

They rounded the bend. Thomas kept his hearing focused, listening for coyotes in the foothills behind them, or the low whoosh a wind raider coming in overhead might make. He heard nothing but the click of their mounts' hooves on the rock and sand track or the occasional retort as one kicked aside a chunk of asphalt. Lady twisted around.

"Why isn't this whole? Shouldn't we be riding in a time period when all this flourished?"

He shrugged. "I don't know. Isn't one of your Talents a sense of time? The bones didn't come with a set of instructions."

Not true, Gill said snippily at his left shoulder.

Overriding his voice, Lady said, "That's true." She paused, a small frown line appearing across her eyebrows. "Nothing. It's as though the thought itself repels."

Thomas pondered the dubious rules he knew of the road. That the coyotes could sense them but be physically unable to touch them while the wolfrats could both sense and reach them had no logical basis. Unless, of course, the wolfrats had their own psychic abilities, on some instinctive level. He knew that some animals possessed a keen sense of direction and had been known to travel hundreds of miles through unknown territory to return to their home ground. Could wolfrats sense prey even through layers of time? Why, then, would they ever hunger? The thought of being ravaged by beasts unrestricted by time and place chilled him.

But, as a hunter himself, he knew that not all hunts were successful.

The wolfrat filled an ecological niche as a very successful scavenger/predator of the city ruins. And although he had not heard of packs reported in the foothills, he knew he could not discount them as a hazard along the ghost road along with whatever troops of Denethan searched the coasts.

For now the road was quiet. For now they were safe.

Lady put her hand up and wheeled the mule around. "Off the road!" she cried out, and kneed the panicked mule past Thomas.

Thomas had been dozing in the saddle. He shook himself awake with a curse. The black mare, bit clenched in her teeth, danced a savage dance by the roadside. Then he saw what it was Lady had seen.

Fireballs, low and level, curving across the terrain at them. They sped down at an incredible rate, the wind roaring in their passage. Cindy reared as he kicked her after the mule. He fought her heaving panic to bring her back to all fours and get her out of the fireballs' pathway. The mare squealed. He threw himself forward as he felt her start to lose her balance—and the last thing he wanted to do was have her go over backward and fall on him, him with a vestful of poisons, explosives, and other chemicals. He kicked his feet free to bail out if his weight did not right her.

There was a moment of soundless agony. He could feel her trembling as she balanced on her hindquarters. Could see the fireballs coming in at them like comets. Could feel his hands frozen in an attempt to bring Cindy down, unable to pull his rifle. Could see Lady, riding in under their chins, throwing herself at the headstall to pull the mare down.

They all came together at once as time resumed. Cindy came to earth, tearing her headstall out of Lady's hand.

The Protector looked up, her jaw dropping open in astonishment. "What is that?"

He shoved his boots deep in his stirrups as the

clinking vials stilled. His heart rattled against his rib cage once or twice before settling. He looked up, and saw it also—so massive that the fireballs it had thrown seemed mere specks. It was dark with an orange corona, and it was curving along the horizon toward them. The wind sucked in, hot and dry. His ears popped. He stared at the apocalypse descending.

"Light . . . light, sound and fury." Lady turned her mule and sat, considering the ghost road. The unknown mass grew larger and larger until it threatened to flame up and blot out the eastern sky.

This part of the ghost road had been a highway. He could feel it now, a lane of despair, people piled upon it, rushing to get out, to leave, unable to go anywhere. Beneath their feet was a common grave site the depth of which frightened him.

Lady said softly, "What night is this?"

He wondered if it could touch them on the ghost road. He faced the asteroid. "I think this is the night the world died."

"No!"

"They tried to flee the city. This is one of the roads they took. Too many, trying to leave all at once." He loved her, and he stared at her soft profile delineated by the orange-black mass hurtling toward them.

He twitched the mare's reins. "We can run for it."

Lady brought her mule around to pace him. "I wonder if we'll be able to see them."

The spear that felt like it was piercing him turned in its wound. He stifled a gasp. "Why would you want to see them?"

"I'd give my soul if I could find out what they thought. Do you think they knew anything of what happened to the roads or the cities? Were they fleeing from disaster or driving straight into it?" Lady looked at him pensively. "That's why you like the ruins. I used to think it was because the gadgets fascinated you. How they worked and why and if they still could. You were always bringing back laser disks and the like. But that wasn't it at all, was it?"

"No. I guess we share a morbid fascination. I can't figure them out. Did they know when they spliced such and such a gene what they would create? How could they ignore the damage they were inflicting?" His left hand rose to his scared neck. "Or were they just playing at life?"

"You know the gills were intentional. We all had them a hundred, a hundred and twenty years ago. The ocean was the only safe environment we had left." Lady stroked her mule soothingly.

"Except for the desert mutations," Thomas argued. "And what we don't know about genetic splicing could fill books. The eleven year plague looks like an intentionally adaptive, evolving virus that attaches to the DNA chain. What genius let that loose? If they meant us to survive, they did it back asswards."

She put her hand out and placed it on his thigh. His muscles tensed under her touch. "I don't think they had much chance to plan."

"And I don't think they gave a damn one way or the other. But I'd like to *know*. I'd like to know just what they had in mind when they created things like me and Denethan." He reined away from her, kicking the mare viciously in the flank, as he shouted, "That thing is going to hit in minutes. I don't know what it'll do to us or the ghost road."

Thomas rode vigorously into the twilight, jaw set, his ears ringing with the roar of his own thoughts. He worked alone, he was used to it, and, dammit, he was not used to having his mind laid open like a raw wound for Lady Nolan to probe whenever she felt like it just to see if he was hurting. He couldn't protect her here. Hell, he couldn't even protect himself. He was unsure what they were about to witness and whether they would survive it.

The mare, still unnerved, responded when he touched heel to her, and began to canter over the foothill. It curved and broke away, downhill, back toward the ocean. He heard the mule braying faintly behind him, then nothing, and knew he was alone until they caught up, which was fine with him. Cindy's ears flicked forward and back, trying to sense if he wished more speed or not.

Both mare and mule came to a skidding halt as thunder boomed. The Protectors turned in their saddles. Beyond them was a vast expanse of light . . . thousands and thousands of small lights . . . shining in the night, white light being colored a garish orange as the burning asteroid swept close and filled the sky. Then it impacted. Blade shrank back and threw his arm up to shade his eyes. Then he heard it, a wail that grew as other voices fed it until he knew he must be hearing the cry of a million throats. The ground shuddered, throwing his mare to her knees and staggering the mule about. Then, silence. The night went dark as if nothing had ever happened.

Cindy heaved back up. Blade grabbed for the saddle horn to steady himself.

"Are you all right?" he asked Lady.

"Yes. Did you . . . did you hear that?"

He had thought perhaps the wail had been meant for his ears alone. But even in the dim light of the half-moon, he could see her ashen face. "Yes," he said briefly. "I heard it." He turned the mare on the road. "I don't want to be around to see the rest of it." He kicked his horse into a lope.

The broken track of the Coast Highway intersected with another, a faint, shattered line out of the east, off the sere dark foothills of the interior. Cindy put her ears back and charged ahead, gaining speed as she flung herself down the curving slope. Thomas rocked back in the saddle slightly to balance the mare, but he let her keep the bit. At the bottom, he reined her in, knowing he must wait for Lady to catch up. The sound of the mule's hooves drumming upon the ground drowned out his faint call. Murphy came downhill in a high-stepping trot. Lady's face was flushed when she pulled in beside Thomas. "That's quite a road!"

"Yes," he said. "I believe they called it Deadman's Curve."

Chapter 14

He said nothing to her of his ghosts, wanting to, but hesitating until the time had long since passed when he could have mentioned it without her wondering why he had waited so long. They seemed to hang on him, a clammy fog of misery. If she saw ghosts of her own, she never mentioned them to him either.

They stopped for a break. He got out of his saddle stiffly, feeling like an old man. He chafed his hands for warmth and stomped his feet, icy numb. Lady put hobbles on the mare and mule while he found a freshet of water and filled the canteens. They squatted in a gully eroded by the ocean and the broken road. Lady offered a thistle flower to the mule who gave her a disdainful look.

"They won't eat," she said, "but they're going to have to be grazed or we'll lose them. They're losing flesh. Haven't we been on this road of death long enough?"

"Almost," he said. A cornmeal cake crumbled in his mouth, as lifeless as the scene around them. "I'd like to cover another landing site. We've probably missed one."

"And if you can't find it?"

"Then we've lost the trail. I've no Talent for Seeking. You?"

Surprise rippled over her expression. "No Talent for

Seeking? Thomas, you've more talents than most people have fingers."

He shook his head. "Not me."

She closed her mouth firmly instead of arguing. He broke off another piece of cornbread and passed it to her, along with a jar of honeycomb Veronica had packed for him. She took the jar and put a sticky finger to her mouth wryly.

"It's lost its flavor, too."

"Use it anyway. There might be some value to it." He watched her eat, with dainty yet matter-of-fact movements. She seemed to be unaware of his stare.

Not everything had lost its appeal. Uncomfortably, he got up and walked out of sight.

The urine he released was a pallid stream against the twilight background. As it pooled into the ashy ground, he found himself wondering if it were night or day outside the ghost road. He refastened his fly, thinking about making love to Lady Nolan once more, but not here. Not where he could not smell the salt breeze and flowers in her hair, or taste the mild flavor of her soft skin. Not where nothing cared for the living. Not where his flesh felt like the icy skin of death.

A branch cracked. Its pop shattered the unnatural silence of the landscape. Thomas froze. Then he located the sound's direction and followed it.

He climbed uphill to skirt the draw, and lay on his stomach to look down at it. Below, three figures squatted around a flat rock, drawing and quartering a wild cat. Sprawled beyond them was the wind raider the three had flown to get this far. He stared for a moment, then a pins and needles tingling began in his boots and hands. Blade lifted a hand and spread it before his face. He'd lost the ghost road. Without conscious thought, he'd lost it and now they were vulnerable to the predators below.

Grounded, the wind raider looked like a large, ungainly blot. Without a catapult or jumping off a sea cliff, it would not be possible to get it back into the air. The raiders seemed unconcerned. It had served its purpose by bringing them this far. They passed each other the bloody bits of their kill, unworried about the black rivulets falling between their fingers or the lack of a fire to cook their meal.

He held his breath. As feeling crept back into his body, he tried to focus for a projection. His thoughts whirled unsteadily. He had no strength for an attack, the ghost road had sapped him. It would have to be the hard way. He drew out a blade and a garrote and gathered himself for a leap.

He took out one by landing on it. Its neck went with a pop as the other two were knocked on their rumps, raw meat flying out of their hands. Thomas sprang, burying his knife hilt-deep in the second who had recovered well enough to charge him. As the third jumped on his back, he flung the garrote over his head, found a neck and brought his hands together, tightening the loop as the men atop him and below him began to die.

He shrugged off the dead weight as the thrashing stopped. He skinned back the grimacing lips to find ordinary, if somewhat decayed, teeth. He kicked the ashen dirt in their faces, thinking that this trio was more manlike than he'd grown to expect from Denethan. He cleaned his loop on the dead man's breeches and replaced it in his collar.

The knife was a little messier to retrieve, but he had no intention of leaving it behind. He cleansed it as well as he was able to before slipping it into his boot.

He took one last look at the three dead men before turning to Lady. He put his hand inside his vest where the finger bones seemed to leap into his grip, and his blood went chill.

She was repacking his saddlebags when he came back. She did not seem to have noticed that they had lost the road and gained it again though she looked troubled beneath the sheen of her sunburn. "Trouble?"

"Nothing to speak of," he answered. "We need to hurry. We're running out of time on the ghost road."

She turned a disturbed gaze toward him but asked no questions.

They found one of the landing sites. It was in a lee, on the bluffs overlooking the ocean, its grass yellowing already in a Spring that had begun dry and would likely get drier. Poppies had been broken and snapped off by the weight of the paralight. Lady dismounted, picked up a broken stem and twirled it in her fingers. It spun in her fingers, gray petals and blackened stem. He watched her toss it to the ground and look up at him, one eye darker than the other, both somehow colorless. He had a sudden desire to see color in her gaze.

"How long ago?"

He frowned. As he looked out over the meadow, he could see the present or near present images superimposed on those of the past. He could see Ramos chasing Jennifer across the grass, her white buttocks still slender as a child's, flashing like a rabbit's flagging tail as she raced away from him. He wrenched his sight away from the two naked children and back to Lady.

"Yesterday. Perhaps even this morning. What do you think?"

"This morning. The sap still runs in the flower. I couldn't see it, but I could feel it."

He nodded and held the mule steady while she remounted. They rode hard until they crested the bluffs above Carpin, and he put his hand out to halt her. The twilight revealed his worst nightmare. He took the finger bones out of his pocket to break the ghost road. His hands were like ice and the thought struck him for a moment that, if not frostbite, he had chilblains.

With a roar, sound and scent and color returned to the world. It brought the reek of fire.

Lady's lips pressed together thinly as she looked down on the plains, and ocean, and ruins in front of them. Thin columns of dark smoke rose into the air from twisted shadows at the base of the ruins.

"God," she said. "We're too late."

Chapter 15

"No sunrise this morning," Charlie said, as he reached out and pulled Veronica to his side. The low hanging clouds showed pink briefly, hiding the errant sun. She had not been sleeping well for the last few weeks, and he'd gotten out of bed early to trail her outdoors this morning. She stood on the sweeping expanse of land behind their house, land that had once been groomed as part of the estate. She shifted uneasily in his arms.

"Missing Jennifer?"

His wife did not look at him, her stance and attention aimed northward. But she answered, "Need you ask?"

"No. I guess not. I heard last night that Lady Nolan's gone, as well as Sir Thomas." He loosened his embrace. "The children'll be as safe with them as anyone."

Veronica looked at him. She had aged somewhat but admirably since his first infatuation with her. Gray brushed her chestnut hair at the temples, but her skin stayed clear and firm. There were fine wrinkles about her eyes whether she frowned or smiled, though. Her brow arched. "It would have been safest not to send them at all."

He looked over the expanse, thinking that he disliked the overcast mornings that burned away to too bright afternoons. He liked the days that started out crisp and clear and stayed that way, even though the ocean breeze could have a bite to it.

Veronica stirred within the shelter of his arms. "I didn't come out to look for them," she said softly. "Enjoy the view, Charles. It's likely to be the last sunrise we'll ever see."

He spun her about roughly. "What the hell are you talking about?"

"I'm talking about the attack." She smiled gently. "I love you, Charlie. I loved you when I first met you, and I loved you when you sent Jennifer away, and I love you now. I want you to know that."

Charles staggered back a step. "Who's attacking? When?" He cursed himself for not recognizing the half-trance of a Seeing.

"They're coming, love, and this time, you can't stop them." His wife's eyes rolled back in her head and she collapsed with a weary sigh. He caught her up. "Ronnie! Wake up! Are they coming at us here or at the plant?" But she was gone, passed beyond his awakening.

He lifted his head and bellowed for help.

They left their mounts tethered above, but even that far removed, Cindy spread her nostrils at the scent and rolled her eyes. Lady took her skinning knife from her belt sheath and cut as much sweet grass as she could reach hastily and threw it in front of the animals before scrambling down the slope after Blade.

After the sterility of the ghost road, the stench of the carnage hit them like a fist. The air swarmed with the buzz of flies, and stank with fire and earth. Lady Nolan staggered to a halt, and put her fist to her mouth.

"God," she said, and gagged.

He pushed her away, so that she couldn't see the bodies, and so that he could not hear her heaving too clearly. His own stomach knotted up against his spine. He staggered, unable to control limbs so cold they might as well be stone. Finally and ironically, thanks to the glittering fire, he warmed enough to approach the bodies.

As near as he could tell, at least they've been burned in one piece, thrown clear of the paralight wreckage. Denethan's men had not torn them limb from limb. It was one of the few mercies he could grant their dying. They had not been immolated. They had died first, and the raiders had burned them afterward. Strands of Jennifer's light blonde hair lay streamered over the charred ground, incongruous against her blackened skull. Bones of her hand were entwined with those of the boy's.

Thomas wrenched his gaze away to the paralight. He could see the flashburn along the fuselage. A vial bullet, then, such as the one he'd fired at the wind raiders days ago, had caught them. They'd gone down burning, helpless, wedged inside the paralight's body, seeing their death surge up before them even as they flamed. He hoped they'd hit the ground before the burning had gotten too bad.

With a sigh, he turned back and caught Lady by her shoulders and steadied her trembling form. "They didn't suffer."

His words caught her mid-gulp. "Wha-what?"

He reflected that she wasn't a woman who looked beautiful crying. Her face had gone blotchy and swollen. "They died on impact. Denethan's men brought them down, but never got to them after that."

"T-thank God for small favors." She hiccoughed roughly. "Oh, Thomas." She twisted abruptly in his hands and barreled into him, catching him up in a desperate embrace and where his jacket fell open, his shirt became wet as she began to cry in sobs whose ache he could feel echoing in his own sorrow. But he could not cry as she did, so he stood there and held her. He envied her her emotions.

He could not tag his own so easily. Did he sorrow because he'd failed in his mission? Or because they were children, too young to die any kind of death—or did he mourn the loss of tomorrow's children, to be born without gills or third arms and other mutations. The gills could be bred out, of course. He knew families with several generations gillfree, but it was a very strong recessive trait and one that could return at any time. He himself was such a throwback. And Charles—

He let go of Lady so abruptly that she rocked back on her heels. A shock thrilled through him.

"Charlie's in trouble," he said. "Come on—we've got to hurry!"

She dried her face on her sleeve and scurried after him as he took the slope in leaping strides. "Thomas! What is it?"

"We've got to get back and get back *now*."

She panted to a stop behind him as he gathered up the black mare's reins. He pulled his scarf off his neck.

"I'm not going anywhere else until you explain."

"I haven't time. Will your mule lead blindfolded?"

"I don't know. He's always been sensible—*Thomas, will you tell me what's happening?*"

"We've got to get back. I'm not going to be late this time if I have to walk on water." He pulled the finger bones out of his vest and looked over the span at the Pacific Ocean. The coastline sparkled back at him.

"What—oh, no. You can't be serious. You look half-dead now. And your hands—it's as if you've been frozen!"

"Listen. The ghost road isn't real—it's time displacement. But even by land, we can't get back in time, and I can guarantee you, Denethan's men are still out there between us and the peninsula. We can't take days going home."

"You might as well suggest flying."

He looked over the edge of the bluff as if considering, then shook his head. "No, the paralight's in no condition."

She planted her feet stubbornly. "Do you expect to walk over water?"

His brows went up. "You've lost your senses. I know the area. There's a man-made marina not too far from here. I recognize the shape of the bay and breakwater. It's not been salvaged too badly. With any luck, we'll find a fiberglass boat shell in good enough shape to hold us. I can rig a sail—if you can convince the mule and horse to stay quiet once we load them—can you?"

"Boat back?"

"It's the best way. And if we can do it in ghost time, we might only lose a day or two."

She threw her arms about him and let out a shaky laugh. "It's not the days I'm worried about losing. What about Charlie? I Feel nothing."

Thomas shrugged. "Who's got the worst reputation as Protector?"

"Why, you, I suppose. You're the executioner."

"And if you were going to Protect something very valuable, wouldn't you send your most fearsome Protector to do it?"

"Yes, but—I don't understand."

"You will," Thomas said bitterly. "If we're too late."

Alderman collapsed, his thin chest wheezing. One of the boys darted out and dragged his body back. Charlie saw the movement from the corner of his eye. With the loss of another Protector, he was as good as whipped and he knew it.

Veronica handed him a loaded rifle. "At least they haven't gotten into the plant," she whispered, her gentle voice gone hoarse with the day's fighting.

"No."

They both knew the enemy would use it to bring him down—that Charlie would surrender if they broke through the water station's defenses and threatened to destroy it. The DWP would never let the plant be sacrificed in his place. He had been betrayed and now he was being destroyed.

Veronica rubbed one eye. She let out a tiny sob. "Oh, Charlie! I can see Jennifer—she's waiting for us."

He turned a deaf ear toward his wife, cradled the rifle into position and sighted on a target. It would be dark soon. As he fired and watched the hillside explode, he wondered if the warfare would get better—or worse when night fell. His wife sobbed brokenly at his shoulder. Even if he survived this day, even if he could somehow gather his ragged troops together and win, he'd lost his wife. Her mind was as broken as the sounds of her grief. He pulled the trigger, releasing the second chamber. He handed the rifle to her. "Damn it, Ronnie. Keep loading!"

She stared blankly at him for a moment, then nodded and took the weapon. Her trembling fingers brushed his gently. She whispered, "I love you," then she bent quickly to the open case of vials and began to load the rifle.

The sea on the ghost road was as black as obsidian. Their wake cut white foam into streams behind them. The peaks and valleys of the waves seemed not to move, as though they rode a crystal sculpture of an ocean.

Lady sat hunched between the two mounts, each hand an anchor to their bridles. Her face was pale, her eyes closed, as she concentrated the Talent she had for animals to keep them calm.

Thomas had all he could do to keep the wind from blowing the sail out. He could not ask for better direction. The coastline skimmed behind them and he hung on the boom to keep it from swinging around and clipping the animals. A line to the rudder was wrapped about his wrist as the sailboat plowed across the currents.

A massive gray shape slid close under the dark waves. He looked across the starboard bow, and his jaw clenched. The presence was as long as the twenty-four foot long boat he sailed. It circled, then came closer, pacing them. It rolled, breaking surface, and he looked at dorsal fins and a flat, dead eye.

The shark grinned. Then it dove, disappearing rapidly. Thomas leaned far out, trying to keep it in view, but his rigging reins drew him back. Primeval forces, he thought. If it could get to him—

There was a hard bump below his feet as though something had hit the bottom of the boat.

"Thomas! What is it?"

"Nothing," he said quickly. He ducked under the boom and went to the port side, at the bow.

Foam churned. But nothing appeared.

He spun on his heels and, straining his eyes, tried to see in the murk behind the boat, but all he saw was the dazzling comet tail of their wake crossing that murky curtain, and it blinded him momentarily. The mark on his wrist itched and he rubbed it absently, thinking of the dolphin goddess. The sea roared at him, covering him with foam.

He turned and faced a bottomless pit of teeth. The shark mauled at him, bitting the air before his face. A scream tore from his throat and he felt the abrupt shift of the boat as the mare reacted, throwing herself back wildly. The boom swung, dragging him half behind it before he caught himself and collapsed the sail—the rigging pulling him literally out of the shark's jaws.

"Keep her down!" he shouted at Lady as the woman cried, "What is it?" Her eyes were opened wide, but she stayed down and brought the mare to her knees behind her.

Spray drenched him as something scraped up alongside the boat. "Just think of it as another big wolfrat!" He pulled his knife and cut himself free from the tangled line. "Watch the boom!"

It swung back, but not too close to them, and danced with the erratic movement of the boat.

The sailboat drummed with another blow from down below.

Thomas fished inside his vest. He grabbed two or three vials without looking and scrambled back to the bow. He nicked his wrist and hung over the side, watching the darkness of his blood disappear into the midnight water.

His hand throbbed. The fingers clutching the vials grew numb. The boat skewed sideways against the waves and he knew they were taking on water. Not much, but enough.

Lady saw it rise. She screamed as his vision filled with a gray wall and white teeth, slashing savagely at his hand.

Thomas dropped the vials even as he threw himself

back in reflex. The shark reared up against the boat, forcing its body out of the ghost water, thrashing against the bow. He could smell it and knew that it crossed the ghost road, that it was not held to mortal boundaries. Then it fell back, unable to throw itself into the boat after him. Blade crawled back to where Lady sat, one arm wrapped about the mule's neck, her skinning knife to its throat, her face streaked with tears.

He took the knife from her as she said, "I was going to throw him over. To save you. To make it let you go."

He grinned weakly. "If it had gotten me, there wouldn't have been enough to let go."

There was a flash and a deafening explosion behind the boat. He shaded his eyes and she tightened her grip on the animals.

"I think I managed to give it indigestion anyway," he said.

"How could it—how could it touch us?"

"I don't know. Gillander warned me . . . there are some things the road cannot contain. Basic forces. Pure evil, he said." He stroked her flank, where she could not feel his cold touch upon bare skin.

She made a funny noise, then said, "I think you'd better stop fooling round and start bailing."

"Right," he said.

Even on the ghost sea, Thomas recognized the point where the sea bowls cupped out from the shoreline. They were nearly home. There was a strand of beach not far from the bluffs where Charlie's house reigned, and as he pulled out the finger bones to bring them off the ghost sea, he felt a moment of misgiving.

"Shouldn't we bring the boat in first?"

He nodded. "I think so. Bring 'em to their knees. I don't want the boom to hit them. I've got to tack us in."

Lady clucked sweetly to the mule to bring it down. The mare was difficult—her black knees already scabbed from rough treatment earlier. Reluctantly, she went, with Lady making soothing noises and stroking her muzzle.

Tired in every fiber of his body, he began to fight the sailboat to make it do what he wanted it to.

Denethan scanned the scorched grass, and the massive house, and the bodies lying everywhere. His men ranged through, trotting like hounds across the grounds.

"Take no prisoners," he said flatly. The carnage was not of his making, but an enemy was an enemy.

"No, sir," his fighters called in response. He looked around again, senses probing briefly, without waste. His eyes could tell him about the slaughter here as easily as his Talents.

On the outskirts, where the last charge had finally broken, he found the body of a large, burly man, curled protectively over what had once been a beautiful woman. It appeared that he had broken her neck himself with one swift twist before being overrun.

Denethan ran a nail tip across the insignia sewn over his breast pocket. The DWP. He eyed the corpse. There was no flavor here of the man who'd faced him down earlier, but he had no doubt that this was the body of one of his most formidable enemies.

He touched a boot toe to the carcass gently.

"We'll leave them," he announced loudly. "If there're any survivors in the hills, they can creep out after we're gone and do whatever they want to with the bodies."

He signaled to his troops and they left with him. What he searched for was elsewhere.

Charlie held his breath another few minutes, then let it out raggedly, and opened his eyes. His vision stayed blurred. He was still alive, but would not be for long.

Ronnie had been wrong about him, though. He *had* seen another sunset. Now he lay waiting for . . . what, he was no longer sure. He moved his hand searchingly and found her chill one, and cradled it, rubbing his thumb back and forth across the circlet of gold which had once bound them together. Strange. There had been no looting.

The black mare let out a strangled whinny as Thomas cut her with the reins, whipping her up the curving roadway. The signs of warfare stained his vision everywhere he looked. For a moment he wondered if the ghost road had brought them to another time, but he knew better.

Lady let out a tiny cry as they drew close to the manor house. Carrion crows took flight at their approach. She pulled the mule to a stumbling halt and half-dismounted, half-fell out of the saddle.

"Everyone," she whispered hoarsely. "Did you See it, Thomas? Why didn't you tell me?"

Numbly, he shook his head. Following the signs, he went around to the back of the house and saw where the final breach had been made. Charles' body curved about Veronica's frail one, her blue dress crimson-splattered with his blood. He dropped from the saddle.

The mare shied away from the sandbag barrier and the wooden crates still with vials of ammo cradled within. He stepped over broken bodies to reach Charlie. He dropped a hand on his old friend's shoulder.

The carcass was still warm. He felt a quivering breath go through it beneath his hand.

He jerked the body over, and, as Charlie's eyes came open, he leaned down savagely and cried, "Where're the children, you bastard! Where did you send our real hope!"

Chapter 16

Lady caught up with them. She hammered at Thomas' back, crying, "For god's sake, leave him alone! Can't you see he's dying! Thomas, let go of him!"

But a thin smile, coated with pale blood, etched Charlie's face. "If . . . I wasn't a dead man, I would be. Right, Thomas? And I don't blame you." He coughed weakly and Blade let go of his shirt. His head dropped back to pillow on Lady Nolan as the Protector took his head and shoulders into her lap.

With an expertise born of practice and Talent, she ran her fingers lightly over his face and chest. Then she looked up at Thomas and shook her head. Blade stepped back and squatted down, trail soreness in his legs, his shoulders aching as if yoked to the world. His Intuition had fled him, bled dry by the ghost road, but he didn't have to Truth-read Charlie to get truth. "Tell me something I don't know," he said bitterly to the woman. "Tell me why this man sent his only daughter and another man's son off to be *butchered*. Tell me why he made sure Denethan would follow his decoys by making sure I would draw the lizard's attention."

Charles' lips worked soundlessly. The shiny scars at the sides of his neck where gills had been cut out bulged purple and the dying man gasped for breath. Lady's brow furrowed in empathy. She gazed at Blade with pain in her eyes, silently pleading for his good behavior.

But Charles reached for and grabbed up Thomas' hand. "Be still," he got out laboriously. His forehead shone with sweat. "You know what I did. I . . . only wonder how."

Thomas grasped his friend's neck in a rough caress. "Your gills, damn it all. Your gills! How could Jennifer be genetically pure just one generation removed when we both know of families two, even three generations removed carrying that recessive mutation!"

Nolan sucked in her breath. "They died for nothing? You sent them out to draw Denethan's attention?" The horror of what she'd seen on the outskirts of Carpin flooded her eyes. The blue turned icy, but the brown brimmed with an unshed tear.

"Ramos . . . maybe. But we had our pair . . . didn't want . . . anyone to know . . . needed a decoy. Denethan had been sniffing around lately. Knew he wasn't bottled up in the Mojave anymore. Who but Thomas would find out . . . sent my own daughter out as decoy . . . hoped he could keep her safe anyway. . . ." The dying man's eyes flickered to his friend's face.

"You knew Denethan would follow them if I went after."

"Your . . . reputation. Ronnie's idea . . . internal spies . . . had to throw them off. We thought you were good enough anyway. . . ." His eyes clouded. "Jennifer?"

Thomas shook his head briefly. He said only, "They didn't suffer."

"Veronica knew . . . two days ago. I didn't believe her." Charlie still held the stiff hand of his dead wife. He squeezed it tighter.

Lady said to Blade, "And you knew about this. That's why you drove us to get home!"

Thomas shook his head. "Not about this. Only that the children weren't what we were told. I had no idea about the attack. I did not think Denethan would be ahead of us." He turned away from the astonishment on her face.

His friend's eyes had closed. Thomas raised his free hand to Lady's and gripped it so tightly she could hear bones move. She bit her lip to keep from crying out.

"Keep him here. Just another moment or two—"

Instead of protesting, she nodded sharply. "I—I'll try."

Charlie opened his eyes and squinted, tears running from the corners of them. "It's dark, Thomas. Is it still sunrise?"

"No. Mid-morning, a little later."

"She said . . . we wouldn't see another sunrise. She was wrong . . . everyone dead but me. Denethan kicked me . . ." He moved his hand feebly, rubbing his rib cage.

Lady pressed her right hand to his forehead and bowed her head in concentration. The strain began to show on her already tired face.

"Charlie," Thomas leaned close and whispered urgently, "Did the children get away? Who were they?"

"Alma and . . . Stefan. But I told you . . . already, didn't I? I was . . . waiting for you . . ."

Lady whispered, "I'm losing him."

Sweet-eyed Alma and blond Stefan, whose genes had sailed all the way from the other side of the world. Thomas rocked back. "Where?"

"To the College Vaults." Too spent for words, his old friend closed his eyes tightly. After a shuddering breath, he added "We didn't plan to send out Alma and Stefan . . . until after searches had stopped. The way would have been clear then. . . ."

Blade nodded and then added, because Charles could no longer see him, "Yes, except that it led back to you again. You old fool."

"Yes." To Lady Nolan. "I'm cold. Can't you keep me warm?"

"No," she whispered. "Not now."

The frame of what had once been a massive, vital man seemed to shrink as he trembled from the cold. Then he coughed again, and drew a long, painstaking breath. "We were betrayed." Then, "Ronnie?" He put a hand up, brushing Thomas' face without knowing it. "Thomas, I've . . . got to go. Ronnie's waiting . . . and there . . . Jenny. . . ."

The Protector lifted Lady's hand from the man's forehead saying only, "Let him go." He pressed his fingers to his temples, trying to shut out the death rattle, so he could think of what he had to do next.

Lady didn't give him a moment's grace. "Give me a hand."

She shut the open eyelids, the stare already blinded. Then she let the man's head drop gently to the bruised and rust-colored grass. She settled Ronnie's curled form next to him, smoothing out her dress, unable to straighten slender limbs that death had already made rigid. He helped her, unthinking, his hands and movements patterning her own, echoing her effort. When she was done, she took off the long cotton slip from the dead woman and spread it across both their faces to keep away the flies.

"Shall we burn them?"

He straightened, putting his hands to the small of his back. He stared at the battle scene, the carnage, the carrion of what had been a sturdy community making a comeback. Crows flew overhead, skimming the roof of the manor house, headed for the slaughter in the front yard. Their harsh calls jarred his effort to think clearly.

There were too many dead. He shook his head. "No," he said. "Just Charlie and Veronica. I'll take care of them later." He walked away, taking stock of the fallen, trying now to note more than their faces, if they had any left, bloating under the sun. Lady Nolan followed after, her steps hesitant, and he knew her thoughts as well as if they were his own: someone, somewhere, might still be alive. Charles had lived this long. She did not note, as he did, that someone else had already walked through here, dispatching mercy strokes to a fallen enemy.

He found two of the Protectors, Alderman and Wyethe, huddled together. They were old men and it was an odd thing to him that, in death, they looked much younger than he could remember them in life. Lady went to one knee beside them. She gently caressed Alderman's bald pate which had sunburned before he'd died. Blade wondered if Wyethe had gone down stammering in his mildly confused way.

"Leave them," he said. "We're lucky most of the wedding guests had gone home already along with several of the Protectors, or there'd be more dead."

He walked in the back of the house. Furniture was overturned, and there were one or two bodies in here. But the house had stayed mainly intact, though it held the sticky sweet smell of blood going bad. He looked about, examining the inherited richness of a DWP's life, of the continuity of a lifestyle going all the way back to the Disasters.

Lady stayed in the doorway, beveled glass French doors framing her. Only one pane had been smashed. Its shards bediamonded her dusty boots. "It looks like they didn't even touch the house." She ran a hand up the framework.

"Nobody's touched the bodies outside, either. There's been no looting." Why, unless Denethan had been interrupted? And if he had, by whom? The approach of the two of them would scarcely frighten off an army.

"In spite of everything, I'd kill for a hot bath." Lady's face flamed a little as Thomas twisted to look at her, but he said nothing. Life went on and though she'd blurted out feelings neither had expressed aloud, the two of them still lived.

"We forgot the plant." She paused inside the house. "Maybe I won't have hot water, after all."

The refinery and pumping station. He looked to her. "Denethan couldn't kill the rest of us more completely than to shut down the stations."

"And he had little chance of getting through its defenses unless he took out Charlie first."

Stepping gingerly over the corpses and congealing pools of blood, he went to the kitchen tap. He turned it on. It howled once or twice, but water flowed smoothly—clean water. He sniffed it. Odorless. He touched the tip of his tongue to it. Dowsed water tasted better, but this was serviceable. He straightened.

Where was the conqueror? Surely he had more in mind than scattering the bodies of the defeated over the face of the earth. Yet . . . He made a fist. "Where is he? And what is he doing?"

At his shoulder, Lady said softly, "Why destroy what he can occupy?"

"Out of Oz? He'd come here?" Visions of the desert nation moving in while the other counties were too confused to stop them filled his head.

"Why not? God knows the Mojave is a hellhole."

"But he was made for it."

She moved past him, took a glass from a cabinet and poured herself four fingers of water and drank it without stopping to breathe. She looked at him over the rim of the empty glass. "Any other ideas?"

"None I like. I'm searching Charlie's office. We'll move the bodies out and you can take a bath while I find out if the pigeon coop is intact. I need to get messages ready." He paused at the edge of the kitchen. "Don't move around much, just in case—just in case Denethan's booby-trapped the place or something."

Her face lightened. "Now that I can understand."

With a grim smile, Thomas left her peering carefully about the kitchen cabinetry looking for trip-wires.

Charlie's office was redolent with his presence. The great oaken desk, the leather couch, the decanter of "serious" liquor. Thomas brushed a hand over all of it, seeking trouble spots as well as memories. Nothing looked touched or bothered, yet nothing would be the same again. He saw the paneling ajar which hid Charlie's private files.

The open seam told him that here, at least, the enemy had taken spoils. He eyed the seam carefully, saw no traps, and pushed it with the toe of his boot. The wall closet creaked open.

The file drawers stood half-open, emptied. Blade

flipped through the tabs. They'd taken everything—from the post-Disaster census a hundred years ago to Charlie's latest reports on the desalinization plants. Records which, from the DWP's standpoint, were irreplaceable. But nowhere in here would Charlie have committed his plans for the children to paper. Those had stayed in his mind and other intangible places.

Thomas kicked the panel open wider, looking back into the office. The bookshelves looked the same, including Charlie's collection of family bibles—his genealogy trees, hidden in plain sight. The precious and well-worn *The Way Things Work* had been left behind. He let out a grateful sigh.

Then why take everything else?

The Lizard of Oz was more incomprehensible than ever. Unless . . . he remembered Bartholomew's strident conversation. Betrayed, Charlie had said. Not attacked. Betrayed.

Thomas snapped a drawer shut and left the wall closet, closing the panel behind him out of habit. He was not worried about his own past. Charlie's list of enforcements had also been mental. His executions were a matter of public record. But whoever's job it would be to step into the shoes of the DWP would suffer. The manuals were gone, as well as the files—books almost as incomprehensible as Denethan, but the only instructions they had for maintaining the stations. Chemicals mentioned were not all available now—repairs once taken for granted were now all but monumental—but still the DWPs had kept the water moving and kept it pure.

Now the job had passed to someone else, without the information to make it possible. Thomas realized he did not even know the succession. It hadn't seemed necessary.

As Lord Protector, he had to retrieve that information. It was Charlie's legacy and he'd be damned if he was going to let Charlie die without passing on his legacy.

"Here, here." Lady stood framed in the doorway.

She'd put on a robe that had belonged to Veronica. Shorter and wider than its previous owner, the blue robe pooled about her feet and its front revealed an interesting amount of skin. He took a moment to realize he'd made the last of his thoughts public. The Protector said, "That bathtub holds an obscene amount of water. I felt selfish. Come join me. Consider it an anointment for the quest."

"The bodies. . . ."

"I moved them already." She held out her hand. "Tell me how you plan to catch up with those baby killers and I'll tell you how brave I think you are." The robe parted further to reveal an even more interesting view. "And then I'll twist your arm if you don't plan to take me with you."

Life goes on. He felt himself move toward her of his own volition, even eagerly, stripping off his scarf. She tilted her head, looking at his gills.

"Tell me, Thomas. Are those the first things to go erect . . . or the second?"

Chapter 17

Thomas woke to the stare of Lady's blue eye, gone deep and dark as the Pacific, her face moon-shadowed in the waning night. She lay propped on her elbow, one bare breast cupped by the rumpled covers of the bed which nested them both. A tangle of her brown hair dipped over her brown eye, hiding its soul from his view. But he wasn't afraid to face her blue stare this early in the morning. He smiled.

Then he jerked her elbow from under her.

Lady responded by wrapping her legs about him, entwining and pinning him to the sheets. She laughed as he drew her on top of him and then rolled over, stilling her thrashing with his own leanly muscled form. She threw her head back, crying, "I give up!"

"Oh, no, you don't," he answered, tilting his chin down so he could go for her throat. "I've just begun to fight." She uttered a throaty moan and tightened her embrace about him.

Like the Pacific, the consideration of her blue eye could not be taken for granted. Later, she watched him, and through her face was dewy with contentment, he saw the questions beginning, rising like storm-stirred foam rises to the ocean surface.

"Tell me about the College Vaults Charlie mentioned. I thought they didn't exist. I thought they were legend only. Would he have sent the children there?"

He wrapped a corner of the sheet about him like a loincloth. "They exist, and possibly. It's possible they came to get the children and got out before Denethan attacked."

"Been there?"

He did not answer.

"What about Charlie? How does—did—he know they exist? Had he been there?"

"Once."

She drew back, propping the pillows behind her and sitting up, tucking her knees in under her chin, satin coverlet hiding and revealing the most disturbing patches of bare skin. "We didn't settle whether I was going with you last night."

"It's not a question to be settled. I work alone."

"You *did*. That's not a question to be settled either. You're nothing but skin and bones now, and your Talent is all but drained off. I doubt you can even Project well enough to blur your target's vision. You need me. How far are we riding this time?"

"Not far. There'll be no need for the ghost road—besides, the mounts are too worn. They can't take it, and neither can you."

Sharply, "Why not?"

"I'm going In-City. You can't come."

Lady's mouth made an involuntary "O." Then she shut her lips. Her rose-petal, inventive tongue nervously wet her lips. Then she said, "How far In-City are we going?"

Reaching for his breeches, he stood up, the sheet falling from him.

"Nice view," she murmured.

He pulled the pants up over his muscled haunches and turned around to her as he buttoned the fly. "Stop it."

She stopped. For the barest second. Then, "I'm as capable as you are."

"I never said you weren't. It's not your capability I'm afraid of."

"Then what are you afraid of."

He faced her, hands pausing in the midst of buttoning his shirt.

"Tell me! Don't give me this male-female bullshit."

"I'm afraid of the city." He'd heard its death cry. Ghost road or no, he was not sure he could go In-City again without hearing it again. Then, vigorously, because he suddenly had to do *something*, he strode outside and began to drag the dead to hastily created pyres, stacking their bodies. After ten minutes or so, Lady joined him, her face pale, her lips thinned. They worked until dawn, finding it too difficult to make one bonfire, instead lighting ten, in a ragged half-circle about the manor house. He used his anger to set off the flames. Lady said nothing as she came and took his hand. The fires burned hot and the stench made tears come to his eyes, but he held his place. The woman at his side murmured a barely audible prayer. The coyotes and crows and raccoons backed off, chattering their dismay at losing the carrion. Wild dogs crouched down in the hills and watched through their marble eyes.

Lady bathed him a second time when they returned to the house, stripping off his bloodied clothes. She bathed them as well, hanging them out to dry in the rising sun. Then she joined him in bed, trembling in sudden exhaustion. He reached out and pulled the opaque window curtains together, dimming the room to a blue glow. Veronica had always loved the many hues of blue.

She said the first words directly to him since he'd walked out. "It can't be that bad. You explore the ruins all the time."

"Just the suburbs, just the edges—not the inner city, and that was a hellhole *before* the Disasters hit. If Denethan is beginning an invasion, I'll be ducking down every dodge hole I find, staying out of his way." He took her by the shoulders and spoke to her firmly. "There's no clean water under that layer of concrete and debris. I'll have to pack in every drop. And bring my meter and chemical kit to check for radiation and toxins. And torches, because under the first layer it's usually dark. There's nesters and wolfrats and worse in there."

"All the more reason I can help," she pointed out. "Your Talent stretches only so far."

He shook his head. "We already know the nesters have the eleven year plague. I'll go—it's enough that I go, knowing that when I come back, I can't take the chance I might father an aberration. I can't take you in with me—I can't expose you to that."

"It's my choice."

"Then you're not thinking clearly. Lady, we're both Talents. If either one or both got the plague, think of the abomination we could have for a child."

"I can handle an extra arm or gills."

He closed his eyes and took a deep breath, then opened them and returned her gaze. "Suppose the abomination wasn't obvious. Suppose it wasn't external, *but internal.* What kind of monster might we bring into this world?"

Her breath sucked in. Then she shook her head stubbornly. "I'd know—and so would you. Besides, who says I'm going to let you father my children?"

"I say. We've been working on it."

She reached up and cupped the side of his jaw in

her creased hand, and her mouth curved gently. "No, Thomas. We've been working on love."

"Don't change the subject."

"I'm not. Isn't this what all this is about—our love for our people, our hope that we can help in whatever way we can, as well as our love for one another?"

He let go of her in exasperation.

"I'll just follow you."

"I need you to carry the word about the massacre."

"We have pigeons for that."

He pointed a finger at her. "If I take you—if—you can't argue with a word I say. Our lives may depend on it."

She smiled widely. "Don't you depend on that either. At least I have enough sense to know when not to break up a winning team." She pulled him down in bed. "Now sleep at least for a few hours."

The pigeons left Charlie's house, circling once on the morning air to catch their bearings, their wings slicing through the thin, blue smoke funnels of the still burning pyres.

Lady shaded her face to watch them go. "Alderman and Wyethe each had two apprentices," she said. "I've suggested to the counties that it might not be a bad idea to have two Protectors instead of one. We've no business weeding out Talent." Sleep had smoothed out her forehead, but there were dark blue bruises under her eyes. She had washed her trail clothes and changed back into them. She held the mule's reins in her work-worn hands, hands that he could vividly remember caressing him in the night with surpassing gentleness.

She turned to the mule, twisted the stirrup in her capable fingers, and put her boot toe in. With a jump, she was mounted.

Blue smoke from the fires swirled about her momentarily. She waved it off with a tired smile. "Beauty always draws smoke," she said and waited warily for his retort.

Thomas did not. He gathered up Cindy's reins, while glancing at the ten pyres. Now, tired as he was, he was glad they had done it. He grabbed the saddle horn, clucked the black mare into motion, and did a flying mount.

He looked at her. "Ready?"

For one heart-stopping moment, he saw fear in her eyes, and thought perhaps she'd come to her senses and was going to back out. Then she winked.

"After you."

Chapter 18

Charlie's gauges were barely used, well crafted, the glass covers made by an artisan glassblower whose crystals were works of art, signed indelibly by a curlique of glass sculpture where they were sealed off. Those sculptures, a dolphin here, a fox head there, made it difficult to encase the gauges and they were often framed in wood which had been hand-carved especially to fit the gauges. Barely used, but not barely loved. The wood had been rubbed and polished so often it shone. Thomas cupped the compass, thinking of the first time he and Charlie had used it. With the exception of the radiation meter, he packed away the other gauges in their case. That, he hung about his neck, entwining the thong gently about his scarf-protected gills. The compass he slipped inside his uppermost jacket pocket. The finger bones, as if precognizant, had already moved there. Angrily, he pinched them out and replaced them in a lower pocket.

He thought he heard an angry clink of ivory against glass as Cindy moved down out of the foothills.

Lady drew even. She had her hair drawn back with

the two hairpins he'd given her. "Are you going to have trouble covering two trails?"

"No. No, I don't think so. We know Denethan is after the children. It's as likely he's the one who stripped Charlie's office."

"If not?"

"The children are most important. Charlie would have told them how to get there if he had to send them off, but the College Vaults are hidden damn well. I have to hope their escorts got to them first. But they can't know about the massacre or that Denethan's on their heels." He sat back in the saddle, thinking of how he and Charlie had first ferreted them out. The fables of vast, underground caches of society had always been around, and beyond the Fire Ring and In-City, little surveys were being done by some of the counties. Charles, in his role as DWP, had been the first to come up with concrete clues as to the reality of the underground. Though it was not part of his system, he'd been able to track a massive amount of water usage to otherwise barren foothills in Claremont.

The two of them had gone north and swung around east, avoiding L.A., looking along the fringe boundaries where Charlie had charted water activity. They'd found what they were looking for, narrowly avoiding a guard of soldiers that made the DWP Forces look like amateurs. Then, they'd been invited down the maw itself. The invitation had excited his old friend. He had found truth in fable—perhaps the old world wasn't completely dead yet. He responded to the invitation with enthusiasm. Charlie had had the guts to go in—he hadn't. At the time he'd told himself it was more important to guard the DWP's back, to ensure that once he got in, he would be sure of getting out because they had no idea what or who they were going after. Charlie returned from his meetings pensive and silent, never telling Thomas what had transpired except to say, "I think our genetic program is ahead of theirs," an odd thing to conclude when it had been legend that only purebloods were entombed in the

College Vaults. But Thomas had not seen or talked
with legend and Charlie made it clear upon their return that the matter was never to be discussed. Charlie
thought he'd done a good enough job to give him the
title "Sir" when they returned. Now, seven years older,
Thomas knew better.

Lady read something in his face. "If necessary, we
can split up."

He reined the black mare about sharply, blocking
the mule's path. "Hell, no. I've got enough on my
mind wondering how to take care of you with you
right here."

"You may not like the idea, but it's still an option if
we need one. We can't afford to leave out any
possibilities."

And, damn it, he knew she was right. But he didn't
tell her so. He just seesawed the bit ever so lightly in
the mare's mouth and she backed up to let the mule
by.

Lady looked at him. "I can see you throttling down
anger as if it were some kind of beast and your will
was a club. I remember you before Gillander died, a
gangly boy who used to watch when he thought I
wasn't looking. You weren't angry then. Where did
you find all that rage? Do you cultivate it on purpose?"

"I think of it as skill."

Her shoulders swayed easily with the mule's swinging walk. "Then you acquired it. From where?"

"You mean from whom. I was furious when Gill
died. I thought that if any of the Protectors had known
how to fight worth a damn, it wouldn't have happened. If I could have fought well enough, it wouldn't
have happened. So when I heard about this . . . man
. . . who knew a hundred ways to kill, I asked Charlie
for leave from my studies to go find him."

"What did Charlie say?" She brushed a stray bit of
hair from her forehead.

"He told me the man was a murderer and if I
wanted the bounty, to go for it. That I'd find him
nesting in the ruins about twenty miles south of here."

She gave him that two color appraising look of hers. "How old were you then?"

"Fifteen. I'd just turned fifteen and I was scared shitless. I mean, it wasn't like I was going out to find a master who would teach me everything he knew, even though that's what I wanted him to do. And it didn't seem likely I could talk him into it."

They were companionably silent, as the two beasts picked their way across a four-lane-wide track, broken and incomplete, that abruptly disappeared about twenty yards from them in a yawning chasm.

Lady made a face at him. "Tell me about the murderer. Did you catch up with him?"

"Yes and no."

"Sweet heaven," she muttered fiercely. "What happened?"

"Well, I not exactly caught up with him."

"You must have learned something from him!"

Thomas smiled at her. "It took me a year and a half, trailing him. Every time I got close, he'd try to kill me. I'd survive it, and I did my damnedest not to forget how he'd done it. That was how I learned. My apprenticeship was one of survival. After fifty tries or so, he took me in. He was a nester. I learned everything else I could."

"Then what?" Her attention was rapt.

"Then, when I could best him, I brought him back. Charlie read him his rights and I executed him."

"Jesus! You can be a cold bastard."

He wrapped the reins tightly about his left hand and stroked the worn leather. "No," he said slowly. "An angry one. Everything that I learned on survival, I learned from that murderer. Everything good in life, I learned from a harmless old man who died because he could never be as ruthless as that murderer."

"I'm sorry."

"Don't be. You asked a question, you have an answer. And I'll give you something more—I don't want you coming with me because that murderer told me the surest way to kill a man: take him In-City."

His muscles tightened and the black mare, taking it as
a signal, strode out ahead of the mule, pointing her
muzzle from the ruins' edges toward the area known
as In-City.

Thomas knelt down and examined the tiny, rough-
shod hoofprint. "Donkeys," he said. Excitement flickered through him.

"Wild?"

"This far past the fringe of the ruins? I doubt it.
There's no reliable forage deep inside there, and burros know that. I think we've crossed the trail we've
been looking for."

Lady's face lit up jubilantly. The expression glowed
in her eyes. "We're close to finding them so soon?"

"Maybe." Thomas straightened. He pointed out the
probable pathway the donkeys had taken. "The prints
are deep enough that I think they're laden, but don't
go congratulating ourselves yet—nesters use burros,
too. There's thistle and gorse and foxtail growing abun-
dantly on these outer boundaries."

Lady gave him a look he could not interpret as she
countered, "but if it's them, to have caught up so
soon—"

He mopped his brow against the noonday sun. "It's
not impossible. Charlie probably gave the escort instructions to lay low. If so, the kids wouldn't have left
until late yesterday, from whatever bolt hole he told
them to hide in."

"How do you know that—"

He mounted and turned Cindy's head toward the
donkey track. "I don't. But I know what I would have
done in Charlie's shoes."

"Well, you could have told me. I was a little worried about . . . wasting time."

He looked back over his shoulder to catch her blushing. "Wasting time? Lady, I could have come up with
about five different things to call what we did most of
last night, but wasting time wouldn't have been one of
them."

"That wasn't what I meant."

"Forget it. I know what you meant. Believe me, as nice as it was to sleep in a real bed with you—I wouldn't have been there if I thought we were behind by several days. I can't afford to be led around by my dick."

That turned her blush to a deep rose. Her lips, slightly swollen from the night's activities, set themselves in a firm line. Thomas turned back around in the saddle to hide his smile, thinking that he had finally had the last word with her.

The scribe bowed low, as only his sinuous form could let him. The movement bothered his aging form, but he did not heed his aches. He had served long and well—and would continue to do so until it was impossible to serve at all. Denethan turned as the scribe's action drew his attention.

"What is it, Micah?"

"We have lost a second pack to the wolfrats."

Denethan frowned. "How many have we left?"

"Two trailers, sir, although one of the war packs could be used—"

"It will have to do. I presume you have better news for me than that."

Micah's inner lids closed in pleasure. "Yes. The pack was closing in on spoor—donkeys, trekking westward, just off the Fire Ring. Your packmaster feels they're not wild burros, although they could belong to squatters."

Denethan got up from his camp stool. "Any guess where they're headed?"

The elderly scribe shook his head. Years of desert weather had given his skin a fine patina like that of burled oak, and etched years both lean and plentiful into deep wrinkles. The movements of the children sent out from the DWP's home had baffled both him and his leader. They had predicted northward, along the coast, the decoys having gone that way also. "I cannot say."

Denethan sighed deeply. "Neither do I. They can continue west or cut north . . . or even cross the Fire Ring into In-City. Send another pack of trailers out—we can't afford to lose them now."

"The nesters—"

"If we run across nesters, kill them. They're outlaws in the local society and I doubt they'd be much more useful to us."

The scribe undulated upward, placed the palms of his hands together, saying, "Yes, sir," and backed away to leave.

"Micah—"

The scribe turned at the tent doorway.

"Have the packmaster get that pack warded before he takes it out. Anything might help."

The scribe nodded understanding and left Denethan alone in the canopied tent. The man resettled himself on his camp chair, letting the heat of the day swirl about him as he thought. He scratched his neck gently, picking at the tiny warts that made a kind of necklace, swearing gently whenever he ruptured one with his nails. There were others who would be out after the peninsula children soon—he'd no doubt of that. He couldn't afford to let anyone else find the pair first, for any reason.

His claws paused in mid-scratch. The DWP might even have been in contact with the College Vaults. No . . . surely not.

But it might be one explanation for the course across the expanse of the L.A. basin, a desperate action for two who were supposed to be, and remain, genetically pure. Denethan was a mutant. He held no good will toward the College Vaults.

He reached the tent fold and threw it open. "MICAH! Get that packmaster and send him in, *now*."

The patch of green in between two leaning giants had gone wild, to seed, and had wilted now in a too dry winter. The mule and the mare cropped savagely, pulling out the grass by its roots in spots, as Thomas and Lady watched them.

"I would not have believed," she said softly, "that there were no lawns, no trees or flowers then. I know you warned me, but I wouldn't have believed it." She and Thomas had scythed as much grass as they dared, two large, ballooned bags lying on the ground at their feet. The animals would eat again when they pitched camp.

"There may have been. It got crowded, as I understand it." Thomas tilted back his head, and watched a falcon span the two spires of the buildings. "This was probably quite a coveted area. This little courtyard park may have been worth as much as one of those buildings."

"How did they *breathe*?"

He only smiled indulgently. Late afternoon shadows cast a deep purple over the backs of the two mounts. "Maybe they didn't." He straightened. "We're getting close to the Fire Ring."

"Do you think they would've crossed it? What about frightening the children?"

"I don't know. Alma has been hearing stories about the burning hills all her life . . . but Stefan, well, his mother kept him fairly isolated. I know, because she worked as chief supervisor for the tanner in my county. After she died, Charlie took him in. So he might not have the superstitions—"

"It's not superstition—it's common sense."

"Most of the hill fires are out now. Oil doesn't burn forever."

Lady took her hairpins out, shook her hair free and massaged her scalp vigorously, the luxuriant mane of her hair flying. Then she combed it back with her fingers and replaced the pins. Thomas watched her, thinking that her brown hair caught the fire of the low sun. What would she look like when they crossed the Ring?

The foothills of lower L.A. held an immense underground reservoir of oil or had before the asteroid that sheared off Nevada had also taken part of L.A. with it, and in the process had set those reserves on fire. That disaster had further damaged an already dying culture. Now the thin lines of black smoke that flumed over the lower city were nearly gone . . . and so were the reserves. None who had lived in Thomas' grandfather's era had been able to put out the fuel fires.

Thomas stirred. Already his eyes stung from the invisible fumes of the ring.

"We'd better get moving."

Lady pursed her lips. "Murphy's had enough, but your mare's still losing flesh. She needs to be grazed tonight, if we can, and save what we cut for tomorrow."

"She may have to eat a burning tire." He thinned his lips and whistled to the black horse. She tossed a dainty head, lips stained green with grass, but came to him. The hollows above her eyes had deepened, and her flank was showing more rib than he liked.

The mule threw up his head and his throat stretched in a silent bray, body quivering as Lady reached for his headstall. She froze.

Thomas heard the howl on the wind. "Yip-yaroo."

"Shit!"

Grabbing up Lady's bag of grass, he tossed it to her. She shouldered it and mounted the mule with difficulty, though it had frozen in a stretch for her. He tossed his own harvest across the mare's flanks before taking to leather.

The mule gave him a wild look, the whites of its eyes showing. Lady curbed him into sensibility. Thomas beckoned for her to ride after him cautiously, and they exited onto the streets.

Beyond the cupped buildings, they could hear the full-throated cries of the coyote pack. They hunted as the wilderness predators they were—silently, with only an occasional yaroo to the packmaster to indicate their direction, making it more difficult to calculate their presence. Thomas's jaw tensed as he listened, then he leaned toward her. "They're not after us. They're ahead of us, outflanking us, and the sound is going away."

Lady shook her head. "How can you tell? The echoes. . . ." She paused. He could see concern for the two children they were following dawn in her eyes. "How can we get there first?"

"I don't know." Thomas cast about. Most of the buildings in this area were fairly intact structurally, though of little worth since almost everything that could be salvaged had been except for the framework itself. If they had been brick, those would have been gone, too, though few large buildings held more than a brick facade. He pointed. "Maybe we can be a close second." He put his boot heels to the mare's flank and she leaped forward.

Chapter 19

As Thomas hunched over the mare's withers, he settled her pace down. He had no desire to founder her after grazing. Cindy shook her head in disagreement, then set her ears forward alertly. He reached out and loosened his rifle in its sheath, keeping the rawhide thong loop over it lightly. Cindy jumped a broken curb and the rifle rattled but stayed in place. He did not thumb open the firing chamber, deciding the event called for darts rather than his dwindling supply of vials. He didn't want to be handling those darts with their sharp tips until he had to. Scant blocks later, the buildings disintegrated into neighborhoods that must have existed in squalor even before the disasters. Fractured gaps opened the walkways where gas lines had exploded, gouting out foundations close to them.

The mule kept up with Blade's mare, its long ears

sweeping forward, then back. Lady's hair streamed free of her hairpins.

They caught up with the echo of the coyote pack. Thomas brought his horse to a skidding halt, and stood in the stirrups. He saw their dun and dapple shapes hurtling over the asphalt and rock, dodging broken beams. At their heels rode a man-shaped figure, reining a stocky pony recklessly through the ruins.

Thomas' lips stretched into a thin line of satisfaction. He shrugged off his grass catcher and motioned for Lady to do the same. He kicked Cindy back into a run, letting his knees guide her, trusting to the mare's own fine sense of agility to protect them as he pulled the rifle loose and knuckled open the firing chamber. Deftly, he plucked darts from his inside pocket, taking care not to touch their points.

They were fletched with mockingbird feathers, stiff and insolent as the creature itself. He flipped the chamber cover back into place and wound the rifle back with his right hand as he cradled it, picking the reins back up with his left. He swept a glance over his shoulder to check on Lady. She'd pulled out some pouches and vials of her own, the bag ends sticking out through her fist, a sturdy slingshot of some size planted in the crook of her thumb.

They were not exactly armed for bear, but close.

The dark funnels of the burning hills hung over them. His eyes smarted and his nose rebelled at the stench of crude. Skeletons of great towers, drums, and catwalks hung canted from their foundations, rusted against the blue-black smoke. He could see low tongues of fire licking about the structures. They angled in crossways to the hunt. Now, in silhouette, he could see the shaggy forms of running donkeys, slim figures bent low over their necks. The children and their escort. The donkeys wouldn't run far, that he knew. Behind them, fleet and tireless, came the coyotes and whipping their heels, the desert mutant packmaster.

"They're running into the Ring!" Lady shouted, her breath thin and wheezy. "They'll be cut off."

The donkeys, gray coats whitened in contrast to the smoke curtain they were plunging near, ran toward a dead end.

Thomas let out a whooping yell. The coyotes swerved, and the packmaster's pony stumbled as the rider twisted to look at them. Thomas put the rifle butt into his shoulder, steadied to focus his thoughts and the chamber, and fired at the lead tracker.

The coyote went down, rolled, and got yelping to his feet. His packmates swept by him. He put his head down and caught up.

Thomas did not wait to see if the fletched dart hung from his flank. He sighted down the barrel as Cindy thundered closer to the pack, and fired his second. Then he reined back. The psychic effort of targeting the fletches left him in a cold sweat. He rubbed the back of his hand over his mouth. He breathed deeply.

This coyote went somersaulting, tail over muzzle. Again, the wave of trailers broke around him. The predator got to his feet limping and shook off the poison of the dart, as the packmaster galloped past. He lunged in his master's wake.

Perturbed, Thomas kneed Cindy into a parallel run. Awkwardly, afraid to use both hands, he reloaded the rifle.

Lady shouted, "What does it take to put them down?"

"More poison than I've got!" he answered.

"They must be warded!"

That made sense, if Denethan wanted to give his trailing packs some extra protection over dangerous ground. He said to her, "Then that's your territory! I'm spent." Spent, hell, he was as weak as a babe.

She nodded curtly. Twisting in her saddle, she pulled out a bag of herbs and targeting charms to aid psychic focus. He aimed and fired again, rapidly, determined to make enough of a nuisance of himself to draw the pack away from the two flagging donkeys in front of them. His second dart clipped the desert pony. It went to its knees with a high-pitched squeal, throwing its rider to the dirt. It tried to get back up, but the right foreleg flopped about under it and it collapsed, rolling and thrashing. Thomas would have felt for its suffering, but the poison was swift and the pony died as Blade drew even with the stunned packmaster.

A shrill whistle split the air as the lizard man scrambled to his feet and charged at Thomas. The pack turned as one and came back, slanted eyes aglow with the thrill of the chase. Cindy shuddered under the weight as the packmaster jumped her, intent on grabbing Thomas out of the saddle. Blade retrieved his shuriken. He went limp and let the long, hooked fingers of Denethan's man grab him and pull him down. As they hit the ground together, he came around with a slashing backhand.

The blade touched nothing earthly.

Thomas saw crimson as the packleader put his forearm about the Protector's neck and began to strangle him. As his vision wavered he glimpsed Lady and heard her through the roaring in his ears.

With a cry of triumph, Lady pitched her bags of herbs and charms, into the midst of the coyotes. The poignant smell of garlic and pepper flumed upward. They gave startled yelps, leaping aside. As if in answer to his pack's defeat, the packmaster tightened his armhold. Thomas made a croaking sound. His vision darkened.

Lady kicked the mule into a charge, her image blurring as Thomas felt his senses collapse. She swung her foot out of the stirrup, and slammed the packmaster in the back of his head as hard as she could. As the being went down, she broke a packet of herbs over his skull and rode past.

Thomas sneezed. He went facedown in the dirt, eyes watering. At her shout, he rolled out from under the enemy's slack form, massaging his neck. He took a deep, shuddering breath as the coyotes attacked. He projected multiple images just to slow them down a little. The vials inside his jacket clicked invitingly.

The mule let out an angry squeal. Flashing teeth

and scarlet tongues filled Blade's vision as he drew his wrist knife.

The pack leader singled him out as the mule's charge daunted the others. Thomas gripped his knife tightly. With a snarl, the coyote launched itself at Thomas' throat.

Thomas slashed at the coyote's grinning jaw. His action met with thin air. He ducked, going to one knee as the coyote's rank breath grazed his face. He smelled of carrion and Lady's mixture of pepper and herbs. "Get those wards down!" he shouted at Lady.

"I'm trying," she retorted over the noise of a mulish trumpet of fierce joy. Murphy lashed and stomped every yellow hide he could reach. They circled him cautiously, waiting for an opening to pull him and his rider down.

The pack leader came after Thomas again. Thomas had no doubt that the desert wolf intended to tear him to shreds. Blade got to his feet as the coyote went for his legs. His answering knife stroke was buffeted away by an unseen force and he lost his knife in the gravel as the coyote's jaws locked about his ankle. Sharp white teeth punctured his boot leather as if it wasn't even there. He dared not throw a vial, for both he and Lady were in the midst of the enemy.

"Lady!" he shouted a last time.

"Got it!" Lady cried in triumph. A cloud of dust cascaded over them as Thomas tried to kick free of his attacker. He clubbed a fist down on the side of the coyote's head. The beast yelped and sprang away.

About then, the remaining pack members, tired of dodging the mule, came to their leader's aid.

Thomas jumped for the packmaster's whip curling out from under the mutant's body. He snapped it in their gleaming yellow eyes. The coyotes bit and yowled in frustration at the cracking whip.

Lady fought to control her furious mule. She slung another packet into the midst of the pack as the beasts threatened Thomas. The next pop of the whip brought satisfying yelps of pain. Thomas transferred the whip to his left hand and grabbed for a throwing star. He aimed it at the pack leader's bristling throat. The predator went down with a gurgling moan. The coyotes on either side of him plunged away in startlement.

He crouched down and retrieved his knife. A big yellow brute was going for Murphy's hamstrings. He threw the knife and pivoted away, hearing it thunk home. Charlie's feisty black mare decided to charge into the festivities, her reins flying. The five remaining predators ground their bellies in the dust and snapped at Cindy's hooves. Blade reached for his boot knife and carved up one more before the pack gave up and split apart, circling and yipping in fear. Then, as one, they wheeled away back in the direction they had come, nearly invisible dun shadows streaming across the hill.

Blade retrieved his wrist knife and one shuriken. Retracing the struggle, he found two of his feathered darts as well, pulling one out of the painted pony. He knelt by the packmaster, Lady riding guard over the still form.

She made a face as Thomas clucked between his teeth. He straightened. As he dusted himself off and replaced the weapons he had reclaimed, he said, "Took you long enough."

"Somebody in Denethan's camp is very good at warding. I'd keep that in mind if you ever want to try to walk in at night."

Thomas winced as he put his foot in the stirrup to mount. The coyote bite sent a thrill of pain through his ankle. He tried to ignore the pain, thinking of matters at hand. There was no sign of any other attackers—or of the children.

Lady tucked her disarrayed hair behind her ears. "Where'd they go?"

He didn't know. But he looked toward the horizon where he'd last seen them. Lady followed his gaze. She made a sound of horror.

He'd last seen them crossing the Fire Ring.

Chapter 20

"You can't be serious." Lady glared down at him as he rigged the retrieved grass catcher to hang over her saddle horn. She leaned back, hips tight against the cantle as if she did not wish his hands to mistakenly touch her.

"We haven't any choices and I'm not letting you go alone."

"We're so close—"

Thomas pulled the strap tight and met her angry stare. "No one will follow them across the Fire Ring. The smell of burning pitch is so intense, they can't be trailed, and it's near dark. Denethan hasn't got time to send in replacements yet. They'll be safe enough."

"I can't just let them go. . . ."

He put his hand on her knee. "I know where they're going. I have a pretty good idea when and where they'll turn north. We'll intersect with them."

Lady looked in the direction he had indicated. "But that means we've two or three days more riding."

"The fires will slow them. Lady, inside the Fire Ring, they're as safe as they would be riding with us."

"Then where do we go?"

His neck corded up as he swallowed through a dry mouth and took his hand off her boot. "About as deep In-City as anybody would ever want to go." Maybe she heard the fear in his voice, maybe not. At least she stopped asking questions.

The torch smoldered in her hand, its light staining the dusk. "How much farther?" she said, letting the reins drop so that Murphy could pick his way carefully.

"Tonight? As soon as I find a place that's defensible. I don't want our backs to the chasm if I can help it."

"The moon's up already." She shuddered, looking at the immense crater where the asteroid had struck. Its far edge was beyond sight and its rim still showed fire-scarring even after all these years. "I thought I heard wolfrats trailing us."

"You did, but I dropped a discouragement of powdered cayenne back there." He eased his weight, leather creaking under him, and Cindy groaned softly.

The mule flicked his ears. Then Murphy snaked around so quickly Lady grabbed for the saddle horn to keep herself atop. Thomas wheeled Cindy in the same direction.

There was no mistaking the flickering of slanted red eyes as the new menace came trotting toward them, nails clicking on asphalt. Lady sucked in her breath.

Blade slipped his hand inside his jacket, reaching for a vial. Instead, he grabbed the finger bones and fisted them, and the twilight world suddenly stilled around him. His mind whirled and his bones went chill.

"Ah, m'boy," Gillander said softly behind his ear. "Sometimes you summon the ghost road—and sometimes, it summons you."

Noise. He reeled in his saddle, as the fabric of his reality stretched and curved, and vertigo snatched his vision from him. Lady Nolan gave a soft cry and he knew he'd brought her with him—that much he could be thankful for. He threw out a hand, catching the soft cloth of her sleeve. She fumbled back and their hands pressed together tightly. He uncupped the bones and wished them back, to no avail.

"I thought you said no more ghost road."

His sight sharpened and his balance returned abruptly. "I lied," he said, unwilling to let her know of his lack of control. He braced his palm on the saddle horn and let his senses trickle out, feather light, testing the area around him.

As if she knew what he was doing, Lady said, "I could hardly move that knife. It's as if Talent can't work here."

Her voice broke his concentration, and he clenched his jaw with unvoiced anger. He'd had no more success than she. But he knew why. The compass slung around his neck still worked as he drew it forth and held it. He looked to Lady Nolan as she brought the mule even with his mount. "That way," and he pointed. The corner of his mouth quirked as he added, "We're not talking ruins anymore."

They stood on a bridge of nothingness, a golden sparkle above an immense chasm. It stretched across the abyss which pulsed and writhed below, a living thing of molten lava. Thomas looked back. Tiny slits of red flashed in the darkness. He did not know how the wolfrats had followed them, or if they had ventured into a level of hell where the beasts ruled.

"We've got to keep moving. I don't know if we're on a ghost road or not—if this is the past or a resonance of it—"

"Resonance?"

He shook his head. "An echo, a ghost, something with the ability to leech away both of us. This looks like the night the world ended. But we can cross here."

"I'm with you." She bent and ripped off a length of hem, dismounted, and blindfolded her mule.

Thomas took off his jacket and used his shirt. The black mare shuddered and stepped after him reluctantly. She would not have been any happier if she'd seen the golden smoke and ash trailing from every footstep she took.

They walked into the night. The bridge muffled the hoofbeats of their mounts. Thomas stayed cold, despite the exertion it took to walk the arcway. Every step required immense concentration as though he plowed through snowdrifts chest high. Beside him, Lady's breathing was harsh but steady. Suddenly, she slipped and let out a short scream. Her torch fell away.

He dove for her, belly first, and caught her wrists. Below her, the torch seemed to drop forever before it hit. The chasm reacted with a boiling hiss and a lava-like wave spewed upward. She hung over the vast pulsating mass below, her eyes wide. "Thomas?"

"I've got you. I won't let you go." The veins and sinews stood out on the back of his arms. "Can you TK?"

"I don't know. I'll try." She closed her eyes, shutting her soul away from him. If he dropped her now, he would be unable to see the terror in her eyes.

Blade clenched his jaw and heaved upward. Her weight grew lighter as he did, and he flopped her back onto the span. She lay there a second, panting. He let go only when he knew she was secure and could not slide back over the rim.

He hadn't had the strength to help. His fingers had been almost too numb to grip her arms. Thank god her Talent, though weakened, was still there.

She got to her knees. "Let's go."

"Can you walk?"

"Do I have any choice?" She gave a bittersweet smile. "It's too far to go back."

They slogged on endlessly until it seemed they must have walked for an entire night. Dawn had to be edging over the horizon from somewhere. Lady staggered, holding onto her stirrup. Murphy came to a stubborn halt. The mule shook his head, ears flopping noisily. "He's got more sense than we do. We're going to have to rest them."

Thomas eyed the waning night. "And ourselves." As he reached up to take off the mare's blindfold, she butted him in the chest and he dropped like a stone. The torch rolled harmlessly onto the bridge and lay there, smoldering. It threw almost as much light as a lantern. Lady came to his side. "Thomas!" She put her hand to his forehead. "You're like ice."

In contrast, the warmth of her hand was a brand across his face. He waved her away.

"What's happening to you?"

"I fuel the road."

"With what?"

"Dammifiknow. My life, I think."

"Then get us off it, now."

He looked into the miasma boiling underneath the thin fabric of the golden span. He looked back into Lady's eyes. One blue, one brown. "I can't," he said. "I didn't willfully bring us this time and I don't know how to get us back."

"Shit." She sat down next to him. She pulled her denim riding skirt off her slim hips and threw it over him. It came billowing down, filled with her warmth and her woman-scented, musky perfume. His teeth began to chatter. She lay across him, hugging him.

When his shuddering stopped, she brushed his hair back from his forehead. "Tell me how it is you do it."

"Do what?"

"Open the ghost road."

He reached inside his jacket. The bones came to his fingers reluctantly and he pulled them out.

Lady looked at what he held. "Is this a focus?"

"No. Yes. I'm not sure. This isn't a paranormal Talent."

"Then what is it?"

"Witchcraft?"

Her laughter died in her throat. "I—" she stopped. "You've always been fey, Thomas, in a way none of the rest of us are. Who else could use a pebble to project a fog? Dowse for water and never have to worry about its being clean? Know unerringly the right and wrong of things? Truth-reading is one thing, but it doesn't make justice any easier to deal out. When I Read someone, I know only if they've lied, but not what the truth is. I've seen you execute a man without blinking, because you knew it was the only thing to do."

He could barely hear her now. He felt transparent, fading.

Lady could feel him slip away, as surely as if he had gone over the rim of the bridge the way she had earlier. She reached out with her mind and caught him in her thoughts, anchoring him. As she did, she could feel the terrible toll of the ghost road.

His mind was like a great, raw wound. She could feel Denethan in it, like a festering thorn. He'd never been rid of his foe—did he even know they were still linked? She shielded him as well as she was able and when she'd finished and opened her eyes to look at him, a hint of color had returned to his face.

She took a deep breath. "I can't lose you now." She grabbed for Murphy and the mare, who stood listlessly, muzzle to the strange golden fog that encircled their hooves. She threw down their grass catchers so they could eat something. She pulled her pack down and set up her tiny brazier, set a spark of fire among the coals with a snap of her mind and made herb tea, sweetening it with a last bit of honeycomb.

With an exquisitely carved teaspoon, she fed him every last drop. Then she picked up the hand still curled about the grotesque bones. He was cold as stone, as death, as . . . evil.

Hesitantly, because she was afraid, and dammit, she, Lady Nolan, had never been afraid since the day her mentor died—hesitantly, she opened his fingers and touched the bones.

The screams of a thousand thousand dead echoed in her mind, a vibration so powerful that it could be tracked through the darkest night. The voices screamed as one, and separately, in fear and hatred and confusion.

"Dear God!" Lady dropped his hand, unable to bear the vision. No heaven or hell or rest for these people, this past. Now she knew what he meant when he talked of resonances, of ghosts, of echoes. "Thomas?"

He stirred slightly. His eyes moved behind his lids and she wondered whether he only dreamed or was caught in a struggle against the ghost road's pull. Lady took a deep breath, preparing to meditate, and offer whatever aid she could give.

Murphy's snort interrupted her. She came out of trance with a jerk, already in a half-crouch and facing the part of the bridge they'd crossed. Red slits bobbed in the darkness.

The wolfrats had trailed them. She could hear the gnash of their teeth. Wind their carrion scent. But how? How did they get here? How did they traverse the fabric of this delicate universe Thomas had woven? With the Sight, she picked them up as smoke and crimson.

Thomas moaned. She looked back to him and gasped. He had tossed off her skirt and lay on the bridge, no less golden or ethereal than it. She smothered a sob, ran a hand across her face to clear her vision, and he looked his weather-beaten self again.

"I won't lose you! I won't!" She grabbed for him, for his beaten leather jacket and pulled it up. Vials sewn into slim inner pockets met her fingers. She grabbed two out. The diamond ring fell into her hand as well. She scored the glass for easier breakage, slipped the ring onto her finger. She picked up his torch where he had dropped it and held it like a weapon. She put her body between the pack and the mounts and Thomas.

"Come and get it," she said. "If you dare."

The wolfrats edged closer. She could see them now, their hides mangey and scarred, gray, mousy, piebald and white, their nails grasping for purchase amid the strange weave of the bridge. They snarled and squeaked and huddled behind one another, watching her with eyes that glowed red.

"Don't be shy, boys." She sent a fire-spark behind them. It spouted up like a firework candle, rarest of joys, and sent the wolfrats leaping at her.

She kicked the first one in the side of the head. It fell, skittering and scrabbling, off the rim of the pathway. She tossed the vial, heard it shatter as it hit, and green-white gas boiled up. She buried her face in her sleeve and over the crook of her arm watched two of the beasts convulse and pitch off the bridge, twitching and writhing as they went.

The gas cloud dispersed as the two remaining wolfrats shrank back, noses twitching, tails whipping about them like frenzied snakes. Then they charged as one and she didn't have time to throw the second vial.

Chapter 21

As the rats rushed her, she saw a third crouching figure rise up from the shadows. He stank like the rats, but she saw the face, the beard—a wild man like none she'd ever seen before. He gave a shout and the rats swerved. She twisted to keep them in front of her, but that put her flank to the nester. Hair sizzled and flamed as she swung the torch. The piebald beast spat as it scrabbled to get away from her.

The nester edged forward. Lady swept the night between them, the torch leaving a trail of sparks to drift on the still air.

"Don't," she said. "I won't think twice about killing you."

Orange light glinted off his fists, a knife in one of them, and an unfamiliar object in the other. *Oh, Thomas,* she thought. *Where are you when I need you?* There was no one in the seven counties who was his equal with a blade.

A wolfrat darted at her, rearing up and pawing the air with sharp nails and long yellow tusks. She swung the torch at him, but kept her eyes on the nester, sensing that he was directing the beasts' movements. She backed up a step, heard Thomas moan at her heels and knew she'd retreated as far as she could. The wolfrats hunched low, their hungry eyes burning in the reflection of her light.

"Gi'e him to me." The wild man spoke, his voice

scratchy, low and guttural. She barely understood him. His teeth were broken husks of yellow in his jaws.

"No."

"He don't belong to you."

Lady watched his hands. He didn't hold the knife for throwing, but for gutting and for that he'd have to move closer. Still, it would take but a flicker of movement to reposition the weapon. As for the other thing, she had no idea what it could do, but he held it as though it, too, were a weapon. It bore a slight resemblance to a zip gun.

She held up the vial. "It's a horrible way to die."

"Who says 'm alive? This is the dark road, i'n't?"

"You know about it?" She moved slightly as she spoke, forcing the rats to circle back, moving them between her and the frenzied man.

The wild man danced on one bare foot so callused its sole was like horn. Then the other foot. His odor fairly steamed from him. "He's marked," said the wild man. "The road runs where 'e does. I been told to mark him agin—so th' road's ours."

He gave a whistle and the rats charged her. With a curse, Lady moved back and tripped, her weight crashing across Thomas. He erupted upward, throwing her free. Recovering, Lady dove toward the rats as they came for Thomas, and thrust her torch into their faces.

They exploded into flame like dry straw. With mewling cries, they clawed and tumbled at one another. Regaining her feet, Lady kicked them over the edge of the bridge. Her underpants caught fire and she dusted the sparks out, unable to help Thomas who danced hand to hand with the bearded man.

They strained against one another, eyes glinting like those of wild animals with reflections of the torchlight. Thomas momentarily pushed his opponent back, his tanned face pale, his lips pulled back to bare his teeth.

"I hate to disappoint you," he said. "But I've already been marked a second time." He twisted his wrist, and the crescent scar of the dolphin's teeth, still pink in healing, came into view.

The wild man gave a cry as if he'd been struck. With a roar, he broke loose, knocking Thomas back. He raised the hand with the unfamiliar weapon. Lady cried out and threw the vial just as the weapon smoked and popped loudly. The bearded man disappeared in the white firelight of the magnesium mixture. Engulfed in its searing light, he staggered backward off the bridge and screamed his way into the abyss.

Thomas went to his knees and then fell, and ivory bones clattered out of his hand as he did so.

The golden span disintegrated below them. With screams, nickers, and brays of fear, they fell.

He blinked his eyes open. It was morning again, and they were sprawled in a broken concrete ring, the streets of yesterday barely spider tracks upon the face of the world he was most familiar with. Blood pooled under his arm and it hurt like hell to move it, but he did, as he sat up.

Lady got to her feet. Her jaw dropped in dismay as she knelt down and began to tug his jacket off. He fingered the hole.

"God damn it."

She slapped his hand away. "Help me get this off before you bleed to death."

"Can't bleed to death—a weapon like this doesn't even exist now. Look at this. It pierced both sides of my sleeve—"

"Meaning it went right through your arm. Help me with this thing or so help me I'll cut it off."

With a wince and a curse, he shrugged the jacket off. His upper sleeve was soaked, clinging to his bicep, and he saw a blossoming of flesh with a tiny purple center crying tears of crimson.

Lady made a sound through her teeth. She ripped the bottom half of his sleeve off even as he said, "Hey! That's my best shirt."

"Now it's your second-best shirt. Why don't you try focusing on getting that blood flow to clot up a little while I take care of the rest of this?"

He took a deep breath. The air was clean, quiet. The noise in the ruins was generated by pigeons, sparrows, and an occasional red-tailed hawk keening past. The wind whispered through conduit towers. Even the squeak of wolfrats down below sounded familiar. Home. He closed his eyes for a second.

"Hey! Don't you pass out on me."

"I'm not." He winced and hissed through his teeth as she tightened the bandage. Her efficient hands wrapped the cloth about and knotted the ends in several places. Their gazes met as he said, "I'll remember this."

"See that you do."

Suddenly, to his surprise, both her eyes brimmed with tears. She rubbed them away quickly. She got to her feet, dusting off her long traveling skirt and donning it. "It's just through the flesh. Keep it clean and you should be fine."

He moved his arm. "It hurts."

"Of course it hurts, you idiot. You were shot. That looked like an explosive projectile to me, like one of Charlie's old guns."

"You're probably right. Want to go back and see?"

"No."

"I missed most of what he said to you. Was he a talkative fellow?"

"No." She hugged her stomach as though it hurt. Then she turned to him. She brushed her fingertips across first his brow and then his wrist. "This is supernatural, not paranormal."

"All that supernatural is, is paranormal that can't be explained or tested yet."

"He told me *you* were the road, Thomas. It goes where you take it. You . . . polarize the forces that move upon it. Primeval, good, bad . . . you glowed in the night as though you were woven of the same fabric as the span."

"Should have unraveled me and made a fortune out of gold yarn."

She spat. His face closed then. "I was dying, Lady. I

didn't expect to come back, but everywhere I looked in that long dark tunnel, I saw your face. You brought me back. I felt peace, I could have had it for the wanting . . . but you anchored me. And then you fell on me and knocked the crap right out of me and I came to, choking for my life."

Her eyes had been brimming, then her mouth quirked. She threw her head back and laughed, laughed until the tears rolled down her cheeks and Murphy started braying.

His mustache twitched. "That's better," he said. "None of this mystic stuff. We're In-City and we need to get out."

The finger bones lay on the concrete between them. He scooped them up and pocketed them. "The ghost road runs on psychic emotion. Misery, mostly. Somehow I can channel it, manifest it. I can open up and give it direction, expend it. Maybe I'm releasing souls from some nether region, freeing them to go where they have to."

"Now who's getting mystical? What about the marks?"

"Current flows between poles. Maybe . . ." he shook his head. "How the hell do I know? We've got to get out of here."

Lady wiped her face again. "How do you feel?" she asked, her voice carefully neutral.

He moved a pace. His swagger had given way to a stagger and he looked as though a stiff breeze would topple him. He held his arm stiffly. The wind whistling through the eroding skyscrapers bore a trace of winter, edged with the promise of rain to come. He pulled the compass from around his neck and cupped it in his palm. Lady was looking expectantly at him when he glanced up.

"Well?"

He shrugged diffidently. "Can't tell. I suggest we just get on our horses and ride. We're still In-City, though I'd say we're several days closer to where we want to be."

She stalked off to her mule, muttering, "And what if we're several years later?"

He pulled his jacket on gingerly. The torn flesh under the knotted bandage had started to swell a bit. He ran his right hand over his inventory. He had less than a third of what he usually carried. The knobby ends of ivoried finger bones met his touch as well. "Let's get out of here." As he rode past the broken foundation where a single spire pointed upward like an index finger, he saw the painted sign of a nester border slapped upon its cornerstone. His eyes narrowed, but he said nothing to Lady. The murderer he'd brought to justice might be dead, but his clan lived on, and now he'd met them on the ghost road, too.

In the shadows as they passed, a hunched-over figure emerged, watched cannily until they'd gone, and then went to the pool of blood still liquid and warm upon the ground. It dipped a finger, then sniffed the blood. Then, with a grin, it ran back into the shadows, intent upon fulfilling a mission.

The sunlight was slanting across the cityscape when at last they halted. Lady swung down immediately, unslung her water bag and cooking pot and filled it for the mule. The mule sucked up whatever he could get, then she did the same for the black mare. Thomas brought out his case of gauges and checked the meter for toxicity and other readings. He frowned as he packed them back away.

"How bad is it?"

"Not good. But if we can avoid eating or drinking from the immediate locale and get out of here in a reasonable period of time, we should be all right."

"What's a reasonable period of time?" She slapped the mule's wet muzzle away affectionately. "Don't slobber on me!"

"Two months."

"I'd say we can make it within your time frame unless one of us gets planted here first."

He grinned at her wry tone. "In which case, it's a lost cause anyway, right?"

She gave both mounts a refill of water, then tied her bag off. "That's all, greedy guts." Her tenor changed. "We're going to have to find water soon . . . and grass."

"It's better for them to do without."

"You can't starve them!"

"They'll absorb the toxins quicker if we can even find grazing. I hadn't planned on the two of us eating much but what we're carrying, either." At the thought of eating, his stomach clenched. "Break?"

"All right." She dropped the reins, ground-tying both animals. "Tortillas and jerky sound lovely right about now."

He scrounged through the food pack. "I even have some dried apricots."

"A gourmet! What luck." She caught the package he threw to her. "Or do you say that to everybody you wine and dine?" Without waiting for an answer, she perched on a cement block and began to unwrap the packet. He watched her, trying to remember what it had been like on the trail from Orange County to the wedding, alone, without her. The memory seemed vague and unreal.

He pushed such thoughts away, knowing they were dangerous. Dangerous to become attached, to become dependent, as he'd been with Gillander, his mentor and friend. His way of life did not encourage commitment. He turned his back so that he could not see her while he opened his own packet of rations. The last of the lemon drops fell to his hand. It melted on his tongue with bittersweet poignancy. While he ate, he turned his thoughts inward to encourage the healing of his arm. In-City, the slightest disability, be it physical or emotional, could be fatal.

Chapter 22

Lady put her hand to her mouth and Murphy danced uneasily under her, shying away from the smell of blood as the dessicated animal swung in the breeze, hanging from the end of a tether. "What is that?" she asked, turning her eyes away.

"Nester totem. It's marking clan boundaries." He kneed the mare closer. Cindy chuffed at the scent of death and minced closer to the building. His sight blurred as he leaned forward to read the sign. After a day of riding his left arm pulsed with an angry throb and the blood loss kept him light-headed. He had said nothing but could feel Nolan's two-color stare on him constantly. She was a Healer and drained by the ghost road or not, she had to know what he was feeling.

The painted sign swam back into focus. Not only was this a clan boundary, but it marked feud territory. He looked down the broken city block, where the road inclined steadily, until a green and gold foothill met his eyes. He pulled a folded piece of hide from his vest.

"What is it?"

"There's water up there," he answered briefly. "We're close to the College Vaults. This clan marking tells me the reservoir is in disputed territory."

"We're sitting in the middle of a nester war zone?" Her voice gained an edge.

"Look," and she did so, despite the garish sacrificial totem behind his shoulder. "They're outlaws. If they could work together toward mutual interests, they wouldn't be outlaws."

Her mouth tightened. "I know that." Then her tone softened. "How about some tea and hardtack?"

He swung down. "More than that. I know it's still light, but we need to make camp here."

"Need? Here?"

His mouth tightened. "I need," he said.

"Ah. Wisdom comes to the boy." She dismounted easily. "I won't argue with that, but does that *thing* have to hang around?"

"Afraid so. Actually, it's the best protection we could have. This is as close to neutral territory as we're going to get until we hit the vaults."

"It'll draw wolfrats." Her voice was partially muffled as she turned her back to him and busied herself with her bedroll and saddlebags.

"Should, but I've never seen one of these do it yet. They're poisoned. Maybe the wolfrats sense it." He reached up for his pack and the answering throb in his arm shot through him. For a dizzying moment, he clung to the stirrup.

"Thomas!"

"I'm all right," he answered. His mouth felt cottony. His vision went dark, then lightened. The mare bore his weight quietly. He could smell her heated skin, see the spidery tracings of her veins through her hide. Of all the animals which had survived the disasters, horses had changed the least. He straightened up as his head cleared. Her tail came around smartly then, lashing at him as if to disprove her good humor. He smacked her fondly on the rump. "I'm all right," he repeated. He hoisted his saddlebags and pulled them off, ignoring the thrill of pain in his arm.

Lady knelt by her tiny brazier, igniting a spark among the coals that burned but were never consumed. She coaxed the rocks into a dull glow before taking out her battered teapot and filling it from her water supply. Then she sat back on her heels and mopped her brow on the sleeve of her blouse. "A good night's rest," she remarked, "will do us both a lot of good. In the morning, I'll be able to work a Healing."

"Save it."

She glanced up at him. "You've lost color as well as

blood. Heroics won't do either of us any good. Can you set up wards?"

He thought about it. The effort set his mind spinning again. It was as if the ghost road was magnetic and he a lodestone, set into a whirl trying to align true and find north . . . affected long after leaving it. "Not yet," he admitted finally. "But it's getting better." He watched her sprinkle her tea leaves and herbs into water that slowly began to steam.

"We can't use the road anymore."

"I don't intend to. We should be able to meet up with Stefan and Alma tomorrow, unless I've lost all sense of time." Their gazes met briefly, then Nolan looked back to her teapot. She thumbed the lid into place.

He pulled his map out of his vest again and smoothed it over his thigh. His jeans had gone stiff with dirt.

"Tell me," Lady said, settling back as her tea brewed. "Tell me about the College Vaults."

His brows met before he could answer and she added, "You don't like them."

"I don't know them. Charlie was the only one who went in." They dealt with Intuition, it was their bread and butter, yet he felt himself flushing as he continued, "When he came out, he got his gills cut away. He never said why, but it was as if he felt alienated by them." He put his hand to his neck and seemed surprised to discover he still wore his long scarf. "Maybe I do know why."

"But the Vaults are real."

"Oh, yes."

"Then why don't they help us?"

"That's not their purpose. Their purpose is to survive, just as ours is. The Vaults were cut into this mountain to provide storage in case of earthquake or war, the labs and other equipment were haphazardly added later. They can't manufacture the past any more than we can, or so Charlie told me."

"And you believed him."

"He believed what he said. Why shouldn't I?" Blade

took up the hot tin mug she handed him. The fragrance of the tea filled the late afternoon air and for a moment, the stink of the totem could be forgotten.

"It's written in your eyes." She blew steam off her mug gently.

He shifted his weight. The concrete under his lean haunches was cold and too hard. "I don't like handing the children over to them."

"He must have had his reasons. Perhaps better medical facilities. If the Vaults have always stayed this isolated, then perhaps the eleven year plague is only an ugly rumor to them."

"Maybe. I don't believe Charlie did what he did out of the goodness of his heart. The DWP was a businessman. He expected something from them."

"Any idea what it could be?"

"No, but I'm going to ask when we get there." Thomas paused to sip his tea. He bared his teeth. "Hot."

"But good." She sat back with a sigh and looked about the city block. The jagged foundations were not fire-charred as others had been, but were toppled and devastated nonetheless. "We're almost out of In-City."

"Just about."

She laughed throatily. "My Intuition's coming back. I can feel you itching, Thomas, just sitting there. You're thinking about the ruins and what they hold."

He hadn't been as far as he knew, but now that she mentioned it, yes, he had to admit it was true. He hid his smile in another sip of steaming tea.

"What do you look for?"

"Artifacts."

Nolan shook her head. "No, I mean *why*."

"Artifacts."

She shied a piece of concrete at him. He ducked, but she'd already missed on purpose. He set the mug down beside his bent knee. His throat closed for an instant, then he answered, "I look to find out why they were human and I'm not."

She looked as stunned as he felt. "We're human."

"Not. Not like they were. Even Stefan and Alma aren't. Maybe I can't explain it, but I know I'm different. You're different. Look at the photos I found in the ruins . . . the pictures in Charlie's family . . . it's more than gills or second eyelids."

Lady sat silently, both hands wrapped about her mug. She did not meet his gaze this time. "We've got the eyelids bred out. And almost the gills. If you hate them so much, why not do what Charlie did?"

"Because it's more than just your neck. It involves your bronchials and throat and lungs. And because I like swimming with dolphins. But I look at the nesters as they regress back to the first days and I wonder if we would look like that to true humans. Like animals instead of people."

A flicker of a glance. "You always stood up for the mutations."

"It's why we're alive today. But the nesters are another matter. They're asking to be hunted down and scourged out, like vermin."

She threw her empty mug down. It rattled next to the brazier, a new dent in its side. "If they're so much better, why aren't they alive today instead of us?"

"But they are. They're in the College Vaults." His voice had gone chill. "And I'm afraid to find out what I've always wanted to know." He folded the map up. "I could do with another cup of that to wash down the hardtack. Got enough water for it?"

"If you've water for the animals."

"I do. And tomorrow, we'll have fresh water, reasonably untainted."

Lady did not reply, but bent to pick up her cup and fill the traveling pot a second time. Thomas stretched his legs out carefully and got up to tend the mounts. They nosed his hands eagerly and rolled reproachful eyes at him. He stroked their necks and soothed them with promises of grass in the morning. Murphy brayed in disbelief and tried to stomp on his booted feet.

"Oh, thou of little faith," Thomas mocked him. He hobbled the beasts loosely. His wound sent a freshet

of heat and pain down his arm. Tomorrow would
bring Healing and answers and perhaps fresh wounds.
Then, once the children were clear of Denethan's snares
and he understood the deal Charlie had made with the
Vaults, he would find the raiders who'd taken Charlie's papers, the lifeblood of the water system, and
avenge his friend's death. The children would draw
them near, he knew that, and how close he dared let
them get depended on how much stronger he could be
in the morning. But if Lady knew he intended to use
the children as bait, she'd kill him for it.

He awoke to a sound in the night, and by the gleam
of a silver bright moon through the cityscape, saw a
knife being held to her throat and knew he wouldn't
have to worry about it.

Chapter 23

He killed the man before Lady could waken and blink.
She lay quietly, a sickly-sweet smelling rag to one side
of her face. He kicked it aside, even as he looked the
night over for the rest of the enemy. The silver moon
was at its brightest and hung over the ruins, making
shadows as sharp as blades.

"Lady, breathe! Wake up!" He checked his collar
for the shuriken he had left and loosened his knife in
its wrist sheath. The hilt of his boot knife rested comfortingly against his ankle. He cut the hobbles away
from the mounts and gave a short whistle to calm
Cindy, his mustache tickling the edges of his mouth.
The black mare jerked her head up and moved a bit
closer. He scratched her chin with one hand as he
reached for his rifle with the other, keeping his

feet planted on either side of Lady like a shield.

A second later the mule lifted his head and his nostrils flared. Murphy filled his lungs for a bray, but did not wind it. A stone rolled from the broken ceiling of a building, bounced down its side, and clattered into the street. Man and mule looked up.

"Now just where did that come from?" Blade mused. The mule's long ears flipped forward and back.

Carefully, he stepped back with one foot as he cradled his rifle and dropped two darts into the firing chambers and wound it painstakingly. He left the rifle balanced across his right forearm, almost negligently. His left arm smarted as he moved about, but he never took his eyes from the shattered rims of the concrete canyons. His Intuition flooded him. The enemy stalked him out there and he could feel it almost better than he would see it when it happened.

He set his jaw. A shadow leaped form one eave to another—he caught its arc in the corner of his eye, too late to raise his rifle. Instead, he kept his rifle loose as though unaware of the movement. He watched the mule to see if anyone was approaching their rear. The animal seemed to be more concerned with the buildings across the street. Its ears pricked forward.

Blade saw it at the same time. Rags flying as if he were winged, the nester came at them with a bellowing charge. He dropped in his tracks as Blade fired, a mockingbird fletch blossoming in his throat. He drummed his heels once or twice and died, yells frothing from his mouth into silence. Ghosts shifted rapidly in the buildings behind the attacker.

How many they sent after him depended on how many males they could afford to lose from this clan.

Thomas lowered his rifle from his chin. "I wouldn't if I were you," he called out.

"Marked man," a rough shout came back. "We've feud with you."

He could not see the challenger, but the words sent a chill down his back, and the drawn scar over his brow twitched in acknowledgment.

The mule stared intently to its right. Thomas looked there as well. Half a building seemed to have an extra column. He opened the firing chamber and dropped another dart in, knowing a single fire wouldn't do him much good. Before he could thumb the cover over, the nesters hiding by the column charged.

He put the rifle up, knowing the danger if he fired without the chamber closed—his ammo could well fire into his own face—but he had no time. Blade sighted and dropped the two nesters, one halfway across the street and the other within a body length of himself. The mule put his nose down and sniffed suspiciously.

The second one took a longer time dying, his dart having been used on a coyote, the poison diluted. Blade held no sympathy for the youth. He searched his vest and pulled out a flare vial. He couldn't put up a stand here in the open. They'd undoubtedly sent for an archer and he was a tempting target.

A fourth nester saw the disadvantage and took it, charging in on his left flank with a yell. The mule never saw it coming.

Thomas threw his wrist knife and heard it thunk home. But the nester wrenched it out of his chest and tossed it clattering to the street. With a defiant yell, he bounded at them.

Blade let him come, carrying the battle to them, and stepped out of Lady's loose embrace, garrote in hand. A foot kick to the chin, striking the nester and sending him reeling, an easy twist to the right and Blade was behind him, garrote tightening. He wasted no time, collapsing the windpipe permanently and releasing the man. The nester dropped to the broken asphalt and writhed there, unable to breathe, contorting until he died.

There was an anguished wail among the street shadows. Blade looked up. A girl. She'd not come after them, and he'd have to leave her alive to point the way, for he hadn't time to deal with her as well. He pulled Lady off the ground. He wasted a precious handful of water, dashing it in her face, bringing her eyes into focus.

She gave a violent shudder as he threw her into the saddle.

"Can you ride?"

She gathered up the reins with one hand, "I—I think so. Thomas, what's happened?"

He retrieved his knife and rifle, wiping the knife edge on the closest dead body. "Never mind. We've got to get out of here." He swung up, took his bearings, and slapped the mule into motion ahead of him. "That way."

A vial broke near them. The mule swerved as flame roared up. Cindy leaped through the wall, and heat blistered Blade's face. Thomas swore between clenched teeth, wishing he'd been wrong. The nesters had held them down until the real hunters could be sent for. Now he would be facing weaponry and ammo equal to his own—superior, if their supplies were any greater than his dwindling reserves.

His left arm began to throb in time with the drumming of the mare's hooves. The coyote toothmarks in his ankle itched aggravatingly as sweat ran down into his boots. Lady's face was deathly pale. She coughed and clung to the saddle horn with both hands, letting the mule pick its way.

Thomas trusted to the clever beast's instinct as he twisted in the saddle. He could hear other horses behind him, and got a glimpse—wall-eyed, ewe-necked wild stock, small and scruffy, tough as nails to have survived on the borders of the city. Their riders hunched, riding bareback over their withers, fists knotted in tangled manes. He turned back and listened to Cindy grunt with every stride. They had only minutes left before they were going to be run down.

He jammed the rifle butt into his armpit. He checked the street to make sure the stretch was relatively flat, before turning and standing in his stirrups to fire. The flare flashed white-hot, scattering horses and riders. One went down, rolling.

Thomas had to sit back before he could see if the fallen horse tripped up others. He heard a high-pitched whinny, truncated, behind them.

Lady looked back over her shoulder in panic. She'd lost a hairpin, and her hair streamed about her face. She clawed back strands of it to see.

"Thomas!" she cried.

"Keep running!"

If caught, she'd be raped and enslaved at best. He'd be cannibalized. He didn't fancy either of their futures.

The mule hadn't been bred for fleetness. It stumbled and began to drop back until he rode even with it. Then it lagged still farther. Lady threw him a terrified look.

"We can't keep up."

They turned a corner at flagging speed.

He drew his reins between his fingers, long leathers, and snapped the ends across the mule's cream-colored butt. The beast's ears flattened and Murphy kept running doggedly, but Thomas could tell he was breaking the mount's wind. Then they'd have nothing left but dog-meat.

"Thomas . . . stop."

"No! Don't quit on me!" He whipped the mule until its cream hide was red-striped and still the beast kept slowing, and Cindy adjusted to its pace.

". . . Make a stand," Lady panted.

"Nearly out of ammo," he yelled back.

Understanding fear showed in her eyes as she looked over. Thomas risked another look behind as they rounded a corner.

He saw a lizard man riding to the fore.

Damn! He had to have known. Denethan's raiders had infiltrated the nesters.

"Keep going," he ordered Lady.

"What—"

"Don't argue! Keep going!" He pulled on the near rein, forcing Cindy into a wide circle. He might go down, but he'd take out Denethan's man and as many nesters as he could, giving Lady a clear run at safety. A vial smashed to his left. Black, choking smoke came pouring out. His eyes teared immediately. Cindy faltered. Her nostrils were flared wine red, and froth ran from between her lips, and her black hide was spattered with foam.

But the cloud worked both ways. They never saw him until he burst out of the smoke, firing his rifle as he came. The lizard man went down as his pony was hit. He rolled lithely out of its way and disappeared behind a rusting steel beam. The pack scattered, splitting up. Thomas fired a second time and a noxious cloud, a nasty yellow-looking thing, took three of them. They died with their tongues hanging swollen and black out of their mouths.

Thomas reined in Cindy and dismounted, curbing her behind him, to face a wall front made of marble, pocked by the smog and years, but still standing. Its entryway was small and intimate. He wondered briefly what sort of building it had been, knowing it did not matter. It sheltered him now, protected his rear, and gave him a chance to keep anyone from going after Lady.

The pain of his wound stabbed at him as he tore down the saddlebags and searched through them for his extra two throwing stars. The nesters and lizards were going to find this as expensive a blood feud as they'd ever begun. The mare stood where he'd put her, head down as she sucked in air and trembled.

He listened as the nesters placed themselves. They'd figured out where he was and surely knew as well that they'd have to rush him one by one. A grim smile thinned his lips. He might actually have a chance.

He laid his shuriken out on the pavement in front of him, neatly in a row, their fractured circles of death framed by his two knives. He pulled out three vials. Two were flash-bombs. The last, a vial of poison. He squatted and pulled the cork, bathing his weapons liberally. The remaining garrote he kept coiled at hand.

The first nester died laying down a line of pitch, but he fired it before he breathed his last. The night was bathed with its orange smoke. Thomas wiped tears from the corner of his eyes with a dirty hand. The pitch burned well, well enough to bring smoke into his nook, but not well enough to smoke him out. He wondered briefly whether Lady had gotten away when a second figure wavered at the corner of his vision. Thomas reached up, caught Cindy, and brought her to her knees. The mare went down with a squeal as an arrow arched overhead and shattered against the marble wall. He gingerly picked up a throwing star.

When the rippling curtain of smoke and heat stirred again, he let fly. He never saw the man fall, but he had the pleasure of listening to his gargled screams before he died.

The third attacker cost him both his knives—a tall, rawboned woman with her hair tied back and a ragged scar high on one cheekbone. The first knife missed her, but the second did not. Thomas wiped at an oozing graze in his hairline—her arrow had been high, but she'd come closer than anyone.

He thought he heard a massing behind the veil of smoke and threw his flash bomb. That left him very short of ammunition. One more vial and his garrote, and his rifle for clubbing if they let him get down to hand-to-hand combat.

There was a scraping along the eaves overhead. Thomas glanced up, saw nothing, but the hair on the back of his neck prickled uncomfortably. Cindy's ears flicked once or twice, but the mare was too exhausted to do more than stay where he'd snubbed her down. Blade wondered who'd gotten above him and thought of the lizard man at about the same time he jumped.

The raider let out a hissing shout of joy as they met. Thomas kicked, the raider caught him by the heel and twisted. Thomas took the energy and rolled with it, coming back up with a backhanded slash to the face. The back of his hand grazed teeth too pointed. He had a split-second to worry about venom when the raider kicked back and his left arm exploded with pain. Blade reacted, his vision red-misted, barreling headfirst into his opponent's torso.

The raider laughed, his hands closing tightly about Blade's neck. The scarf twisted and tore under callus-scaled fingers. His gills fluttered for air and found it as Thomas drove both fists into the lizard man's balls—they weren't built any different there, he thought with satisfaction—and broke the weakened hold about his neck. Each staggered back, taking the other's measure.

Then the lizard man spoke, his lips lifting to reveal his sharpened teeth with every word. "The packmaster you killed was my brother." The dun and brown speckled face of the mutant took on a malicious delight. "It is said a man who dies In-City haunts it forever."

Thomas thought of all the thousands who'd fueled the ghost road. "You might be right," he said, and attacked.

His uppercut set the raider back on his heels, his second eyelids closing a moment in bewilderment. Before Thomas could follow up the advantage, the mutant kicked, driving Thomas' right knee out from under him. As Thomas went to the pavement, his hand swept across the coiled garrote. The raider gave him no time, a rugged one-two in the ribs sending him sprawling back, grunting with pain.

He tasted the flat sweet taste of his own blood on his lips. Everything hurt. He rolled and got up, slowly this time, and heard shouts at his back. Cindy got to her feet with a piercing whinny. Reinforcements for his opponent were deciding whether to brave a rush.

The mutant hit him in the jaw. Thomas felt the blow clear through his spine as the back of his head smashed into the marble wall. His ears roared and his eyes went dim. He put his hands up in defense and caught the lizard man around the neck with his garrote as he drove in for the kill.

He pulled tight as his sight came back, but it was no good. The raider had both hands under the loop, his tough hide defending him, and Thomas had lost strength from the beating he'd taken. His thoughts reeled and he wondered if he could hold the lizard man long enough to use as a shield for getting out of there. The black mare let out a squeal of fear and shied away.

They rushed him without hesitation.

Chapter 24

Thomas strained, the cords of his neck standing out with the effort. But it wasn't good enough. He couldn't dredge up the strength to pull the garrote tight. The trail had beaten him long before the desert mutant had gotten to him. He dragged the man back with him, putting his back to the marble wall. He could feel its coolness even through his leather jacket. He faced the nesters as they came running, triumph written across their faces. The line of pitch spread on the street flickered and burned out as they jumped it and got him in their sights.

Glass shattered at his feet. Thomas swore and ducked away as the white-hot, stinging cloud brought cries of pain and fear. The raider tore himself free and went to his knees, coughing. Blade kicked him hard in the throat, and staggered back, hiding his face. He could hear Murphy's derisive bray, chiding him for his weakness.

Through his tears, he looked up and saw the cream-colored mule being herded out of the night, riders on either side, Lady tall in the saddle with her chin high.

He reached inside his jacket for the last of his vials. There would not be many survivors once he threw it. His fingertips grazed finger bones as he did so, and he wondered what his chances would be of reaching her first if he took the ghost road.

Her voice pealed out of the smoke and fire. "No,

Thomas," she called. "Enough. They only want me."

His roar of denial choked in his throat. He clawed his way near and went to his knees, cupping his hand about the bones.

"Thomas! *Enough*. They came for a Healer, and I've agreed."

"I won't let you do it."

Lady paused in the meadow. Grass swirled about her boots and licked up the hem of her riding skirt. She was dewed by the morning, and the sunrise lent its color to her cheeks. "It's already done and you've no choice. Besides, you'll be right in there with me." The pastoral beauty of the nester campsite framed her, and at the far side of the meadow, a hide-sewn tepee awaited her.

"We're talking plague here," he said, as he finished wiping down the black mare's nostrils. She'd bled from them, but seemed recovered now, though she might never be the same again. He'd come that close to running her to death.

"You don't know that."

"I know," and he pointed the rusty-colored rag at her, "that they were willing to kill me to take you. And while you've been meditating, I've been watching them deposit bodies inside there by the litterful."

"You laid waste to half the able-bodied men in their clan."

"And if you searched their belongings, you'd probably find goods looted from half the men missing from your county."

She came close enough to put her hand on his. "Enough, Thomas. This is not for you to judge."

"No. You're right. I'm just the executioner." He took a deep breath. "This is delaying us. We're going to lose the children. We won't be able to get to them before Denethan does. Everything we've gone through will be wasted. Every life, for nothing. Ronnie, for nothing. Charlie, for nothing."

The gentle coolness of her skin soothed him into

silence as she held his hand close. "Come with me."

"No." He would not become one with the press of hair and flesh inside that tent. With the stink of their retro-manhood and the reek of their crude hide clothing. His arm flamed fiercely and he knew she wouldn't have the strength to undertake another Healing for at least two days after this, but he would not join their pack.

"You don't need to fear them. They've respect for the strength you showed in defending me. They've forgiven you their dead and crippled."

"I don't fear them!" He tore his hand away from her. "I don't fear them."

"Hate them, then."

"That." He picketed the mare. "They'll steal us blind if I go into the tent with you. I like riding with a saddle, how about you? Old Murphy's spine looks like it might be real uncomfortable bareback."

"We're guests here." She gave him a glacial look from both brown and blue eyes.

"They're not even—" He bit his words off and swallowed them.

Lady waited a breath or two, then finished, "Human?"

"Don't put words into my mouth."

Lady gave a strange, one-sided little smile. "I don't have to," she said softly. "I can hear some of the thoughts in your head, remember?"

A Talent he didn't have. He shielded himself and paid attention to Murphy. The mule was travel-worn, as were they all, but his wounds from early on had scabbed cleanly. Both mounts were contentedly cropping spring grass. From behind his shoulder, Nolan said, "Your arm needs tending," and she laid a hand on it.

Shrieking pain brought him to his knees. Sweat rolled down his brow. He doubled over, gasping for breath. Lady dropped down beside him. "Oh, love," she whispered. "I didn't know." She looked up. There were nesters appearing from nowhere. "Take him to the tent with the others."

He couldn't stand up to defend himself as they gently pushed his kneeling form onto a litter and carried him into the tent. He had a brief glimpse of blue sky with white mare's tails flicking across it, and then the stench and darkness of misery claimed him.

Someone bathed him. The water was barely warm, scented with orange and lemon peel. He winced as they touched his wound. The bather made a titching sound, distinctly female.

"Infection cleared, but there's a lot of Healing yet to be done."

Another, huskier voice, one he knew well. His eyelids flickered as he thought of waking to glare at her. "The energy in the Healing tent was too diffuse for him. But he'll live. He's like that mule of mine, too ornery to do anything the easy way. He's awake now."

Thomas opened his eyes. There was a young girl leaning over him. Her brow was heavily boned, and a faint brown mustache lined her upper lip. Her hair was braided back, a wild brunette mass plaited into submission. Her eyes sparkled in dark delight as his gaze met hers.

Nolan cleared her throat. "I don't think," she said, "that the clanman's daughter is a suitable conquest."

The girl looked up. She smiled widely, showing teeth a mite too sharp. "You flatter me," she said. "He'll have nothing to do with me, anyway. We know the Marked Man well. If he could, he would bring every last one of us to the counties and to a death sentence."

Mindful of the lap that pillowed his head, Thomas said nothing. The girl washed his face quickly, then moved him onto the grass. She left with a rustle of hide and fur.

Thomas tried to sit up, but Nolan held him down and slid over, her lap pillowing him instead. She picked up the washcloth and continued to bathe his torso.

"How do you feel?"

"Groggy."

"The incense and drugs in the smoke do that. It makes it easier for the patient to accept Healing. Herman is now the head clansman here. You've made him a happy man—you eliminated his rival earlier."

"Good." With a grunt, he sat up. He looked at his upper arm. Pink and purple flesh was still angry, but the heat had nearly gone. He flexed it. "Thank you," he added dryly.

"My pleasure." She dropped the cloth into the basin of scented water. "Herman says to tell you that Denethan has not crossed the In-City boundary yet and those you trail are a half-day away."

"He's not only happy, he's helpful," Thomas said and shrugged into his shirt.

"Look at me."

He refused.

Lady watched him get to his feet, waver, and stood herself. "I did what I had to do."

"For animals."

"For people. People more affected by what has happened to our world than we are. I see people here who can't cope with our Talents, who fear us as though we were the Devil himself. I don't know if they were driven away from the counties or ran, but I do know they found themselves within a system they couldn't comprehend." She reached out and spun him so that he had to face her. "And even if you are right, refusing to help them doesn't make me better. It sinks me so far down on the evolutionary ladder that I'd have a hell of a time climbing back up."

He looked into her angry face. "What about the plague, Lady? Just what sort of Healing did you do inside that tent?"

"There's been no talk of plague yet in this clan. Is that what you're worried about? Your precious sperm count?"

Now it was his turn to grab her. "No, dammit—I was worried about you!"

"It's my body. I'll just have to deal with it." She shrugged out of his hold, walked a few paces away to a tree where Murphy stood in the shade. She pulled his reins off the picket line. "I thought you were in a hurry."

He found his jacket hanging over a shrub. The inside pockets were woefully empty but for his finger bones. His shuriken, however, had been cleaned and replaced. He clenched his jaw, thinking of the bodies they'd been pulled out of.

Over by the cooking fires at the meadow's end, where nesters sat and talked and worked their hides, he saw a massive man stand and begin walking across the grass toward them. He was a redhead, his uncut hair a tangled mane that caught the sun and twisted its color through every strand. His homespun shirt and hide trousers were crude in every sense, but he walked with the pride of royalty.

Thomas swung aboard the black mare. She held her head well, but she walked without any spring in her step and he knew she needed more rest. He nodded his head.

"Here comes Herman."

"We've been promised free access over the In-City border to the track that leads to the reservoir."

"Why doesn't he camp at the reservoir? We're talking a day's journey at the most," Thomas said.

She frowned at him. "I asked him the same thing. He says it's death."

Blade frowned back. It hadn't been death for him and Charles, but he did not dispute her as the massive nester walked up and grabbed a headstall in each hand. Now that he was close enough to smell the man, he was close enough to see silver threading the fiery red. Herman let out a laugh that smelled of sour beer.

"I'll walk you to the road," he said, "as promised." Cindy came as coaxed, but Murphy tossed his head stubbornly and Lady had to shake her booted foot threateningly within his eyeshot to get him to move.

Herman strode at a hunting pace. They left the nester grounds far behind them, and the sun moved to just off midday in the sky before they slowed for breath. Thomas listened to Cindy pant and to Herman standing calmly and thanked whatever gods listened that this nester had not been among the ones he'd met. The behemoth pointed along the edge of the ruins. "There."

Thomas nodded. He had his bearings and Herman had taken them where he was supposed to. He gathered up Cindy's reins. She responded to his knees and moved down the slope onto the track.

He twisted in the saddle. Herman stood, grinning hugely, his massive hand still wrapped in Murphy's headstall.

"Let her go."

"I think not." Herman's lip curled back. "We need a Healer."

Blade's hand slipped inside his jacket, found a shuriken.

Lady leaned down and put her hand on Herman's shoulder. "This is not the way," she said evenly. "I am more than a Healer, I am a Protector. My honor binds me to return to my county." She gave Herman pause, and more than that, she blocked Blade's throw.

"We have feud with the county," said Herman.

It didn't matter which county. Nesters feuded with all of them. "I know," answered Lady calmly. "But we know you need Healers. There will be some who will want to come and help, if you promise their safety."

"Water rights?"

She shook her head. Herman's brow knitted. Then, "We have water enough, right now. I will think this over. If Healers come, we would have to let them go back again."

"If they wanted to. Back and forth, as they needed to."

"No bounty hunters."

She looked at Thomas over that bountiful head of hair. "No. Right, Thomas?"

He shifted weight. "It's your treaty."

Herman looked at him, skepticism in his hazel eyes. Then he pointed a blunt finger. "You are an enemy and yet our friend has marked you, so," and he made a slash mark over his brow. "We don't understand this."

"Neither do I."

"You have the power to walk in dreams. You would be wise to know if you walk toward good or evil." Herman let go the mule's bridle. "Thank you, Lady Nolan, for the Healing." He turned his back on them to prove his bravery and stalked away.

Thomas sat in faint surprise at the nester's proposal. He had never known a nester to do anything other than take to satisfy the moment's needs. Nolan reined Murphy over to join him when Herman paused, half-blending into the scrub brush, and began to turn around as if he'd forgotten something.

A rifle whined. One, two. He heard Herman thud to the ground before he could react.

No one was visible. Then, from a jagged rooftop overlying the track, a young man dropped to his feet, white-blond hair ruffled. He carried a rifle in one hand and grinned.

"Well, Sir Thomas. How was that?"

Blade felt color return to his face. He grabbed Murphy's reins from Lady's numbed hands and snubbed the mare over. "That was some shooting, Stefan. Now let's see how good you are at burying the evidence."

Chapter 25

Stefan didn't need any help burying the body. He had his own detachment which materialized shortly after he began digging. Although Thomas appreciated the assistance, he knew instinctively he did not like the six escort guards from the College Vaults.

He could not read their body type under the uniforms, but they were taller and more muscular than he
and he was no small man among the people of the
counties. Neither did they have the fluid grace his
double-jointedness and martial training gave him. He
doubted they were pure-blooded. The gene pool would
be too valuable to waste on patrolmen whose duty was
to kill or be killed. He relaxed a little at that thought.

Lady traded glances with him and he thought that
neither of them had to be psychic to read the body
language of the captain and his five partrolmen. Thomas'
stomach turned and he knew why Charlie had come
home quietly and had his gills removed. From the
gloves they wore to the stances they took, they acted
as Thomas did himself when dealing with a contami-
nant. Lady frosted them in return with her one blue-
eyed gaze and did not thaw even when Alma joined
them.

Bruises of weariness shadowed the girl's pale face.
She rode her donkey as if every movement were agony. Lady helped her down and sat quietly with her as
Herman, the head clansman for one great and glorious
day, was buried.

"I'm sorry," Stefan said quietly as the last shovelful
was turned. "He looked as if he'd been menacing you
and then when he turned to circle back—"

"A mistake," Thomas said. "Regrettable and un-
derstandable."

"I sent my men on back-track. No one has noticed
he's missing yet." Remmick's speech was as stiff as his
posture. Big-voiced, like his stature.

Thomas met his glance in passing. "Too bad you
weren't in charge when the boy took aim."

"I was in charge. It's my failure as well. I told him
to target you . . . in case it was needed." Remmick
took a deep breath. His chest swelled the khaki jacket
of his uniform. The cuffs of their trousers were tucked
into their boots. The holsters on their lean hips were
filled with a kind of weapon Thomas had only seen—
stable ammo had not been found for guns of this type

and he had only briefly admired their killing beauty. "So you're the gutsy bastard who drew Denethan's packs off our heels."

Thomas did not smile at the tone of grudging respect. Nothing the captain had said had pleased or amused him yet. "We did a job, but nothing permanent. Denethan's going to cross our paths again before we reach the College Vaults." He looked at Lady and Alma. Their heads were bowed close together and from the sudden redness in the girl's face and the pinched look around her eyes, he knew what the Protector was telling her.

Thomas said to Remmick, "After you picked up the children, raiders attacked the DWP settlement. There were no survivors."

Stefan sucked in his breath, sharp and quick.

The captain's eyebrows arched. "None? That is most . . . inconvenient."

"Yes."

Stefan made a cutting motion through the air with the side of his hand. "Never mind. We'll start a new county, building on what Charlie left us." His blue eyes drilled Thomas. "You taught me to cut my losses."

"Indeed. And where will you find what Charlie left you? His office was gutted as well."

Remmick stirred. "We'd be well on our way, then . . . Protector."

"Not until I'm done with them."

Stefan looked from the captain to Thomas. His eyes narrowed. "What do you want from me?"

"You know why Jennifer and Ramos were sent out?"

"To draw attention from me and Alma leaving."

Lady spoke up, her voice commanding attention, as she walked up, an arm about Alma's shoulders to steady her. "They gave their lives for you."

"Jennifer's dead," Alma repeated, in a stunned echo.

"It was necessary." The Russian's blue eyes stared down Blade. "You were supposed to prevent that."

"Bullshit. I was sent after to draw attention as well."

"That, too. But you were supposed to be the Protector, the one who could stand against all odds—"

"Stefan!" Alma's voice was high and pure, edged with her sorrow. "They *died* for us. There isn't a county of the seven which can manage without the information taken from the DWP."

The blond youth jutted his chin out. "And what do you want from me? Tears? They won't help now."

"I came across In-City after you, not just for the two of you. You'll draw Denethan . . . and he's the one I want, on my ground and on my terms. If you're game enough, puppy, to do for your counties what Ramos did for you," Thomas said quietly.

Stefan rose to the challenge. "My counties? My counties lie across the ocean, holding the bones of my mother's parents. I was born there. *I would have survived there,* but she was always afraid. She didn't think she was strong enough, but she was. We were the only ones who made it across. It was one of your counties which killed her. I don't think I owe you anything."

Thomas was conscious of the guardsmen gathering around them. He smiled at Stefan. "Are you telling me you're not game enough?"

"Not for suicide."

"And I agree," Lady put in. "I won't be quiet while two jerks have a piss-off to see who's bravest." Behind her, Alma gasped. Lady didn't miss a beat. "Nothing right now is more important than the life these two have the potential to conceive. Damn the water lines. Let somebody else run them. Bartholomew is probably setting up details right now. His legacy can wait until you deliver the children."

Remmick shouldered in between Thomas and Stefan. "Listen to your woman, Blade. If we have Denethan closing in, standing around is the last thing we need to do." His words put a flush on Lady's face and she closed her mouth with a nearly audible snap.

Blade leaned inward. "You, captain, have the opportunity to ambush Denethan when he least expects it. Can you afford to lose it?"

Remmick lookedly coolly down at Thomas from his

bulky height. His dark eyes were flat and chill. "Denethan does not worry us."

"He should. How far have we got to go—half a day's travel?"

The captain nodded.

"If he's close enough, and I think he is, he'll wonder how we disappeared. He won't leave any stone unturned to find us, and that puts him at your doorstep. Then, Captain Remmick, he becomes your problem. *That* will worry you. He's a mutant. He's got no love for the old race or anything else remotely human. So let's detour and put an end to the matter."

Remmick slapped him in the ribs, saying, "Your arsenal appears to be depleted."

"But yours isn't."

"No. And, for the moment, it isn't about to be. I have my orders from the dean to escort these two in safely. The rest will have to wait. You have my word I will bring this matter to the dean's attention." He snapped his fingers. "Mount up."

Uniforms in a blur of motion separated Thomas from the others until only he was left standing. It did not matter that Remmick rode a desert ass like the others, his boots nearly trailing the ground. With a grudging shrug, Blade swung up on the black mare. His bicep gave him a twinge of pain, a reminder, as he settled into the saddle. With a last look at the nester's grave, he reined the mare after the troop, but Denethan remained in his thoughts. Under the new clarity of Lady's Healing, he realized Denethan had not been out of his thoughts since they had fought, like an ulcer that festered until it was a great raw wound, and she'd Healed that . . . now they were knit together. If he wanted his foe at hand, all he had to do was tug.

Thomas smoothed his mustache. Considering the possibilities, he rode drag to Remmick's point.

Midday, inland, with heat beginning to shimmer off the foothills. Thomas wiped his brow with the end of his scarf and wished he had not lost his hat. He could feel the sun through his thinning hair and beads of sweat trickled down his neck and temples. Stefan pulled his donkey out of formation and dropped back. His fair skin bore the stamp of too much sun, and he frowned as he looked at Thomas.

"I'm not a coward," he said.

"Never said you were." Blade watched the guards ahead. If their ears could swivel and flick toward a conversation the way Murphy's did, he'd swear they were endeavoring to listen. He was not surprised that Stefan gravitated toward him. He had taught the boy shooting, he knew how the lad thought. Confronted directly, bull stubborn, but give him time to think about it, and he would eventually swing around.

"You thought it." Stefan sighed.

"Perhaps." Thomas stood in his stirrups, stretching his legs and back a little. He looked back at Stefan. "That was a good shot."

Stefan made a slight face. "One I never should have taken. But I never thought to see you sharing the track with a nester."

"Herman," Blade said absently. "His name was Herman." He focused. "What is Remmick like?"

"Efficient. Like you and Charlie on a bad day. We've been running the hooves off these beasties." Stefan thumped his donkey's neck. "Is everyone dead?"

"Everyone who hadn't left the party. Oletha, Alderman, Wyethe, Veronica . . . several of the mayors." Shellyann's dead face passed through his memory. They'd found her protecting her son's lifeless body. "Most of the children got away . . . at least, I don't remember seeing the bodies."

"There's that, then." Stefan busied himself plucking at the stiff, wiry mane of the donkey. "We must have gotten out just in time."

"Just," he answered. "Charlie was still alive when I found him."

"I'm sorry," Stefan looked at him quickly.

He could see the truth in the young man's face. "I know," Thomas returned. "We both are. But it's possible Remmick is right. You have another allegiance now."

"Alma is my allegiance." The young man's eyes brightened. Thomas felt something in his thoughts soften at the other's emotion.

Stefan lowered his voice a little. "Have you been to the Vaults?"

"Yes. Once."

"What are they like?"

Five levels, beginning a hundred feet underground. Set into a mountain so cleverly that not even nesters could tell real rock from sculptured entrance. The reservoir behind the mountain peak could not be seen from the entrance, but it had sparkled like a giant sapphire as they'd ridden past it. There were no outward sentries that Thomas could see, but Lady had leaned toward him as they approached and remarked, "Every hair on my head is standing up."

His had been, also. Technology he was unfamiliar with scanned their presence. Before he could answer, a deer bolted across their track. Her tail flagged as she bounded through the underbrush and disappeared. Remmick signaled a patrolman.

"Bring her down. Venison will taste good tonight."

The patrolman vaulted off his donkey and went on foot, his long strides quick and sure. Remmick also dismounted. He went to a place on the hill where rock had broken through the dirt, its gray stone face a map of strata and geological pressure, thrust upward by the very force of its own existence. It was then, Thomas saw in dull surprise, that the outcropping was false. Sculpted by a master, but fake nonetheless.

Remmick paused in front of it. He put a hand palm down on the rock. It split as though a messiah had parted it. Thomas watched bemused as stone slid back to reveal metal and the silvery gleam reflected the sun's rays.

It also struck him that his Intuition to Truth-read had fled at a very unfortunate time.

Chapter 26

The interior cavern was cool and hushed. Not until they entered it did Blade realize the afternoon had been filled with birdsong. Now he heard nothing but the shuffle of their own booted feet and the hoofbeats of their mounts. A sign proclaimed STAGING. Three freshly uniformed men met Remmick and saluted.

He answered them. "The password, gentlemen, is new blood."

Thomas watched as the three opened up an interior door to a narrow-necked corridor. Remmick's five patrolmen then gathered up the reins to the donkeys, Murphy and the black mare.

"Take them to stabling," ordered Remmick. "See they're given hot mash tonight and are well-rested. Take care of the mare, she's a good specimen. Have Mendes type her in the morning." He waved to the interior corridor.

One of the three stopped him politely. "Sorry, sir. The dean knows you're here. We've been requested to do a weapons check."

"Ah." The massive man considered, then gave a nod. "Sir Thomas?"

Blade spread his hands amiably. The aide who'd spoken paused a moment as if gathering his nerve, then stepped forward and began to pat him down. Thomas stood impassively. If he had not spent most of his weaponry, this pup of a sentry might have something to worry about.

The aide patted his inside pockets down several times, then turned to Remmick. "Sir, there's something in his pockets which may or may not be a vial, but it—it keeps moving, sir. I can't seem to get my hands on it."

The artificial light had lent a pallor to Remmick's face. His cold gaze raked Thomas, then he showed his teeth in a smile. "Some of these Protectors use a bit of TK, lieutenant. He's playing with you. Sir Thomas?"

Puzzled, Blade opened his jacket. The only things remaining in his pockets were Gillander's finger bones. The ivoried knobs of their ends stuck out of a seamed niche. They seemed stationary now.

The lieutenant stared for a moment, then nodded, satisfied. He turned to Lady Nolan. "Ma'am?"

Her face pinked, but she said, "Of course, but mind where you put your hands, young man."

The lieutenant patted her down quickly, found two shuriken and a bootshank knife. He handed those solemnly to Remmick who turned them over and over in his hands as though a little unsure of what to do with them. Finally, he said, "A resourceful lady."

"Always," Nolan responded. "This is a tough country."

Without further hesitation, Stefan and Alma were both searched. Stefan had left his bolt rifle with his pack and the lieutenant found nothing more, but Blade could tell from the way Alma looked at Lady that the lieutenant had not uncovered everything.

Remmick pulled some objects off a hook inside the corridor. They were clear, clumsy lens. "Goggles, if you please. We're going through an air lock into a decontamination chamber. It will be flooded with a strange, harsh light. Keep the goggles on to protect your eyes. This is only a preliminary cleansing procedure. You may or may not be subject to others once we reach the Vaults."

Thomas watched the captain pull his goggles on and imitated him. Alma giggled at Stefan who'd suddenly acquired the expression of a bullfrog with bulging eyes. Remmick then herded them into the corridor. Before closing the doors, he said, "Lieutenant, there's a major infestation of nesters in sector Montclair Vee

Twelve. Take some defoliants and clear them out ASAP."

The door closed on the lieutenant's response. Lady reached out and took Thomas' hand. Hers was shaking though she said nothing. Thomas' ears popped faintly as the next set of doors began to blossom open. As sound and light flooded them, Remmick said, "Stefan and Alma have quarters prepared for them. But as the dean is aware of our arrival, I'm sure he will wish to see you as much as you wish to see him."

In a small voice, muffled by the goggles hiding her shapely nose, Alma said, "Can't Lady come with me?"

"I'll be along later, dear." Lady patted her hand. "Save me some hot water. You do have hot water here, don't you?"

Remmick's neck flushed. "Yes, ma'am, we do." As soon as the light faded, he tore his goggles off and bled the doors open. "To the elevators, please."

"Elevators?"

Remmick pursed his lips. "A sort of powered stairs. We're going down into the interior of the mountain." He pointed the way. Thomas followed, but not before eyeing the pattern of corridors they now occupied. A sign pointed to STAIRS in a different direction. He made note of it. Elevators might be mechanical, but stairs were not.

The descent was not entirely pleasant. Alma went very pale and sagged visibly under Lady's hold. She finally closed her eyes, and a fine bead of sweat rode her slender brows. Thomas lost gravity for a moment. His senses reeled as they had not since the ghost road. Surrounded by artificial things, he seemed to have no being. His stomach turned and he knew he was going to be ill in front of Remmick, who would no doubt scorn him further.

Then the elevator thumped gently and its outer door slid open. Two sentries snapped to attention immediately.

"Take these two to their quarters. Arrange for meal credits and let the teaching staff know of the additions to their schedules." Remmick, crisply ordering the two, did not seem aware of Blade's distress.

Lady watched Stefan helping Alma down the curved corridor. His voice drifted back to them.

"I'll take care of you now. Lean on me."

With a half-smile that spoke wistfully of an emotion Thomas could not name, she looked at him. Before she could say anything, Remmick strode briskly away from them in the opposite direction.

Thomas found it hard not to stare as he followed. There were sliding gates that opened and shut automatically at their approach—grills that he knew could be shut down permanently if the operator so wished—lights that dimmed or brightened to the sound of their steps—other equipment that seemed to watch them pass by—things he had seen in the ruins, smashed, half-salvaged, uninterpretable until now. And even now, not all he saw made sense. No wonder Charlie's visit here had fired him up so.

They passed a number of closed doors and one immense hall where Thomas paused to watch more than a hundred men go through their paces. It was the largest *dojo* he had ever seen. He wondered why there were no women present. Women were generally more supple. Lady's attention flashed on it as well, but she said nothing to Thomas.

They took a second elevator marked PRIVATE. It took them seconds to reach their final destination.

The room was spacious, well-decorated and cool, but its air held a slightly musty smell as though stale. He looked up at the large-domed room, the ceiling of which defied the feeling of oppression Thomas felt. He fought an impulse to bolt as Remmick saluted the man behind the desk and was told, "At ease."

The dean was a large, florid man, with veins that had broken into tiny crimson flowers across his aquiline nose. Two chins drooped to his stubbly neck. His eyelids hooded hazel eyes. Gray speckled his thinning brown hair which he, in his vanity, had combed from

just above his left ear over his balding pate to the right
ear. He wore a black overrobe, with a silken purple
sash hanging about his neck. No warmth came to his
expression as he eyed Thomas and Lady. Without a
word to them, his attention flicked to Remmick.
"Decon?"

"Done upstairs, sir. In moderation."

"Good. That's something, at least." He folded his
hands over neat stacks of paperwork. "Welcome to
the College Vaults. Like what you've seen?"

Actually, Thomas hadn't. "You've impressed me,"
he said.

"Good. That's not our purpose, but good all the
same. I understand Charles Warden is dead."

Behind Remmick's khakied body was a wall lined
floor to ceiling with a bookcase and books. The other
two walls were backdrops to paintings, some of them
priceless and thought to have perished long ago.
Remmick knew what he stared at, and returned his
look. Cool. Unperturbed.

As Blade's attention swept the room, he knew the
only weapon he needed to control the dean was fire.
Both he and Lady could provide the spark at will, if
needed. He no longer felt defenseless. "Who carried
you the news?" Intuition prickled the back of his
neck.

"Your own hand, I presume. Some of those pigeons
Charles kept were from the Vaults. We received the
news. Tragic. However, the business at hand is not.
We have the two youngsters whom Warden felt repre-
sented a return to a desirable gene pool. We have
medical as well as educational facilities here which will
greatly benefit them." His hooded eyes closed, then
opened again. The light in them was that of a hungry
falcon. "Warden was a brave and literate man."

Thomas had not known that Charles had kept in
regular contact with the facility, but he did not let the
surprise show. "It will be difficult," Thomas said, "carrying on without him."

"But bound to happen sooner or later. You lead a

precarious life. Outsiders are a bit more mortal than some." The Dean chuckled deeply and tailed off. His tone became crisp again. "Where were you when the attack occurred?"

"On another mission, one which he knew might take me away at a crucial time. He took his chances." For reasons of his own, Thomas did not feel like revealing everything to the dean though he did not doubt Remmick would fill him in later.

"He lost his gamble. By treachery perhaps?"

"Not by me," Thomas answered. His chin went up slightly. "Denethan has been an enemy for some time, as was his father before him."

"Ah, yes. The miscreant from the Mojave." The dean shook his head. He turned slightly in his chair. It creaked under his bulk. "Charles warned us against him when he first visited us, some six years ago. He did well to find us. Men better than he had tried and failed. None used the method he did, though. Our water intake gave us away. We've since corrected that, following his suggestions. He was a generous . . . man."

"Perhaps too generous," Lady said. "The bargain you made with him concerning the children no longer stands. We're here to renegotiate."

The dean gave her a measuring stare. "So the lady speaks," he said at last.

"I do, indeed, and very well. Our community has suffered grievous losses—losses which the knowledge you have hidden away can help to repair most swiftly."

The dean kneaded his heavy hands about one another. Thomas noted the thickness and twisting of the joints. The man paused and said, "You hope to draw us out against Denethan. You ask that we expose ourselves to a world gone mad and savage. I have no good reason to do this."

"Your reason is humanity."

His hooded gaze took in Lady carefully. He said, quietly and deliberately, "your humanity and my humanity are two different things. Honor, perhaps, might dictate our actions." He looked to Blade. "An honorable man would have come to us and solicited our aid."

Thomas grimaced. "Honorable men have more time than the rest of us."

The dean traced a burled pattern on his desk. He looked up. "It matters little now. Denethan cannot find our door unless we will it. As for the four of you, we welcome the children into our colony. There're tests to be done, naturally, blood and tissue typing, but I'm sure Stefan and Alma are everything your counties hope they are. I'll arrange quarters and re-outfitting, and you can be on your way. I don't suppose you intend to partake of our hospitality any longer than necessary."

Lady moved closer to Thomas. She slid her hand into his. "No," he said, momentarily distracted. "Give me two dozen darts and a dozen vials, and I'll be on my way."

"Still Charlie's Lord Protector?"

"I am. And I'll take his massacre out of Denethan's hide."

The dean scratched his neck, fingernails rasping across the stubble. "I don't blame you," he said, finally, "although that mentality is what drove us underground. Surely you'll stay the evening."

Lady's hand gripped Blade's more tightly. "I'd like to stay permanently, with the children."

The dean smiled hugely. "And what could you possibly teach them? My dear, I've forgotten far more than you'll ever know. The outside has lost realms of knowledge. The nesters are little more than vermin. Your instincts are good, I know, but—" he spread his hands.

"I'm a Healer. I'm a Protector."

"Parapsychology is a chancy subject at best—difficult talents to verify and none that can be passed on by mere academia. Surely your county has more need of you than we do."

Thomas could feel her humiliation burning in her.

He closed his other hand about hers. "We can't afford to lose you now," he told her.

She looked at him. Her brown eye brimmed with an unshed tear. The dean interrupted, saying, "Perhaps we can answer your questions tomorrow, give you something to carry back with you?"

"You can answer one now." Blade dropped Lady's hand and swung back to face the massive desk and the man who sat behind it.

"I'll try." An expression shadowed the dean's face and Remmick responded with attention.

"Are you human?"

"I beg your pardon?"

"Human. Which ones of you come from the old lines?"

"Why, my dear executioner, we all do. Every last one of us. Does that interest you? If so, perhaps you'll volunteer for some lab work."

"What kind?" Lady murmured.

"A little blood work, a few skin scrapings. Charles did the same when he was here. He did his genetic homework the hard way, but here we have medical advantages you obviously do not. The more diverse our samples, the more accurate our conclusions can be."

"Conclusions about what?"

The dean licked his lips with the merest touch of his tongue. "We're trying to determine just how aberrant the different counties have become. The plague, other factors. The Disasters didn't create your kind, Sir Thomas, it only set your ancestors free. Labs working on genetic engineering for space exploration were destroyed, but certain . . . tissue cultures were not."

"Aberrant?" Lady repeated. "Is that what you call us?"

"Dear lady, of course not. I mean no offense." The dean stood. For a big man, he was surprisingly light on his feet.

"I've shed enough blood over the past few days," Thomas said dryly. "I might as well shed some for you." With a warning look to quell Lady's rising anger, he took her arm and guided her after the dean. Under her breath, she muttered, "Arrogant son of a bitch."

Remmick marched a pace or so behind them as the dean led them to another elevator shaft and downward again. The grills they passed through were continously marked AUTHORIZED PERSONNEL ONLY. The halls were sterile tunnels, radiating an impersonal beige aura. Their passage through them was muffled as if it were not quite real. The dean led them through a door. Its upper portion was glass, steel meshed for strength. A white-coated man turned as they entered a large, sterile kitchenlike room.

"Dr. Mendes. This is Sir Thomas Blade of Orange County and Lady Nolan of Torrance County. They're part of the escort of our new arrivals. They're in a hurry to be on their way, but they've graciously agreed to donate to our sample pool."

"My god, Gerald. Have they even been through decon?"

The dean said smoothly, "Now, now. Of course they have."

The doctor wiped his hands on the flaps of his white coat then and smiled broadly. "Good. I won't keep you, Gerald."

With an eerie grace, the large man pivoted on his heels. "But," and Lady reached out tentatively, "what if I wished to stay? Surely there's something I could do here of value."

The falcon expression went hard and cold. "Dear Lady. You've been In-City. You've lived on corrupted land. I'm prepared to extend you every hospitality, but your joining the colony is unthinkable. What if you carry the plague? Our population has none of the mutations you could carry. Our program is coming along admirably. At the very least, if we suffered you to stay, you'd have to submit to voluntary sterilization. You're still a moderately young woman. Wouldn't you find that difficult? You're better off returning to your own where you can be appreciated as the unique woman you are."

Suddenly pale, Lady shrank back. "Surely your tests would show if I carried the plague or not?"

"Within a ninety percent accuracy rate," Dr. Mendes said smoothly. He smiled reassuringly. "It's the other genetic coding we have to worry about . . ." the doctor's words trailed off.

Thomas put his arm around Lady, finding her suddenly frail within his hold. "We have work to do anyway," he told her. "I don't intend leaving without you."

She gave him a brittle smile.

The dean wrung his hands. "That's settled, then. Remmick and I will leave you in the doctor's capable care. He'll see you to your quarters and Remmick will handle your affairs in the morning." He left, the captain on his heels.

The doors closed behind them. Dr. Mendes had brown eyes as cold as the corridors of the Vaults. He let out a gust of sound. "Well. Let's get started." He began bustling through a fortune of rare equipment. Charlie would have loved it in here—probably had loved it in here. Lady plucked uncertainly at a button on her sleeve. Mendes turned around impatiently. "What are you waiting for? The sooner you strip, the sooner I can get this over with."

Mendes turned his back again, readying a set of glass tubes on a pristine plastic counter. He opened and closed cupboard doors, adding to his instruments. Thomas was as baffled by the doctor's attitude as by Lady's sudden quiet. It was as though her rejection had taken all the spirit out of her.

Thomas loosened his scarf to free his gills and began to ease out of his battered leather jacket. "The dean mentioned something about genetic engineering and space exploration. What was he talking about?"

"Well, the Mars program for one, and what we called the longship, or the generational program—"

"What?"

The doctor turned. "Just how primitive are you?" His dark skin was flushed with impatience.

Lady moved then. She reached for Thomas' arm. "I think I'd like you to kill him for me."

Thomas smiled thinly. "I think I'd like to do it." He leaned over the counter which separated them from the doctor. "I'm primitive enough to do it."

Mendes swallowed. "I apologize," he said thickly. "I don't work with people often."

Lady softened, saying, "Apology accepted."

Thomas hesitated.

Mendes put in hastily, "You do know about airplanes?"

"Of course."

"That we landed on the moon?"

Thomas shook his head.

"Mars?"

Again, negative motion.

"Ah." Mendes took a deep breath. "Well, we did both. Mars was intriguing. It was felt that genetically altered people, with environmental suits, might do quite well there. And then there were those who fancied altering for ocean exploration and cleanup. Labs were doing all sorts of work. Your . . . differences . . . are the results of those programs. Some authorized, some not. Your changes are not the most drastic by any means. Some labs augmented animal, instead of human, structure."

"Did we go to Mars?"

"Not in that state, no. And the longships went out before the disasters . . . no way of telling what long-range effect the voyage had there until they return . . ." Mendes stalled. "How about stripping down?"

When making love, it had seemed one thing, but now, in the oppressive atmosphere of the lab, quite another. As Lady began unbuttoning once more, he asked, "Is it necessary?"

"No. But we like to make visual records." Distractedly, the doctor pointed at equipment bolted to the corners of the lab. "We put the data on disk."

"Laser?"

"Yes! Are you familiar with them?"

"Vaguely." Thomas finished taking off his jacket. "But this is as far as I'll go."

Lady threw him a grateful look as she merely rolled up her own sleeves. Mendes frowned but said, "As you wish." He took up an instrument.

Lady remained stoic but paled as he took skin scrapings and then a blood sample. She winced at the scraping. When Mendes came to Thomas, he looked at the bloodstained clothing and the bandage.

"What happened here?"

"Wounded in a skirmish."

"I'd better take a look at that." He sliced through Lady's carefully knotted bandage and kneaded the almost healed pink flesh. "How recent was this?"

"Two, three days."

The doctor's eyebrows went up.

"I'm a Healer," Lady said in explanation.

"Oh? Turn this way. I want the camera to catch that. No, angle the arm this way—that's it." The doctor looked back at her. "You did this?"

"It's one of my Talents."

"You're an augmented paranormal? Ah." The doctor turned away quickly, but not before Thomas saw his skin grow ashen under his naturally dark complexion. He busied himself daubing glass slides from their blood samples and running them through a large white machine. It hummed for a few moments, then its screen filled with symbols.

"Good news," Mendes said without facing them. "No plague, as yet. Sir Thomas, you're a bit anemic. Put more iron into your diet."

Lady relaxed with an audible sigh. Happily, she linked her arm through Thomas'.

The doctor pushed a button set into his counter. "That's it, that's all I need. If you'll take a seat in the room through there, I've sent for Remmick."

Lady helped Thomas on with his jacket. "That's everything?"

"Well . . . I could do a visual check for physical

aberrations, but with your eyes and his gills already recorded, it's not necessary."

She nodded. "All right." She walked with Thomas to the waiting room. They stepped inside.

The door snapped shut behind them. She gave a little shudder. "I'd never get used to all this opening and shutting without my controlling it."

"I'm not too happy about it either." He examined the entryway. There was no way of opening the door from their side. His instincts began to unsettle him. The room was as sterile and barren as an elevator. Involuntarily, he steadied his gut for another dizzying drop. Lady sat on the plastic bench against one wall. She tucked her booted feet under her.

"Disappointed?" He continued stalking about the apparently seamless walls. Sprinkler heads overhead appeared to be in good condition.

"About Alma and Stefan? Yes. I hope we get a chance to say good-bye."

"Don't count on it. Remmick could hardly wait to spirit them away." She started to say something else, but he heard a door close on the other side of the wall. He motioned her silent and strained to hear.

She noticed then that they had been sealed in. She joined him against the wall of the chamber.

". . . settled in upstairs. Got what you need?"

"Yes. The girl is pre-menses, so we don't need to worry about plague contamination." Mendes' voice crisp and businesslike. "The boy, however, is from a Russian gene pool. I have my suspicions. He could be carrying a genetic Trojan horse. It's happened before."

The dean's voice rumbled in answer, "As a male, he's expendable. We can carry him for a few years before we make a decision. I won't have contamination, not now, not after all this work. We're nearly pure. What about the other two?"

"In the holding tank. One of them was spiking our ESP testing equipment like crazy. Do you suppose it's possible—"

"Bah! Would they have let you put them into the tank if they could read your mind?"

Thomas began to pry at the sealed door. A fingernail splintered down to the quick. Lady helped.

"What do you want me to do with them? That abomination with the gills is dangerous."

"Kill them," the dean intoned.

Sprinklers began to hiss, dispensing a white, misty cloud. His throat closed almost immediately. He tore his scarf off completely, freeing his gills. Lady collapsed at his feet.

"Kill them," the man repeated. "Then flush them."

Chapter 27

Below the reservoir, two still forms were tumbled into a ravine from an opening that snapped shut as quickly as it had opened. The ravine held water when it rained, runoff that eventually joined a storm drain system that could still make its broken way to the ocean. Now, wet or dry, it was a feeding ground for the wildlife in the foothills and some of the bolder predators from the ruins.

Whatever the scavenger, there would be little recognizable left of the bodies once it found them. As dusk lowered a purple curtain, a large shape loped confidently down the slopes toward the ravine and the insignificant freshet left over from heavy rains the month before. It ran mostly on two legs.

It was not human, but neither was it not not-human. It cast over the ground like a hunting beast until it stopped before the two tangled forms lying helplessly in the brush. It stooped its form over them and listened carefully. As if satisfied, it hoisted one and then the other, filling each shoulder with a burden, and loped to the concrete river that ran to the ocean.

There the beast dropped its burdens. With a black-clawed hand, it traced the chevron mark on the man's brow. It gave a grunt of satisfaction before pulling together branch and brush to form a crude raft. It rolled the bodies onto the raft which bobbed in the water. It watched the two for a long moment, and scratched at its long, russet hair. Then it pushed the raft away with a large, callused foot and watched the voyagers float downstream.

Below the city, dirty water ran like the River Styx to the ocean. Its pipes were massive, concrete and no longer whole, becoming more of a spillway than a pipeline. Animals and other things found their way through the ruins above to the depths where water—even dirty water—and life could be obtained.

A notch-earred wolfrat made his way down a warren run of trash and slime, bits of ooze clinging to his coat. The notch that took off most of his ear scarred into his eye, drew it up and puckered it half-closed. But he did not need his twilight sight to find water. He could smell it. His nails clicked on old plumbing and foundation stonework as he lumbered downhill, his tail dragging behind him like some half-forgotten reptile. The wolfrat shouldered his way through a jagged crack in the pipe. The cement edges tore out more than its share of tufted hair from his mangy hide. The wolfrat's lips twitched in a snarl of pain, unvoiced, for as pain went in the world, the discomfort was minor and unmemorable. As he hung over the lip of the crack to dip his muzzle into the murky water flowing swiftly past, he sensed a movement upstream.

The pipe was massive, and the water it carried past measured untold gallons. The wolfrat's ears flickered forward. Sometimes the water also carried gifts—gifts of garbage still fresh enough to eat. Sometimes the water carried unfortunate critters who'd also come down to drink at one of the various breaches and fallen in. That was how the wolfrat had nearly lost his eye and ear—trying to fetch out a hill cat, spitting and hissing in its fury. The wolfrat lost that dinner, and the hillcat its life, drowning in the dark spinning waters before the pipe spilled it into the ocean. Better, perhaps, that it had allowed the wolfrat to pull it out, and taken its chance fighting for survival in the dry tunnels.

The tattered ears twitched again. Unless the wolfrat missed his guess, something bigger and tastier was floating downstream, coming right at him. The beast braced himself and hunkered lower, claws flexed for grabbing. If the human scent daunted him, it was not for long.

A long shape barreled toward him. The wolfrat tensed, his tail anchoring his tenuous position, nails stretched and elongated, his toes prehensile in their flexibility.

As the smaller of the two figures borne along faced toward him, he reached and snatched. Fabric tore, and fresh cuts welled up with crimson, hot blood scent spattering the water's surface. But the raft bobbed away, bumping up against the curvature of the waterway, halting only momentarily.

The rat lashed out again, fishing frantically. He nearly toppled in his enthusiasm, but his claws caught— and this time held. He drew back slowly, lest the water-burdened flesh he desired break away from him again. He bared his teeth, long fangs beginning to slaver with anticipation. His shoulders hunched as he drew the heavy burden closer to the jagged opening in the pipe. If the creature should begin to fight, he would lose it, he knew. But it stayed limp in his hold.

Hot drool ran down his lips. Then the soft, tender flesh in his grip began to separate and he lost it as it tore loose. With an aggravated squeal, the wolfrat perched a moment on the break in the pipe, then backed out quickly. He raced through the warrens, knowing exactly where the next watering hole was. He pushed his way through moldering earth and arrived in time to watch the raft float away right under his nose.

The wolfrat stayed perched in disappointment for an

instant, then, with a hissing sigh, lowered his head to drink. The water, at least, was relatively fresh as water went beneath the ruined earth.

The dolphin swam in crystal clear seawater, felt the thermals and scents of an outpouring of landwater into her pathway, and made to swerve. She disliked the sting and taste of landwater in her eyes and airhole. But she had been summoned, and so she stayed near the spillway which erupted from the city ruins. Then she tasted a scent she knew, and paused.

The being who had danced with her one moonstruck time not long ago rode that landwater. She circled and searched the spillway, the foam in her wake bouncing upon the surface like gems. She bit the thermal wash, tasting his essence more clearly.

She was not an ordinary dolphin, any more than he had been an ordinary man-thing. She rose and tail-walked a few lengths to gauge where the wash originated from. As she spanned the waves, she saw the two dark bundles flash out of the spillway and rise hesitantly on the crest. Then they began to sink.

The dolphin dove and sped toward the bundles. Her intuition had brought her fishing this coast and now she was about to snag the unexpected.

She caught the raft up and flipped them about in the water so that their blowholes faced upward, tending them like dolphin pups. Her keen hearing brought her sputterings of awareness. She nosed at the two. One bled, a crimson cloud upon the water. The dolphin circled, knowing that the blood was likely to attract deadly hunters.

She nosed at the favored one's appendage, more limp than a fin, but stronger, too, though not for swimming. It flopped about with her attentions. The dolphin sounded unhappily. She searched the lower tides, tasting, smelling, listening. Teeth glistening, she snapped at a barracuda drawn by the blood scent and arrowing past her. It sped away, jaws grinning in defeat. A second tried to bolt past. She punched it and after a flailing wiggle, it, too, swam off, much more slowly, fluid leaking from its gills.

The dolphin surfaced and cleansed her air, blowhole expelling with a spray that danced about her, refracting an iridescent rainbow. She pulled alongside the dark bundles, watching as they floated limply, hanging upon the raft. She took up his wrist in her jaws, gently, as she would take a dolphin pup up to his first surfacing, aware that among her people she was huge and having learned tenderness from experience. Her bite caressed the marks of their first meeting.

She recalled with pleasure the instinct that had drawn her to the sea bowls and her delight on finding a being who shared her love of the sea and beauty and things arcane.

The dolphin goddess shook with fury. What enemy had dared to injure her favorite and his mate? Her eyes blazed, and turquoise sheened about her hide as her aura flared. She emitted a cry in her despair which only her kind and the faraway gods could hear, and shook her favorite roughly as if he had participated in his own demise, too careless to know of the gift she had bestowed upon him.

He fell from her mouth, splashing into the water, and she nosed him in the ribs as she would a reluctant pup into using his airhole. Then she picked him up again and shook him, keening silently in dolphin grief.

His gills fluttered weakly. She shook him again, then heard to her exultation the same struggling sounds a weakened pup might make. Then bad air flushed from him rapidly, expelling with an odor that made her gag in disgust. As he fell from her grip a third time, it was with a thrashing and a growing awareness.

Encouraged, she turned to the mate and shook her, too, her wounds pinking the foam with every shake until the woman made a gasping sob, and her limbs jerked in startlement. She expelled the same foul-smelling bad air, then took a choking breath as the dolphin curled about them both. The goddess opened her jaws in a wide and knowing smile as they reached for her, suddenly uncertain of their buoyancy in the ocean water, and clung to her, and gasped for air. Dolphin prayers are rarely said and even more rarely ignored.

Thomas frowned as he pulled the bandaging tight about Lady's upper arm. "I don't think she did this," he said in answer to Lady's complaint. "This doesn't look like a bite pattern. More a rip or tear."

"Then what did? Did they try to mutilate me after they gassed us?"

"Does it matter? We're here, alive, when we had no chance."

She ducked her chin down, silently. A fathomless expression passed over her face, made a little puffy and swollen from the side effects of the gas used on them. She looked tired and worn and every day of her twenty-nine years.

He reached out, cupped her chin, and gently turned her face toward him. "You're a Healer," he said. "Make sure that doesn't get infected. I don't want things falling off of you."

Her lips quirked. "Any *thing* in particular?"

"Several, as a matter of fact." He smoothed the wispy hairs off her forehead. "I suppose I'll have to find a shell comb for you."

Lady waved graciously over the expanse of beach. "Take your pick."

He settled down in the sand beside her. Their clothes were spread out, drying, and he took his nudity matter-of-factly. Lady had insisted on retaining her undergarments and sat in them now, the paler portions of her skin rapidly pinking. He'd have to get her in the shade as soon as she had warmed. The crude raft—he must have woven it together before passing out when they'd been dumped outside—had broken apart when they beached.

"Where are we?"

"Best guess or for certain?"

Lady let out a gusty laugh. "Best guess, by all means."

"Probably Catalina, though I'm not familiar with this side of it." He eyed the striated cliff wall at their backs. "In high water, I'd say this strand disappears."

Lady shuddered involuntarily. "Are we going to have to swim for it again?"

"No, no. I mean really high water, like when the Santa Anas come up. High tide is going to push us back some, but we'll be all right. It's fresh water that worries me."

"Is there any?"

"Bound to be some. I saw a wild goat or two looking down at us when we came ashore. They're tough, but they still drink. I may have to swim around until I find a cove where the cliffs can be climbed to do some dowsing, but we ought to find something."

Lady rubbed her hand over his lips. "I could go for roasted goat," she mused.

"Me, too. But not just yet. That was a rough swim, hauled by dolphin or not. We were in no shape to make it across the channel. Still cold?"

"A little, but the sun feels good." She shivered again, lightly, despite her words. They lapsed into a long silence, watching the hard brightness of the Pacific as it washed against the sands of their cove. Then, she stirred and leaned up against him, drawing strength from his presence. "I dreamed that I was dead."

He did not answer her, thinking thoughts that were the same, but not wanting to deal with them just yet.

"Are you listening to me?"

"Yes."

"Then talk to me. Am I crazy?"

"If you were sane, you'd never have insisted on coming with me."

She kicked sand over his bare feet. The warmth felt good and he kept his feet buried. But he did not feel like talking just yet. The fan of Lady's hair trailed over his shoulder.

"Did we die? Or were we just unconscious, so far under we never knew what happened to us?"

"I don't know," he said, finally, after a further silence punctuated only by their soft breathing and the breaking of waves upon the beach, and an occasional screech of a wheeling gull. "I just don't know. *Kill 'em and flush 'em.* Why?"

Lady sighed. "So we couldn't contaminate them." She tickled a fingertip over his bicep. "We have to go back. We can't leave Alma and Stef with those bastards."

"That, I know." He looked out over the ocean expanse toward where he imagined he could see the shoreline. It was a long and tiring journey already made once, waiting to be retraced, and with Cindy and Lady's mule lost to them. The waters were coming in, slowly, inexorably, high tide moving up the sands, but he did not see the dolphin arcing upon them. He wondered where she went, and if she was waiting for him to come out and dance with her again. His lungs ached, and charley horses knotted calf muscles not used to marathon swimming.

"What do you have in mind?"

Thomas put his arm about her. The sun-warmed aura of her skin brushing next to his filled his mind with a giddy thought, one that he pushed away for the time being. Getting into the College Vaults a second time would be an ordeal. "We should rest here for a week or two, provided we can find water."

"So long?"

"We've been through a lot. What happened wouldn't have happened if I had been thinking straight."

Lady sat up and looked at him, both eyes blazing indignantly. "What happened wasn't your fault! Those . . . gentlemen . . . tried to kill us!"

He tried not to smile at her. She fairly bristled. "Lady," he said softly. "We're both Talents. They shouldn't have been able to entertain those thoughts within arm's reach of us."

Her lips worked without a sound passing them. Then

she let herself sag back into his embrace. "All right. We rest a week. What then?"

"I'm not sure. I have debts to pay first."

"Debts?" Her voice was muffled this time, as she moved to nestle her face against his chest, and her lips vibrated teasingly against his nipples.

She was seriously interfering with his thought processes. He reached up to her shoulders and sat her back on his knees, a hand's span between them. "You saw the dolphin who brought us here . . . you know you've never seen a creature like that."

Lady's mouth curved sulkily, but she nodded.

"Well, I have. And she marked me. It was the day of the wedding. I can't pretend I understand what she is or where she comes from, but she saved us and I owe her. I think she'll collect on that. I'd like to have it settled before we leave here."

"What if she wants your children?" Lady said softly.

"Lady!"

"All right, Thomas. I'll get serious. I understand. But she just might be a mutation or something."

"No. No." He looked out at the changing tide. "No, she's something special. Man-made or maybe nature-made, but she's something special, and I owe her our lives."

"And then we get Alma and Stefan?"

"And then."

Her face became melancholy. "I hope to God," she said to him, "that there's something left of them by then."

"Me, too."

Chapter 28

Thomas kicked his way to the surface. Lady sat placidly on the driftwood raft which had replaced the old one, her hair loose about her shoulders, looking for all the world like some mermaid out of the long ago past. He sputtered a bit and caught at a log end to steady himself.

"What is it?" she asked, leaning toward him.

"Plastic netting, heavy duty stuff, strung quite a ways along here. It's probably been in place for a hundred years or more."

Her brown eye reflected compassion, her blue eye the ocean. "Why?"

"Damned if I know. A fishery boundary maybe, maybe defense. Anyway, there's a few skeletons caught in it . . . I imagine it's been the death of a dolphin or two. Even a gray whale."

"Do you think this is what she wants, for you to cut it down?"

He ran his hands through his wet hair, slicking it back off his forehead. He'd grown very tan in his weeks on the island, but Lady had woven a grass hat and merely freckled lightly. She wore her hat now.

"I don't know what she wants." He hung in the water, floating. The sea looked calm about them and there was no sight of their benefactress.

"She towed us here. You can't believe she did it accidentally."

"I haven't the tools."

"You have the knife you found in the military cache." Lady wore it now, belted at her side. He'd used it to help rebuild the raft. "The only other alternative is for you to start swimming—and push me all the way to the peninsula." Lady leaned forward so close now she was almost lying on her stomach. "You know, Thomas," she said seductively. "I think you have remarkable stamina in many things. But I don't think you feel like towing me."

He rocked the raft. "Maybe it would do you some good to go swimming."

She let out a tiny shriek and sat bolt upright in the center of the raft. He gazed at her, and let the warm feeling he felt when he looked at her, flood him. No longer did he feel that emotion as a disability. Perhaps it had happened when he'd died . . . perhaps it had happened sooner, a little bit at a time. It was a metamorphosis he regretted no more than the butterfly regretted leaving its cocoon behind.

She said, "What are you thinking? Your mustache is twitching like an otter's whiskers."

"Flattery will get you everywhere. I'm thinking you'd better hand me the knife and I'll give it a try."

She unbelted the tool and tossed it over. He unsheathed it and let go of the raft, letting the waves take him gently.

Below, it took a moment for his eyes to get used to the sting. But he'd been bred for that tolerance, just as he'd been bred to have gills. A strand of kelp, dislodged by the tide, floated past him, trailing its own leaves like a hand across his body. Bubbles streamed out of his gills, a wake of white diamonds bumping into his sight whenever he turned his head. His skin goosefleshed. The water was cold this time of year. It sapped his strength. If the net were too tough, or he became entangled in its loose strands, he was on his own. Even the dolphin goddess feared these depths. She had towed them there and left them in a spray of turquoise water.

He readied the knife as the bright yellow netting reared in front of him. It was still taut, years of the ocean leaving little or no wear on it. Barnacle scale decorated it here and there as he tried to trace its anchorage, and seaweed grew through it as though it were a trellis, but it was deadly and remained that way. The ocean had tried to adapt it into something useful and failed.

The old-timers had tempered a good blade. Made of a metal alloy he could not identify, it was tougher than just about any knife he'd ever handled. Yet he doubted its edge would be much use against the net. He reached an end and followed it down, where concrete and a plastic pole fastened it inviolably to the ocean floor.

Thomas took a deep breath and let himself surface slowly. He looked about. Lady bobbed a little distance away. She watched the cresting waves anxiously. He did not hail her. He breathed a few times to pump up his bloodstream, then dove once more.

If he cut the net loose, or even cut it into smaller pieces, those pieces would still trap swimmers. No, the net had to come ashore where nothing could become tangled. That task was impossible for him. He could not guess the weight, but knew it must be close to several hundred pounds. His best bet was to wind it up and try to anchor it about its original mooring. Such a task seemed monumental as well.

If all he did was think about it, he would go into hypothermia before he could do anything. Thomas gripped the knife tightly and began to saw at a crucial strand. It parted easily. He moved upward, cutting as he went. The last major strand at the top strained. With a cautious move, he cut that free, knowing it would sling loose.

It did, but the ocean's grip upon it kept the reaction moderate. Thomas kicked upward, cleansed and revitalized his lungs, and dove a last time. He found the other anchorage near a kelp forest as the net began to flop about him, going to and fro in the tide. He panicked and thrashed as kelp twisted about his feet. His ears rang as he began to choke, gills unable to provide him with quite enough air. Then he looked up, seeing the sunlight streaming down into the kelp forest as the weed grew tall, seemingly before his very eyes, reaching upward.

Thomas grasped the end of the netting. The tide seemed to be with him as he dug his feet in the sandy bottom and coaxed the net into the kelp, where it could anchor and trellis something good. The tiny fish living in the forest darted about him, in and out of the netting with no trouble.

It took the better part of the afternoon, surfacing and diving, to anchor the net into the kelp bed. He kept the net low, around the base of the plants so that it would not entangle the sea otter population floating above.

Lady called encouragement to him and finally helped him aboard the raft when he quit and tried weakly to crawl out, shivering. She threw a sun-warmed grass mat over him.

"Will it work, do you think?"

He'd explained to her what it was he was trying to do. He gave a wobbly shake of his head as if to say he did not know. His teeth chattered in spite of himself.

"I tried," he finished. He lay down, his head in her sun-soaked lap, and rested, the ocean rocking him to sleep.

The dolphin came at dusk, her wake phosphorescent with the iridescent fire of her aura. She leaped and caprioled for them, nearly capsizing the raft. Lady clung to Thomas.

"Is she happy?"

"I'd say so. She's dancing for us."

Lady murmured, "I'm unused to the ways of dolphins."

Thomas laughed, as if she should not be. He watched as the mammal came alongside, grinning, her eyes shining with the last of the light off the water. He ran his hand along her flank. The beast then dipped away and came up under the tow rope. As the raft shimmied into movement, Lady clenched the bundle of their clothes. Thomas put an arm about her.

"We're going home."

*   *   *

Nighttime. He shrugged into his leather jacket, made incredibly stiff by its debacle in salt water, even though he'd been rubbing a crude plant oil into it the past few weeks. It would never be the same unless he could get his hands on some decent saddle soap. He mourned briefly for all of Charlie's instruments and gauges, lost to the College Vaults.

He put a hand back for Lady. She grasped it.

"How far off the peninsula are we?"

"Not far at all." His hushed tones matched hers. He brought her into a squat upon the grass, damp with winter dew. "This is what I'm going to do." And he told her the plan he'd formulated while building the raft.

She made a forbidding sound through her teeth when he'd finished. "No." Flatly. Finally.

"Listen to me. There's no other way."

"No."

"Lady—"

"You'll get yourself killed."

"We're afoot. Time is against us now. For all I know, Denethan's been laying siege to them."

"I know, I know." Silence. In the darkness he could not quite see her face, but he swore that her ice-blue eye glittered coldly at him. There was a rustle of cloth. He thought perhaps she'd turned her face away. He heard a muffled sound.

"Don't cry."

"I'm not crying, damn it," she threw at him.

A night bird rose at the sound and winged away, keening.

Then Lady said quietly, "And if you can rush the catapults and get a wind raider, what then?"

"We fly to the Vaults."

"What if there're no raiders here?"

He rocked back on his heels. "Then we'll have to walk, I guess. But there's bound to be. He'll have left sentries at the catapults. Those installations are too valuable to him to abandon just because he wiped out the peninsula."

In a very small voice, she said, "I'm afraid of heights."

"Then don't look down." He squeezed the hand she pushed into his tightly. "We've got cover. Let's go."

"All right, but don't take all night. I'm tired."

In the end, it was she who found the catapult. She pulled tightly at his wrist.

"Down!"

He let her pull him down. She crouched next to him. "There."

He saw it then, a tiny carroty flame of fire. Then, blacker than ebony against the night, the catapult tower. He crept closer.

His gamble had paid off. Two immense batwing shapes rested on the crest near the tower.

"Two of them."

"We'll have to disable one," she returned.

Thomas smiled in the night. Girl after his own heart. "I count four sentries, how many have you got?"

"Five. There's one asleep near the raiders."

"Ah." He looked over the camp. "I can take out those four, if you can handle the fifth."

Silence. Then, "All right."

He knew she could protect herself. But this seemed more like murder than self-defense. He had no immediate comfort for her. They crept down toward the camp, the sweet oil of mesquite filling the air as it bruised and broke about them.

If it had been he on duty, he would have smelled it and known that something moved in the brush. Perhaps they didn't have that much mesquite on the Mojave, or perhaps they just weren't alert enough.

It didn't matter. The outcome would have been the same. He Projected, blurring their vision and reflexes, got the four, quickly, and Lady the fifth.

After cleansing it, he handed her the knife to slash the wings of the extra wind raider. He bent to lift it up so she could reach it more easily.

Five men jumped from underneath the machine and came for him. He heard Lady's sharp cry, cut off, and began to kill anything that came near him.

Blade paused in the grass, head down, breathing heavily, thoughts swimming through his brain. She was dead, wasn't she? And he alive, out of their reach, outnumbered but not outfought. He'd reach for her thoughts in his, but that wasn't his Talent. The only thought he could reach for was that of the enemy.

What right had he to be crouched in the darkness, alive?

"Blade! Are you listening?" The deep, masculine voice pealed out in the night.

Thomas swallowed hard. His throat hurt. His heart felt as though it could burst. The enemy shouted for him, but he had not intention of listening.

Whatever the enemy said it would be lies.

"Blade! I know you're out there."

He turned his back and began to wend his way through the undergrowth, painstakingly, having underestimated the enemy before. He was wrong about his feelings. He'd disabled himself. He deserved defeat.

"You're getting old, Blade! You set off at least seven wards crossing the hill. How many more will you set off getting back? You're not getting out of here alive. I've got her, Blade. If you want her, come get her."

He closed his mind and continued to work his way toward freedom.

Lady sat, her feet bound, and a ward tied about each wrist. The fetishes rattled whenever she moved. "You won't get him," she said. "He knows better."

The tall man at the edge of the firelight stood looking out into the darkness. At her words he turned back toward her, amber eyes catching the glow of the fire. "He'll come back," Denethan said. "If I have to make you howl on the wind, he'll come back."

"Never! He's a professional."

Denethan pointed a finger at his scribe. "Micah, persuade her to do some shouting."

The wizened old man squinted at Lady. He blinked slowly. "I," he said, "would do what was asked of me."

"You," she said, "should drop dead."

The scribe curled back with a hiss. Denethan pivoted on one heel. "Micah," he ordered.

The scribe reached a leathery hand into the heart of the fire and withdrew a single, radiant ember. He held it toward her.

Lady felt her heart skip a beat. She thrust with her mind, made it spark high enough that the old being dropped it with a hiss. She looked away, but she could feel its heat draw near. "He'll come back," she said to Denethan. "But when he feels like it, and then he'll kill you. For what you did to Charlie, to me, to the county."

"Charlie?" the man said.

She felt the ember's breath upon her face. "The Director of Water and Power. The massacre on the peninsula."

Denethan laughed softly. "What a monster you must think me, but that, my pretty one, was not my handiwork."

Lady opened her mouth and screamed with all her might for Thomas. The night grew still after her outburst. No answer came. She felt the blistering warmth of the coal near her left eye, the blue one, the icy cold one that Thomas had always hated.

"Wait a moment." Denethan beckoned to the scribe. The old man knelt in front of her, glowing sparks trailing from his fingers. How could he bear the heat? He moved the ember back into the fire.

She bowed her head, knowing she was right. Thomas would not return for her, could not compromise his duty in hopes of saving her. He could not. He was what he and Charlie had molded him to be, a Lord Protector, an enforcer, all the deadlier because of his psychic abilities. She had known he could, and would, leave her behind when they'd gone after Jennifer and Ramos. When they'd gone In-City. And now.

Men like Thomas did not seek out partnership. It was a liability. He'd use the ghost road if he had to—and they both knew it would kill him this time.

"Call him again."

Her voice choked in her throat. She shook her head. "He won't come," she said, her voice barely audible. "Not tonight." She dared to look up. "But he'll come back for you some day, and when he catches you, he'll cut your heart out of your chest."

"Yes," Denethan murmured. "I think he might. But that might be too late for both of us."

A figure loomed suddenly in the firelight. "Tell me why."

Lady felt her pulse throb in her throat, and hot tears sprinkled her face as he looked down at her. It was Thomas.

Chapter 29

"Because we're alike, you and I," the desert mutant said, "and we were born out of their dreams, not their nightmares, no matter what that bastard buried in the mountain told you."

Blood-splattered and weary, Thomas swayed on his feet. Then he looked to Lady.

"Believe him, Thomas."

He closed his eyes faintly. That tiny sense of Truth-read came to him, a fragile thread of an ability the ghost road had leeched from him. It told him that his enemy was honorable. He pointed at the wards on Lady's wrists. They parted with a blue spark that snapped. "Show me your hospitality and we'll talk tomorrow."

They slept till mid-morning in a canopied tent of golden silklike fabric that billowed in the wind and captured the rays of the sun. A gold and dust dappled coyote lay in the corner, his head on his paws, eyes watching them alertly, but no one in Denethan's camp bothered them.

He slept on one cot, holding Lady in a light embrace, and the desert raider slept on the second. They had lain down warily, too tired to talk, accepting a momentary truce, after Lady had said, "Thomas—Denethan did not raid the peninsula."

But Thomas had had doubts of his own and that touched on them. So they had agreed to discuss their differences when their heads were clearer, Denethan out of courtesy, he thought, and himself out of necessity. Besides, Denethan was within arm's reach should Blade change his mind and decide to kill the mutant.

He woke, Lady's soft purr upon his chest, and lay there. He kept still, not wanting to wake her. When he finally turned his head to look at Denethan's cot, he found the man watching him, eyes like molten gold. He was not a lizard—he was like the coyote, the hillcat, and then a lizard, but all gold and dun.

"You can leave her," Denethan said quietly. "Fox here will watch her. You and I have much to talk about."

He moved carefully to disentangle himself, but woke her. She yawned and sat up, saying, "You weren't running out on me?"

"Never."

She glanced at Denethan. The man stood by his cot and bowed with liquid grace, saying nothing. They moved out into the sun where chairs and a table had been put out for them.

His men treated him like a monarch, and perhaps he was, a desert lord where no one else dared to reign. His lightly scaled skin was tanned gold, and his hair was light blond, like Thomas' but thick and curled.

His eyes were bronze, catlike, and warmed when he smiled. He was tall and well-muscled, taller than Thomas and more massively built, but exceedingly graceful. He walked barefoot to the conference chairs. His toes were webbed, the skin delicate, with gold tracery upon the folds. His nails were hardened, nearly claws, but, visibly, that was all of the mutant about him. Thomas sensed there might be more. He thought to himself ironically that this was the being he'd called the Lizard of Oz, a green man from an emerald city, but this man had nothing about him that was not gold.

Thomas settled himself, keeping his legs under him and his body loosely balanced. Lady took her cue from him and did the same. She graciously accepted a cool glass of juice from Micah.

In the daylight, Thomas could see much more of the lizard about Micah than showed in Denethan. Just, he supposed, as Micah could see he had gills and Lady did not. He refused the juice when offered, saying, "Tell me why we shouldn't kill each other."

Denethan put an eyebrow up. It arced elegantly over his amused eye. "It would be a waste, I think. We are both excellent specimens of our race."

"And what race is that?"

"A race that was meant to walk the stars."

"Perhaps—except that one of us is a little cold-blooded."

"Thomas!"

The desert lord waved a hand. "Let him talk. He hasn't offended me . . . yet. We are old enemies, and that weave is a very knotted one, but I'm beginning to think we are not the only weavers."

"Why?"

"Because, as Lady Nolan expressed so elegantly late last night, my troops were not responsible for the massacre on the Palos Verdes peninsula. We interrupted the real murderers and they fled rather hastily. Not, you understand, that I had not had similar intentions."

"You did not allow looting."

"I never do. We're not barbarians. We are only desert adaptive. We are survivors."

Thomas shifted slightly. Charlie's last words had spoken of betrayal, not raiders. Had the College Vault escort brought an attack force with them? And Charles, all unaware and triumphant in his dealings, welcomed them? Those who thought of the county settlements as infestations? "Did you see what happened? Could you identify who fled?"

"No. We were on their heels, but not that close. I had my men give the mercy stroke to those who were mortally wounded . . . I could not spare the attentions of my Healer. For that, I am truly sorry."

"Then why were you here? Why did you come back out of the Mojave after, what, ten years?"

Denethan paused. He poured himself a glass of fruit juice and savored half of it, making Thomas wait. Then he set the glass down. "Have you ever been to my region?"

"No."

"But you have felt the hot winds come scorching out of the desert?"

Thomas nodded.

"It can be a cruel life. Some of us are more . . . reptilelike . . . than we deserve to be." Denethan got up. His muscular form rippled gracefully with the movement. "We were mutated genetically—engineered for survival. I'm told that originally, my breed was destined for colonization elsewhere. Mars, perhaps. Arid. Cold, though, horribly cold, and my . . . breed . . . had not been quite perfected. Whatever the reason, we were created. As you were."

Thomas put his hand up to his throat. His gaze met Denethan's.

"You understand." Denethan cleared his throat and added, "There is a virus. . . ."

"The eleven year plague," Lady said suddenly.

"Yes—you know of it?" Denethan did not wait for an answer, her interruption had been enough. "It's devastating my people. The mutations are increasing, almost geometrically. We'll not survive another thirty years and remain human."

He stopped pacing. "I knew of Charles Warden's genealogy program. I came for those children, to take them home. I wanted them to save my people! We had appealed to the College Vault decades ago. Their answer was to destroy my father and decimate our population. Our answer to that was to find an easier country to live in."

"Which we already populated."

"Yes. So and thus, by trial and error, we do eventually find wisdom. I came to the uneasy conclusion that we might learn to live together. But first, the children. Plague has already struck my camps."

"And you just intended to take them."

"Yes. The decoys we tracked up the coast . . . there was an accident. One of my men was overzealous. The craft began to burn. The children panicked when our ship circled them. They chose to crash rather than be rescued. But on examination of the bodies, my men found that we had been duped. We came back, in force, to the peninsula, to find the massacre. Your DWP, it appears, had enemies."

"No one is perfect," Thomas said.

Denethan put his head back and laughed, a booming, hearty sound. When he'd finished, he said sadly, "If we'd been perfect, we wouldn't have needed your children."

"But why," Lady said. "Why all the years of raiding and terrorizing? Why the war ten years ago?"

"Did you not do the same to me? Our hold on the desert is tenuous at best, but never a year goes by that we do not fight other men for our right to live! We have the right to defend ourselves!"

Thomas got up. He shook his head. "Not from us. Not from the counties."

Denethan grew deadly still. They stood face-to-face. Then, almost imperceptibly, the desert mutant relaxed. "We are linked, you and I," he said softly, clearly, so that he might not be misunderstood. "If you lie, I will know it."

They stood, looking into one another's eyes. Thomas felt the uncanny movement of another within his soul—and looked into the earnestness of another's. Never had it been so easy to Truth-read. Or so devastating.

"No one," Thomas repeated, "to my knowledge, men of the counties or even nesters of this region, has ever gone to the Mojave to raid you."

Long moments passed. Then Denethan stepped back. "Then who?"

Together, they answered each other, "The College Vaults."

Denethan began to pace again, running his fingers through his hair. Light motes, bits of gold, spun off as he did. "It has to be. I thought they had done with me. They exist for purity. You and I are monsters in their sight, nothing of humanity remains in us."

Lady added, "They tried to kill us when we brought Alma and Stefan to them. They gassed and dumped us. We were less than animals to them."

Denethan tilted his head to listen to her. "I'm surprised they did not succeed. None of my spies has ever returned from there. No one I know has ever returned from there."

"Charlie and I did, once. And we were going back last night."

This halted Denethan. "You know the way in?"

"I know the way in, all right. I just don't know the way out."

Denethan seated himself. He snapped his fingers, and Micah reappeared. "A tray of bread and cheese, and whatever cooked meat you can find. We have a lot to talk about."

Thomas told him, "First, convince me you are not still an enemy."

From out of nowhere, Denethan drew a knife. He grasped Thomas's wrist and drew it close. Lady made a determined noise, and she frowned, then reeled back in her chair. Denethan paused long enough to glance at her saying, "You have some Talent, but don't seek to fence with me." He sliced the knife across the soft flesh inside of Thomas' wrist, then did the same with his own.

Two thin lines of crimson welled up.

"We bleed the same, you and I," the desert lord said. "I'm not so sure about those inside the Vaults. The man called dean is the same man who ruled them when the Disasters came and the Vaults were closed. How he lives decades past his time, I don't know. But I do know this . . . we are more human who learn to make peace out of war than those who cannot."

Thomas closed his eyes in thought. *Human.* He had been engineered to be the stuff of dreams, of tomorrow, not nightmares. This he knew Denethan believed with all his heart and soul to be true. Could he do less?

With an expression of pique, Lady waved her hand over both wrists, and the cuts healed. "Keep talking," she said.

Denethan ran his hands over the webbing a last time. He pulled on the buckles to double-check the security. "Now remember, when the catapult is released, it brings a disquieting sensation. Keep your wits about you or you'll never get the glider righted."

Thomas nodded, but he could feel Lady at his back, hunched in as if she could make herself small enough to ignore the sensation of flying altogether.

The desert lord eyed them both. "I wouldn't send you out without practice flights," he said, "if I didn't have to."

Thomas smiled. "Remember, I was going to steal this. At least now I get it with a set of instructions."

Denethan laughed. "I'll be behind you at launch, but ahead of you on the thermals. Follow me. I'll signal."

"Right."

The desert lord left the fuselage. Thomas got a clear view of blue sky, all he could see from his angle on the cocked catapult. He felt Lady shivering. "Is this the woman who's cursed me from one side of hell to another?"

"Oh, shut up," came her muffled reply. "Just tell me when it's over."

He felt his smile widen. A desert man leaned over his view.

"It'll be a minute, fella." The mutant showed his too sharp teeth. "It's a good thing his lordship likes you. He had a fella killed this way once. Course, we launched him without the wind raider." He laughed hugely.

Lady muttered an obscenity at his back. Before he could say anything to quiet her, he heard the command.

"Launch!"

The catapult shivered. Then it jarred beneath them. He could feel the tremendous push and the wind raider quivered as it—and they—were thrown into the sky. For a moment, the earth and sky changed places and it looked as if they were going to tumble straight down. Their webbing dug into their ribs. Thomas' head whirled. Then the ship righted as he pulled back on the rudder and the wind filled the batwings.

The solar motor at the rear took hold, humming steadily, pushing them farther ahead. A moment later, the vessel shuddered as the second plane took their draft, then came up under them and passed them.

Grudgingly, Thomas realized that the desert warrior was a master with the wind raider. He took his signals and followed after.

"God," a voice said at his shoulder. "Look down, Thomas. It's beautiful!"

In shock, he followed Lady's suggestion. The panorama below was one of green and brown, laced and quilted by the tracks of the ruins. Lady was hanging over the side in delight.

"How soon did he say we'd be there?"

"Two hours, if the thermals are right."

"Look! Look, there's the edge of the Fire Ring, to the south."

To look wherever Lady pointed, and keep an eye out for Denethan's signals, made Thomas cross-eyed and a little dizzy. The better part of valor, he decided, was to watch the other wind rider. He missed little, for Lady kept up a delighted patter cross-country. He decided that he preferred to have her cowering, but the opportunity had passed.

Denethan had troops in the field, still searching for the College Vaults and the whereabouts of the children. They were hardened, battle-worthy troops, Denethan had told Thomas and Lady, more than equal to the weeks of living In-City. He had sent word ahead where they would be landing and to meet them. As they sculled now over the foothills, he could see the open area where Denethan planned to set down. It was littered with bodies dressed in khaki, and more than a few lizard men as well. There'd been warfare already.

"Who holds the field?" he said to Lady, busy gauging the thermals as they spiraled down.

"Denethan's troops." Her joy faded. "If even one of the College guard got away. . . ."

Their whole attack was predicated on surprise. "Don't even think it," he warned her. He made a warding sign over the plane and followed Denethan's bold descent over Indian Hill, where the College Vaults were buried under several hundred feet of rock.

As they jolted to a halt, Denethan made a running leap and caught the side of the fuselage, braking it to a complete stop. "A born airman," he said, and clapped Thomas on the shoulder.

Thomas did not feel joy. "How many did you lose?"

"Barely twenty. We got thirty-four of their finest."

"Any get away?"

The desert warrior did not meet his eyes as he looked about the browned grass field littered with dead. "None," he said, "that my captain knows of."

Which meant there was room for doubt.

Thomas took a deep breath. "Hell," he said. "None of this was dead certain to begin with."

Denethan caught his expression and smiled in appreciation. He reached into the fuselage for Thomas' rifle and tossed it to him.

As he strode behind the troops, it was a comfort to have a rifle and his old jacket filled with vials again. He crested the knoll and looked down on a brilliantly blue lake. "This," he said, "is the Cobal Canyon Reservoir. Follow me and I'll show you where those bastard get their water. I still remember how impressed Charlie was with their system. He pointed things out in great detail before entering the Vaults."

Thomas knelt by the filtration pump, a vial in his hand. Denethan manned the huge valve. Amber eyes studied Thomas as he thumbed the cork out of the vial. "What is that you've mixed?"

"It's a mild hallucinogenic. We call it amberose. We use it for breakout fever . . . when our adolescent Talents reach puberty—"

"I know," Denethan said. "We suffer it, too. But the drug deals with it?"

"It calms. In some cases, it can bring it on . . . with certain Talents, it's best if they suffer breakout when it can be dealt with more easily."

"Like Firemakers."

"Precisely."

Denethan looked across the basin and said, "There's the signal." He set his feet and began to turn the cutoff valve.

Thomas tapped the vial into the last of the water the College Vaults would be getting for a while.

Lady set her full mouth disapprovingly. "I don't think they deal with Talent. I don't think they believed we could have reliable paranormal abilities. This could awaken the latents. . . ."

"The more confusion the better. We can't go down and get them, they've got to come up and get us. Or at least open up. Now all we can do is wait."

*   *   *

They sat as the afternoon faded to dusk, then all
night and into the morning.

Lady slapped her thigh. "I swear, every kind of bug
left on the face of this earth has had a bite out of me."

"Not quite." Thomas pointed at one crawling up
her bare arm. "I don't think I've seen one of those
before."

She grimaced and squashed it. With the slap of her
hand came a sharp whistle downslope, the arrogant
cry of a mockingbird. Denethan's troops flattened at
the lookout's signal.

"Thank heavens," Lady muttered. Then, "Oh, god,
Thomas, I'm lying on an anthill."

He pointed at a clump of bracken. "Get over there,
get down and get quiet."

She went, with an angry glare of her blue eye. She
got down just as six uniforms crested the knoll.

Thomas had to give Denethan credit. His troops
were finely trained and well disciplined. Not a one of
the six uniforms had bloodstains on them or holes in
them when he and Denethan and four others dressed.
Lady handed him his rifle as he finished fastening the
jacket.

She eyed him critically as he said, "Is my neck
covered?"

"Barely, but anybody close enough to you to tell
you have gills will be dead."

"Isn't that the truth," remarked Denethan. He
shrugged in his too tight jacket. "Keltz—cut that up
the back. Just slit it, I can't move." The fabric gave
way as the raider did as ordered. He rolled his shoulders. "That's better. Ready?"

Thomas nodded. He asked Lady, "Know what you
need to do?"

"Yes. I don't know whether I can do it without a
token, but if Alma's had enough amberose, she might
respond to a summons. But—how are you going to
get in there? There's several hundred feet of rock and

dirt between you and the vaults. How are you going to take them out?"

"We're using the anthill method, one you should be familiar with."

"Anthill?"

Denethan grinned as he slung his rifle over his shoulder. "Stir them up enough, and they'll come get you."

Lady stepped back as shocked as if they'd struck her. "You can't ask me to call the children up through that—call them up to wade through a war zone to get to us!"

"We haven't any choice," Thomas told her. "And it's a risk for all of us—I see no other way." He reached out and took her hands. "I promise you that I'll do everything I can to see they make it safely."

Her lips trembled, but she said nothing else. She knew he would keep his promise—even if it meant trading his life for theirs.

Denethan slapped Thomas on the back. "Let's go."

Chapter 30

"It's a massacre up there, sir," Remmick reported. "They've cracked our outer doors. They're being repaired, but we can't last out a siege if the water is shut off."

The dean of the College Vaults paused behind his desk. He'd been shuffling through papers and now put them aside with a stack of yellowing file folders.

"Arm the expendable breeders, then. Fire them up. Tell them about the abominations that are daring to attack. Do what you have to do to get them upstairs. Then use them as a shield. Send them out in a wave and come in behind them. Get the doors closed how-

ever you can—but I don't want a single attacker left
alive or we'll never have peace again, doors shut or
not. They're animals and they hate us."

The captain nodded briskly in understanding. "And
Remmick—" The guard paused in the doorway. "Be
sure to arm that Russian youngster. This is as good a
time as any to get rid of him."

Another crisp nod.

The dean settled back in his chair. He looked at his
gallery wall where the best of the Norton Simon mu-
seum had been scavenged. The art had been brought
here where it could be used to uplift and inspire the
artists of a new generation.

His fat, freckled lip curled. First, that generation
had to be born. Recent births were promising. He
sighed. He would hate giving up his art collection and
his books, and other, more intangible things. But it
would be necessary to outfit the new, fit rulers of this
country.

Alma lay on her bed, staring unhappily at the bland
ceiling of her room. Her stomach cramped, hesitantly,
tentatively, then violently, and she dug her fists into it.
The hormone shots Dr. Mendes had given her were
changing her—and she lay very still, frightened, wondering if she could lie so motionless that the cramps
would not know where to find her, disbelieving that
her own body could attack her so. She heard Stefan in
the outer room, pacing. She wanted to call out and ask
for a cold washcloth, but couldn't. Something was
wrong with the water system and they had been told to
obey strict rationing for the next forty-eight hours.

Now that she knew she could not have it, her mouth
dried and her lips cracked just thinking of it.

There was trouble above. Nesters making trouble,
they'd heard. Stefan was dying to go see what was
happening, but they'd all been confined to quarters.

Alma put the back of her hand to her clammy
forehead. She hated being underground. She hated
the walls and floors and ceilings. She hated the chemi-

cal smelling air that pushed out of the vents. She hated the lights that never went off in the corridors even at night and shone under the cracks of her apartment door even if she pushed towels in its way. It was never night and never day, always the same.

She felt her muscles tense. Another wave of pain rolled through her. Alma bit her lip and tried to think of anything, anyone, different from here. She closed her eyes and almost instantly, Lady Nolan's face appeared in her thoughts.

Her glistening brown hair looked windblown, and Alma could see both the sky and the earth in her warm, off-color eyes. There was love and tenderness in those eyes. Alma had always been fond of the Protector. Whenever she'd visited Alma's township, she'd always brought comfort and healing and laughter, three things the girl sorely missed now. Alma was drifting into sleep with the dream of Lady Nolan when their apartment door opened.

She heard Stefan question the intruder eagerly. She did not wish to awaken, but something was happening. She struggled out of her misery as Stefan ran into the bedroom.

He carried a rifle across his chest and thrust it toward her. "We're under attack. Denethan's lizard men have come to wipe us out like they did the peninsula."

"Stefan!"

"This is my chance! They treat me like a child here, but they need my help now—"

"Fighting?"

"Yes! Upstairs."

Alma said, in a tiny voice, "I want to go with you."

"But you're sick. It could even be breakout fever."

"Let me go."

He looked shocked. "Alma. They're killing mutants up there."

"I want to go with you." She grasped the rifle. "I was dreaming of Lady Nolan—she was standing in the open, grass about her ankles, the wind in her hair—"

He tossed his head, a shock of white-blond hair falling across his forehead as he did. "She didn't even come say good-bye to you," he said.

"That's not the point! This place . . . there's no windows, no doors. I want to breathe again!"

He looked at her, plainly not comprehending. With a twist, he freed his rifle. "I have a job to do. Stay where you're told." He "about faced" and left, his issue blues straining at the backs of his shoulders.

Alma waited two seconds, then followed him down the corridor.

Denethan braced Thomas while he loaded and wound both rifles. "It's a bottomless pit."

"No. It just seems like it. We've cracked them open like an eggshell and they know we won't go away. They've got to get rid of us."

The desert lord scanned the hillside. His men lay in heaps by the oaks and furze bushes, the choppy grass turning rust-colored with blood. "They're close."

Thomas handed both rifles to Denethan, then loaded his own. His shoulder ached where the stock kicked with every firing. "One more volley and I'll be close enough to get in. From there, we're home free."

"I still think we should just drop a couple of vials down the air shaft—"

"No." Thomas checked his ammo belt. "I'm an executioner. I kill when I'm told to, when it's part of a judgment, *but some of those people down there haven't done anything wrong.*"

Battlefield grime dimmed Denethan's golden beauty, as he looked down at Thomas, eyes narrowed. "You heard them as they died. We're less than dirt to them. *Mutants*. The only victory we can bring out of here is to do no less to them than they would do to us."

"We have an agreement. We need Stefan and Alma, and there may be others hidden below. Denethan, I've been inside the dean's quarters. It's wall to wall with books and more. I've seen the medical labs . . . maybe we can stop the eleven year plague. The doctor talked about longships that went into space and will return. Can it be true? Think of what we can regain! We can't destroy ourselves all over again."

Denethan grew silent, his thoughts hidden by his scale-patterned face. Behind them, where Lady sat loading other rifles, her face wrinkled in sudden concentration. "Thomas—I have her. I think I have her."

"Where?"

"I—I don't know." The rifle fell from her slack fingers. "Thomas! They're massing a suicide attack!"

Denethan sprang into action before Thomas could stop him.

The Protector stumbled to her feet. Blade caught her as she swayed. Her skin went chill with the effort of her summoning. Her teeth chattered and did not stop even when he draped his battered jacket over her shoulders.

"What's going to happen?" she whispered.

He looked unhappily over the battlefield, remembering past skirmishes, as Denethan brought his men into position. "A bloodbath," he said.

All he had to do was stay in one piece long enough to bring the four of them out of it alive.

He caught the sense of it the moment he spotted the rainbow of colors among the uniforms. Dropping to his knees along the wings, hoping to outflank the attack and slip inside, Thomas paused and yelled to Denethan. "Stop! They're civilians trying to draw our fire! Look for the khakis!"

If the desert lord heard him, he gave no sign. The *shoop* of rifles firing filled the air. Bolts and darts brought down the first wave of men, their fellows behind staggering over fallen bodies, their pale faces filled with determination to get to the mutants. He heard their cries, their shouts of hatred and knew that Denethan was probably right. There would be no quarter given by those from the Vaults. They fought against abominations, not fellow men.

A hole opened in the flank nearest him. It was now

or never, for he saw the khaki colors massing in behind the civilians. Thomas got to his feet and made a dash for the Vault doors.

Denethan ran with him, and Thomas saw the colored vial in his hand even as he threw it.

"God, no," he cried, as the gem like glass hurtled through the air. It smashed as Thomas pulled his shirt up over his neck and mouth, and threw himself to one side.

The toxic cloud dispersed almost immediately in the air. Inside, in the mouth of the vaults, bodies toppled like empty shells. Denethan clawed at his arm.

"Come on!"

Thomas threw off his hand, and got up, as angry as he'd ever been, but the desert lord was moving. He set his jaw and ran after him, leaping bodies that flies were already settling on. As they moved into the Vault, a khaki-uniformed troop faced them. An iron-jawed captain led them.

Remmick stared. "You!"

Thomas put his hands to his neck. "I'm a little hard to drown." He blurred Remmick's vision, to hinder his movements. Denethan gave him no chance to say anything further, as he jumped the two closest men, blade in hand.

Remmick blinked, pivoted and fled. Thomas would have gone after him, but he found himself with an empty rifle and very, very busy.

Alma caught up with Stefan in the stairwell. Her pulse pounded and she grew sick to her stomach, but she reached for him and held on.

"Don't go out there! Not yet!"

"Alma! What are you doing here? Let go of me."

She clung determinedly. "Not yet, please. Listen to them. . . ." Hoarse cries and shouts echoed down the stairwell. "They're not fighting up there, they're *dying*."

"I'm supposed to be with them!" Anger flashed in his blue eyes and he shook her off, roughly, as bootsteps echoed on the overhead rungs. Remmick jumped in front of them. The Vault captain's eyes lit in recognition.

He grabbed for Alma and pulled her to her feet even as she let out a protesting cry.

"It's you he wants. It's you he'll get, if he pulls out." Remmick looked to Stefan. "I need your help."

The blond youth hesitated, then nodded.

"I've got the doors repaired now—we can get them closed, but I need a strong pair of arms."

Stefan stood up taller. "I'm your man."

"All right. Come on." Remmick steered Alma in front of him, taking the stair rungs one at a time with Stefan leading the way.

Lady massaged her throbbing temples. She could hear everything, piercingly, even the sound of her own breathing and the blood rushing through her veins. The screams of the dead and the dying. The epitaphs, the curses, the hatred of the fighters. A man toppled at her feet. Her vision blurred, she could not tell if he was friend or foe. She brushed her hand over him, his wound stopped pumping blood and he lay quietly. Would he live? She had no way of telling. Her Talent drew her elsewhere—drew her as inexorably to Alma as she had summoned the girl to her side. She stared at the fighting ahead and knew she'd never make it—but she had to. She drew Thomas' jacket tightly about her, pinching it shut at her neck. It smelled of leather, the sea—and him. Her fingers slipped inside, snagging on one of those countless pockets, and ivoried bones slipped into her hand. Lady closed her fingers about them. Only the ghost road could take her where she wanted to go. Not understanding why she did it, Lady shrugged out of Blade's jacket, before ducking her head and invoking her path. The cries of the dead and dying fueled her way. She shuddered, rejected it, and fought for a new road. Heedless of the battle, she made her way to the steel vault doors.

The tide of khaki-clothed men forced them back and outside once more. Rifles emptied, knives came out of sheaths and blood flowed crimson. Thomas shrugged off his newest attacker and downed him with a sharp left foot to the jaw. On the follow-through, he spotted Denethan in serious trouble. A knife in the ribs eased the situation greatly and the lizard man finished the other two guardsmen with thrusts of his own.

"Pull back," Thomas said. "They're slaughtering us." He stood in the massive steel framework of the doorway. It began to shudder and sing while they stood upon the tracks. He tried to recover his focus to use his Talent, but there was little time for it. He was nearly drained. His hands and feet were better weapons than his mind.

"Shit!" Denethan leaped aside. "Get out of here!" He yelled to his remaining troops. The ones who could fled for freedom.

The Vaults began to close. Thomas felt a whisper pass him, a chill being, a ghost brushing his side. He started. The hair prickled on the back of his neck. Denethan grabbed him and towed him out, throwing him down behind a barrier of dead men.

"Cracked open like an egg, eh?"

He had no answer. The doors ground shut, tearing heads and limbs from bodies, crushing bone within its tracks. He shuddered to hear the noise. Then, two people wide, it stopped, unable to compress its fleshy barrier anymore.

Denethan looked at him, and raised an eyebrow. Thomas shook his head.

"Sir Thomas! I have a proposition for you!"

Remmick appeared in the doorway, just enough of him to present a tempting but difficult target. The captain looked about, searching for him. "You'll never get in."

"And you'll never get out," Denethan bellowed back.

"Every den has a bolt hole," the captain returned. "Don't be too sure of that. And you'll never have what you want."

"How can you possibly know what we want?"

Thomas shouted. His hand went up automatically to his shuriken, then he swore quietly, for he still wore the uniform of the maintenance squad.

Remmick jerked, and a pale form filled the void of the doorway.

"That's Alma," Thomas said quickly.

Denethan yelled, "Hold your fire!" for the girl was completely exposed by Remmick's actions. The desert lord rolled to his left and began loading his rifle. "Damn his hide."

"To hell with the girl," Thomas lied. "We want revenge!"

Remmick twitched. The girl went to her knees amid a wash of blood and gore. She began to cry. The captain reached out and tore her tunic from neck to navel.

"Take a look, Blade! She's unblemished! We already know she hasn't been contaminated by the plague! And her DNA's as pure as it gets nowadays. You want the human race back! You'll need a good little breeder like this! Put down your arms."

Denethan mentioned a physical impossibility and muttered, "If he's human, we don't need it." He got into firing position and looked at Thomas, bronze gaze narrowed. He sighed at the expression he read. "All right. I'll cover you." To his men, he ordered, "Put down your arms."

"You're killing them!"

The desert lord smiled grimly. "They swore a blood oath to me—we to each other—and they'll die for it. They begged for the right to follow me here and die for it! We're not animals. That's what makes us human, eh? The will to live and die for one another? Now get going!" And he stood, rifle hidden behind a muscular leg. "All right, captain. No weapons."

Remmick looked suspicious. "Where's Blade?"

Thomas crawled on his stomach, slowly, painstakingly, getting close enough to rush the guardsman. Denethan said, "We're the only ones left."

"Lizard man, I saw the Lord Protector when you rushed the door."

"Then he's probably in that gore you're standing ankle-deep in. But we'll take the girl."

Remmick's gaze flickered nervously over the area. "I heard his voice!" He started to pull Alma back inside as he yelled, "Stefan!"

The boy answered weakly. He tried to pull himself to his knees from under a pile of death. His blue uniform was charred and streaked with blood. With a cry of defiance, Alma turned on Remmick, beating and clawing at him, the shreds of her clothing about her waist, pale skin streaked with the blood of the dead. He clubbed her, once, and she collapsed with a groan over the tracks. The whining doors convulsed and began to shut again. Thomas was close enough now to smell the machinery burning.

The Lord Protector leaped. He caught Remmick by the collar. The captain responded, and Thomas felt fingers like steel crushing about his arms. He reached out with his power, his Intuition, and did not touch a mortal being. This . . . thing . . . was artificial.

The air lock and inner doors opened, filled with the dean's bulk. The man smiled at Thomas as the captain drove him to his knees. The black-robed man leaned over and picked Alma up, slinging her easily over his shoulder.

"Take him outside to finish him, Remmick. Then download. I don't want you functional if captured."

"Yes, sir."

The being holding Thomas with inhuman strength made no response as Thomas kicked him with all his might. The dean paused in the elevator, and laughed.

"You've no idea what you're dealing with," the head of the College Vaults said. "He's not even close to human." He was still laughing when the air lock doors shut him and Alma away.

Remmick dragged Thomas down. In his blurring vision, he saw Denethan grabbing Stefan, dragging him away from the massive pulleys. But the door still rolled on. The two wrestled, scuffling into Remmick, breaking loose the grip of one of his hands upon Thomas. Thomas tried to brace himself on the tracks as Remmick reached for him again.

The four of them fell into the narrow opening, squeezing between the doors. Denethan, with a cough and gasp, dragged Stefan out and clubbed him into submission. The desert lord then grabbed up a rifle and swung it across the back of Remmick's shoulders. Thomas felt a bone break as the guardsman continued to squeeze, carrying him across the ground like a sack of meal. There was a pause, and Denethan swung again, harder.

The plastiflesh shell of Remmick's face fell off. Thomas found his image reflected back at him from a smooth obsidian surface. There was no loosening of the grip around his throat. But he was gilled. His lungs were meant to hold air for ten or twelve minutes at a time. What he had to worry about was crushing, permanent damage. He thought of Denethan's mindstorm, and its crackling levin-bolts. Out of his thoughts, he conjured one. Fire danced on the obsidian surface, obscuring his reflection. The being, whatever it was, began to convulse with the power overload.

Denethan said, "I've got this one." He slipped his knife blade in the base of the captain's neck and backed off.

Sparks arced. The thing threw Thomas violently across the clearing, staggered about, and then collapsed onto the bloodied grass. Thomas hit the ground hard, and stayed down, panting, momentarily unable to see. He fought for breath.

"What was that?"

"An android. I've seen a few before in the desert labs. Never one powered up. Can you get up?" Denethan towered over Stefan's quiet form.

A siren cut into the sudden silence. A single, piercing note. Denethan was reaching down to help Thomas up. He froze. Klaxons shattered the noise of the battlefield.

They heard the muffled explosion. Indian Hill danced, quivering, as a massive wave rippled through the dirt and rock. Thomas staggered to his feet in disbelief.

Then someone shouted, "Avalanche! Run for it!" as the side of the mountain began to cave in.

Denethan scooped up the unconscious boy as Thomas began to hobble for his life.

"Lady!" Nowhere did he see her. "Lady!" He stumbled across his jacket on the ground, turned inside out, the pockets empty.

Gillander's bones were missing.

He remembered, then, the feeling of gooseflesh he'd had . . . like a ghost slipping past him.

She was trapped inside the exploding mountain. They'd learned the hard way that time could not protect them . . . weapons and death were just as real on the ghost road. His agony tore out of his bruised throat. "Lady!"

Denethan reared up beside him. "Sorry," he said, and swung.

The dust and smoke hung across what had been the entrance to the College Vaults like an impenetrable curtain when the ground stopped dancing. Denethan squatted next to Thomas. "Well," he said, "That's that. They'd rather blow themselves up than be tainted."

Thomas ached all over, but nothing hurt as badly as the knowledge he'd lost Lady. He said nothing.

Denethan moved past him, knife in hand, and put it to Stefan's throat. "Judging from past experience, this little bastard's no better than the rest."

Thomas kicked out, sent the knife spinning, and lay back, groaning, as broken ribs ground, and his right arm flopped lopsidedly. The expression in Denethan's eyes let Thomas know he was very close to being killed as well.

"Leave him be," Thomas said, suddenly very tired.

"He's been taught like the rest of them."

"He grew up in my county. The short time he spent in their hands can't poison that."

Stefan moaned and thrashed on the ground. Denethan looked down. He then looked back to Thomas. "You'd better hope not. He's not human like us." He moved away.

Thomas rolled and got to his knees. The truce with the desert lord was ended. He was only as safe as he was strong. Denethan respected strength. Strength and survival.

He limped toward the mountain base, where dust still poured from above, like blue and gold smoke in the air. He didn't want to live without Lady. He'd looked inside himself and found that which wanted a home, a base, a pairing. He'd found a solution to the bittersweet loneliness that had plagued him at a wedding party a lifetime ago.

The air shivered. He could almost hear the despair of the dead. He saw a shadow among the settling motes. It grew stronger, coalescing.

It was a woman, short but feisty, her head held high as she carried another woman, smaller, slenderer, in her arms.

Lady came walking out of the side of the mountain.

Chapter 31

"This means I get the pick of the litter."

Alma blushed, wrapped in a dress made of the gold-spun silken canopy Denethan had used for his tent. The gold brought out her coloring, peach toned, her dark brown hair still curled, but not short and gamine as it had been. She'd matured over these last weeks, Thomas thought. The young lady raised her chin and said softly, "Children don't come in litters," answering the big, scaled warrior. "But we will send our second son or daughter to you for fostering. I promise."

"Done." Denethan swung on Thomas. He clasped the man's shoulder none too gently. "I still stand by my offer. A dozen of my finest to go home with you."

Blade shook his head. "No. Not yet. But an ambassador in the spring will be welcome."

"Politics is a tougher battle than war."

"I know. But I'll have some help."

Lady sat on the cart seat next to him, holding the reins as two ponies stamped their eagerness to be off and away from the stench of funeral pyres. Denethan nodded. "Take care, my friend." He straightened in his saddle, made a sign, and his legion rode after him.

Lady adjusted Thomas' sling. "That one may come as ambassador himself."

"I'm expecting it," he answered. He leaned back on the cushions. "Let's take the long way home."

Stefan snorted. "Getting soft, old man."

Thomas looked over his shoulder at the back of the cart. "At least," he said icily, "I did not take all of my lumps in the head."

The boy blushed as rosily as his new bride.

Lady clucked and the cart jolted into movement. She caught Thomas staring at the debris of the hillside which had once contained the College Vaults. Those were ruins he'd have to come back and sift through, though not for a definition of humanity. He thought of medical equipment, books, and priceless paintings. Surely some of them would have survived in the deeper tunnels.

She sensed his uneasiness. "What is it?"

He made a diffident movement, cut short by the sling on his arm and the strapping about his ribs. "He's an old fox, the dean—and I never met a fox or gopher yet who didn't have a second hole." He grasped her hand. "Why didn't the blast touch you?"

"The Ghost Road's more than paranormal, it's elemental—keyed to the person who walks it. You're an executioner. You used death to fuel it. But you were dispassionate about it at first and the road could only drain you. It couldn't touch you until you made the lives you took personal. Then you were corrupted, adding to its energies. It could draw on you and wound you with ever increasing effectiveness. I, on the other hand—"

"You are a Healer."

"Exactly. I took up the bones and couldn't use them, not as you had—I was diametrically opposed to the flow. So I reached for life." She waved a hand over the hillside which was littered with scattered ruins as far as the eye could see into the haze. "For every death, there was a life born down there once. Then the ghost road was mine. Oh, it drained me, too, but it had much farther to go, the entire cycle from birth to death. So the blast couldn't reach me once I'd found Alma and taken her."

"Elemental. And my totems?"

"Oh, that's a mystery you're going to have to solve. But a worthwhile one. There's magic in you, Thomas."

He shook his head, then murmured, "Thank god you were able to summon the road."

She smiled prettily. "Oh, I had help. A crusty old soul who likes to give advice from behind your left ear. You'd call him a ghost. I'd call him a psychometric resonance." Lady considered him a moment before saying, "Lord Protector, you need to find a successor to the DWP, and your county lies waiting."

"I know. And thank god for Macaulay's *The Way Things Work*. We may have lost the rest of Charlie's papers, but that still survives." He leaned against her slightly. "Dying is easy. Staying alive is the hard part."

Her lips brushed his scarred brow. "And I've never known you to do something the easy way."

He smiled. "Got any lemon drops?" he asked, as they followed the long path home.

DAW

Cosmic Battles To Come!

Charles Ingrid

☐ **THE MARKED MAN** (UE2395—$3.95)

A recurring plague was decimating mankind, linking to the DNA structure to create truly terrifying mutations. Desperately, a small group searched for a way to breed the shifting bloodlines back to a "pure" human form. And while they experimented, Thomas Blade and his fellow Lord Protectors, gifted with powerful psychic abilities, stood guard as the last defense against the forces of the mutant Denethan, who had sworn to complete the destruction of the "true" human race.

THE SAND WARS

☐ **SOLAR KILL: Book 1** (UE2391—$3.95)

He was the last Dominion Knight and he would challenge a star empire to gain his revenge!

☐ **LASERTOWN BLUES: Book 2** (UE2393—$3.95)

He'd won a place in the Emperor's Guard but could he hunt down the traitor who'd betrayed his Knights to an alien foe?

☐ **CELESTIAL HIT LIST: Book 3** (UE2394—$3.95)

Death stalked the Dominion Knight from the Emperor's Palace to a world on the brink of its prophesied age of destruction. . . .

☐ **ALIEN SALUTE: Book 4** (UE2329—$3.95)

As the Dominion and the Thrakian empires mobilize for all-out war, can Jack Storm find the means to defeat the ancient enemies of man?

☐ **RETURN FIRE: Book 5** (UE2363—$3.95)

Was someone again betraying the human worlds to the enemy—and would Jack Storm become pawn or player in these games of death?

☐ **CHALLENGE MET: Book 6** (UE2436—$3.95)

In this concluding volume of *The Sand Wars*, Jack Storm embarks on a dangerous mission which will lead to a final confrontation with the Ash-farel. *Coming in 1990*

DAW

C.J. CHERRYH
THE ALLIANCE-UNION UNIVERSE

The Company Wars
☐ DOWNBELOW STATION   (UE2431—$4.50)

The Era of Rapprochement
☐ SERPENT'S REACH   (UE2088—$3.50)
☐ FORTY THOUSAND IN GEHENNA   (UE2429—$4.50)
☐ MERCHANTER'S LUCK   (UE2139—$3.50)

The Chanur Novels
☐ THE PRIDE OF CHANUR   (UE2292—$3.95)
☐ CHANUR'S VENTURE   (UE2293—$3.95)
☐ THE KIF STRIKE BACK   (UE2184—$3.50)
☐ CHANUR'S HOMECOMING   (UE2177—$3.95)

The Mri Wars
☐ THE FADED SUN: KESRITH   (UE1960—$3.50)
☐ THE FADED SUN: SHON'JIR   (UE1889—$2.95)
☐ THE FADED SUN: KUTATH   (UE2133—$2.95)

Merovingen Nights (Mri Wars Period)
☐ ANGEL WITH THE SWORD   (UE2143—$3.50)

Merovingen Nights—Anthologies
☐ FESTIVAL MOON (#1)   (UE2192—$3.50)
☐ FEVER SEASON (#2)   (UE2224—$3.50)
☐ TROUBLED WATERS (#3)   (UE2271—$3.50)
☐ SMUGGLER'S GOLD (#4)   (UE2299—$3.50)
☐ DIVINE RIGHT (#5)   (UE2380—$3.95)

The Age of Exploration
☐ CUCKOO'S EGG   (UE2371—$4.50)
☐ VOYAGER IN NIGHT   (UE2107—$2.95)
☐ PORT ETERNITY   (UE2206—$2.95)

The Hanan Rebellion
☐ BROTHERS OF EARTH   (UE2290—$3.95)
☐ HUNTER OF WORLDS   (UE2217—$2.95)

NEW AMERICAN LIBRARY
P.O. Box 999, Bergenfield, New Jersey 07621
Please send me the DAW BOOKS I have checked above. I am enclosing $_____
(check or money order—no currency or C.O.D.'s). Please include the list price plus
$1.00 per order to cover handling costs. Prices and numbers are subject to change
without notice. (Prices slightly higher in Canada.)
Name _____
Address _____
City _____ State _____ Zip _____
Please allow 4-6 weeks for delivery.

DAW
Epic Tales of Other Worlds

TERRY A. ADAMS

☐ SENTIENCE   (UE2108—$3.50)

The true-humans looked upon the D'neerans, the only human telepaths, as not quite people, not quite trustworthy. Then their exploratory starship made first contact with real aliens—and suddenly the fate of all humanity rested on the mind skill of a single D'neeran!

☐ THE MASTER OF CHAOS   (UE2347—$4.50)

With the unexpected arrival of beings from the far-off planet Uskos, the telepathic Lady Hanna must embark on a mission of peace to the stars. Here is a galaxy-spanning tale of cultures in collision, of a man seeking a key to his long-forgotten past—and of the human-seeming creature which threatens the futures of Uskos, of Hanna, and of a world out of time.

JOHN BRIZZOLARA

☐ EMPIRE'S HORIZON   (UE2365—$3.95)

Invaders from the Andromeda Galaxy return to reclaim a former colony planet, now occupied by the Terran Interstellar Empire. Vastly superior, the aliens brush aside mankind's defenses, and put an end to the Empire, which has long been on the verge of collapse. They offer mankind immortality, matter transport, and the power to convert consciousness into a higher form of energy. Does mankind dare accept their offer—or is there a catch?

DORIS EGAN

☐ THE GATE OF IVORY   (UE2328—$3.95)

Cut off from her companions and her ship, attacked and robbed, anthropology student Theodora of Pyrene finds what began as a pleasure trip becoming a terrifying odyssey on the planet Ivory, where magic works. For all her studies and training are useless, and she is forced to turn to fortune-telling to survive. To her amazement, she discovers that she is actually gifted with magical skill—a skill, however, that will plunge her into deadly peril.
